Not Far From Roswell

Edited
by
Kelly A. Harmon and
Vonnie Winslow Crist

Pole to Pole Publishing
Baltimore

Not Far From Roswell
Copyright © 2019 Pole to Pole Publishing

Published by Pole to Pole Publishing
Edited by Kelly A. Harmon and Vonnie Winslow Crist
Cover design: Kelly A. Harmon
Cover layout copyright © 2019 Pole to Pole Publishing
www.poletopolepublishing.com

ISBN: 978-1-941559-36-9

Library of Congress Control Number: 2020930652

Not Far From Roswell

In the deepest sense, the search for extraterrestrial intelligence is a search for ourselves."

~ Carl Sagan

Table of Contents

Sunday Drive

Gregory L. Norris

*F*ew *words inspired such joy among the family as those* Dad spoke on Friday nights in the mid-1960s when he returned home from the job that kept him away for the rest of the week.

"On Sunday, let's take a drive!"

Oh, the anticipation through the rest of Friday night and the dragging slowness of Saturday. But the wait was worth it, and Saturday allowed for mundane necessities like washing the car so that its fins and lights glowed in Sunday's sunshine, and the shiny grill of the family's armored land-boat mirrored the smiles of all assembled within its illusion of safety.

James, his science magazine opened, on the right side of the backseat, Polly on the left, holding her favorite doll and the diary she got for her eleventh birthday to record the day's adventures, Mom in the front looking stylish in her pillbox hat with the length of veil, and Dad seated behind the wheel, that comforting smile on his handsome face, his sharp black suit hung up for the day, clad in a shirt without buttons, relaxed khaki slacks, and his favorite hat.

"Where are we going, Pop?" James asked.

"Wherever we want," Dad answered, a cigarette dangling from his lips that Mom prepared for him using the car's dashboard lighter. They exited their neighborhood of cookie-cutter ranch houses and tended lawns, where most neighbors were hard at work following church services to rake the first of autumn's falling leaves, and drove north, north, north.

Everything interesting always happened north.

§

They passed the big sign, the one for Wanda's Diner, which no longer was open for business down near the river. James tensed.

"What is it, son?" Dad asked, eyeing the boy from a corner of the rearview mirror.

"I was just thinking about that time we ate at Wanda's," James said.

Dad laughed. "In what life? Wanda's served its last burger when I was your age."

"But—?" the boy began, only to stop himself from finishing the thought.

The sensation returned, real for one second, gone the next. Hot fudge atop cold chocolate ice cream, the extremes in temperature and the two tastes so exquisite as to be made unforgettable. And hadn't there been someone else with them? In the space of that long-ago memory, James recalled that the backseat in this very car was once more crowded. Didn't he used to ride on the left? No, the *center*.

Then it was gone, and the vibrant leaves glittering beneath a cloudless blue sky the color of comfortable denim seduced him.

They motored north, windows cracked, no one speaking, the family all smiles.

§

Oh, the wonders seen on previous Sunday drives! There was the hot air balloon ride, and the time they watched the military test-fire rockets in the mountains. They weren't supposed to be there for that breathtaking event, but Dad knew just where to travel, what back roads to take, where to creep out of sight for the best view possible at dusk. And if they'd gotten stopped, well, he said he knew just what to do. Something hidden in the trunk brought home from his work in New Mexico. No worries.

On this day, one so bright it nearly blinded them, Dad pulled over to the side of the country road. An old man, looking quite happy according to his wide smile, sat on a lichen-encrusted boulder, part of an old farmer's wall.

"My good man," Dad called past Mom to the man. "Could you tell me about the local attractions?"

The old man stood and tromped toward the car, stirring sunlight en route. He leaned down at the window. "You'll want to visit the fall carnival. Few miles up this very road. You'll know you're close when you reach the covered bridge."

"Did you hear that, children?" Mom exclaimed. "A real covered bridge!"

"Over the bridge, through them woods—you can't miss it," their new friend and tour guide said.

Dad thanked the man and drove forward. They passed fields of corn and pumpkin being harvested by a small army of workers. Beyond that, it was apple orchards, the fruit that covered the tress glowing like gems and sweetening the air. On the far side of the orchard, past the trees at roadside, it was mushrooms. Gigantic, multi-colored mushrooms in fantastic shapes. They hung from branches and covered the ground. Workers harvested them, too, but the shadows cast by the trees lent them the appearance of phantoms.

Darkness engulfed them. James looked up and realized they'd reached the covered bridge. Polly chortled in glee. James closed his science magazine—the words blurred long miles earlier and he'd been trying to read the same sentence without success.

"Would you look at that?" Dad sighed in a dreamy voice. "What a sight!"

They drove through the covered bridge, arriving at a field where other cars sat parked and a spirited celebration of life and the season played out a short walk beyond a trampled down field, past the edge of a line of trees. Colored leaves drifted across this panorama like confetti and scattered in the pleasant breeze.

James sucked in a deep breath and then just as deeply expelled it. The air was crisp from leaves and rich with a host of other tantalizing smells—gear grease from carnival rides, cotton candy, and hamburgers roasting on a grill. Polly continued to giggle at James' left. From the direction of the carnival grounds, more laughter rose up. The boy's skin broke in gooseflesh and a chill teased the fine hairs at the nape of his neck. Even before the shiver tumbled, Dad was out of the car. Mom followed. James hesitated—the shudder spilling down his backbone had paralyzed him. He caught Dad's disapproval through the windshield and jumped out of the car into a day too bright to be anything other than a blessing.

Polly skipped at Dad's side, one hand clutching her doll, the other in Dad's much larger grip. James noted that Dad wore that ring, the gold one with the big square garnet stone and the funny markings. *Hieroglyphs*, he remembered—after all, he was going to be a scientist when he grew up, curing old age and solving the world's problems, few of which seemed present today.

They neared the break in the line of trees and approached a ticket booth. A man in a shirt with red and white stripes stamped the backs of their hands. James winced. He looked down to see a red star in temporary ink tattooed across his skin. It stung. He shook it out. There was too much fun promised by what awaited them at this autumn carnival to give in to the pain.

James realized he was several steps ahead of the rest of his clan. He turned back. Mom was in Dad's arms, looking as though she'd fainted. And Polly? James saw the doll sitting in the grass, its fake eyes always opened now wide with a look that could only be horror.

"Where's Polly?" he asked. No one answered because no one seemed to hear him, and for a terrible instant James was sure he was dreaming the entire scenario, as the words came out, slowed down, sped up. "Where's Polly? *Where's Polly!*"
After that, he was laughing and being swept away by all the many joys to be found at the carnival.

§

James wandered down a kind of concourse where games were being played and calliope music pulsed. Over his head, wildly screaming enthusiasts rose in open-air cable cars, their legs kicked over a hundred feet of empty space.

It must be the closest thing to flying, he thought.

"Can we—?" he asked.

"We can do anything here," Dad said, holding up his hand, showing that red star, which triggered a connection in James' overwhelmed mind. How much that stamp on their hands resembled the symbols on Dad's garnet ring.

They ate at a line of grills set along covered picnic tables—corn on cobs cooked atop the coals that tasted so sweet they required no butter or salt; hamburgers roasted to perfection on toasted buns with ketchup, mustard, slices of onion, and briny pickles; and big ice cream sundaes with hot fudge and chocolate ice cream, just like the ones he remembered they used to serve at Wanda's Diner down near the river. Though that couldn't possibly be, because Wanda's closed up shop long before James was born.

He jumped on a car and rode through the Haunted House. The smell of gear grease mixed with a fetor of old wood. Lights flashed, simulating lightning. As the car advanced, something brushed James' forehead—a drape of strings suspended from the ceiling meant to pass for a spider's web. As the car lumbered deeper, it approached dioramas painted phosphorescent Day-Glo colors bathed in black light—the werewolf, whose animatronic jaws snapped as he passed by; the vampire, who sprang out of a velvet-lined coffin; the mummy, reawakened in his crypt. It was all fairly commonplace, three-dimensional reenactments of the creature features that ran on UHF on Saturday afternoons. Effective, but nothing overly scary.

Then the black lights cut out, replaced by one in electric blue. The silly monster dioramas ended. The car traveled into a room and came to a stop. The air there thrummed with an undercurrent that crawled over James' skin. The food in his belly soured. Cold fear embraced him.

"Hello?" he called out.

Silence. There were no more shrieks coming from his fellow visitors to the Haunted House, just that maddening pulse through the air, like a giant's heartbeat, and a sensation from a summer thunderstorm before that first crackle of lightning. The fine hairs on his bare arms all stood straight up.

He blinked, and the empty room beneath the blue lights was no longer empty. A lone figure walked out of the electric glare and moved toward him. James narrowed his eyes in an attempt to identify who it was. The head wasn't right. Nor were the eyes. It was the worst monster of all in the Haunted House. The only real one. Better to just close his eyes completely. Yes, clamp them shut, his inner voice urged. And so, he listened. A moment of intense pain followed before he roused on that other ride, the one on cable cars sweeping high above the ground.

The safety bar slammed into place. The cable car carried him up, up, over empty space. Ten more feet. Fifty. He became even with the trees and soon was above them, looking down on the world and all the happy people who'd come to the carnival on this glorious autumn Sunday.

A smile on his face, gravity tickling his belly, James kicked his legs. One of his sneakers slipped off and he watched it fall, hoping it wouldn't hurt anyone far below his lofty position among the clouds. The cable car led over a fountain, turned around among the trees, and traveled back to its beginning point. It was only a sneaker, he told himself. They'd lost more important considerations on these Sunday adventures far from home. The other sibling that used to sit in the backseat, for instance. He could almost remember her name, see her face in his fractured memory. Almost.

His sneaker was gone. But James didn't worry. He was flying. Oh yes, really flying!

He aimed his face up at the sky filled with sunlight, the boy's smile persisting for another second.

Then he screamed.

And screamed.

§

They drove south. Polly slept as the early autumn twilight descended, clutching at a new doll, a doll won at the carnival. James came out of the fog, helped along by the acrid stink of cigarette smoke and the brisk air pouring through cracked windows.

"We're almost home," Dad said.

James looked up and his father's eye was once more upon him, studying him from a corner of the rearview mirror.

§

"The ring," James said. "What do you mean you don't have my father's ring?"

The funeral director shrugged. "There was no ring when we readied your father."

"Gold, with a square of garnet stone. He never took it off."

"I'm sorry," the funeral director said.

"What about my sisters—Polly or the other one? Did they take it?"

The funeral director regarded him with a curious expression. "Sisters? I thought you were the only child?"

James rubbed his eyes but didn't respond.

They laid his late father out in a black suit and crisp white button down. Despite his age, James's father looked so much like the man in his memory from forty-odd years earlier. The one who worked all that time in New Mexico. The one that had haunted James' dreams since.

§

He returned to his apartment and reached for the pill bottle, only to hesitate. The purple pills were meant to elevate his mood and they did—but they also blurred memories and made thinking difficult.

James put down the pill bottle, checked the door to make sure it was locked, and paced. Dad was dead. Dad in his black suit. *No more Sunday drives*, taunted the little acid voice in his thoughts. Sunday drives? He hadn't thought about the old tradition in…

Decades?

Rain spattered the apartment house. James sat in the chair that faced the front door, resisting the urge to blink until his eyes burned.

Remember, the voice inside his skull demanded.

Dread rose up inside him, an emotion he remembered clearly from another time. The 1960s. Dad was on the road all week, gone to whatever job in New Mexico kept him away from home and family. Something to do with the government. The military? Dad never talked about it with Mom. Mom barely talked at all in those days. She was a shell, a zombie going through motions after something happened, something involving the sister he couldn't remember. In the past, that old dread was tangible. It hung over the house like a cloud even on the sunniest of days. And it thickened whenever Dad returned, dressed in his black suit. How James came to loathe that suit.

On Friday night, Dad's car with the sinister smile on its grill chugged into the driveway. He entered the house, casting a long shadow. James' dread doubled, quadrupled, as his father spoke those cursed words.

"*…Sunday drive.*"

Saturday passed with the weight of eternity. Then it was Sunday, a day worse than James had imagined possible.

They boarded the car. Polly sat wide-eyed, clutching doll and diary, not speaking. Once, he risked a look inside that book when no one was home. It was filled with insane scribbles, some of which looked like the hieroglyphs on Dad's special ring. The rest was graphomania, fragmentary and frightening: *I remember the lights, and the heartbeat of their engines; last night I was up there again, on the roof, and then far, far above it; the blue room—the man inside had the biggest, darkest eyes.*

They passed the sign for the old diner, and fresh fear slithered through James. The sign sat dark in the overcast of that cloudy, frigid autumn Sunday, a thing barely there. Ivy had overgrown most of it, but you could still see the bulbs, imagine the shape they made when lit: circular, a bright beacon attracting hungry, weary travelers to stop and be nourished. For a second, he was there in the old diner, eating. The dark ooze went down like bitter medicine.

"Think of it like a chocolate sundae," Dad said, out of focus in the shadows of the abandoned diner.

In that horrific memory, Polly sat to his left, crying as the concoction was forced into her. And closer, between them, was the one whose name he couldn't recall. Anne Marie? Cheryl? The older sister who vanished soon after their last visit to Wanda's diner on that other rain-lashed Sunday outing.

Mom lit Dad a cigarette. Dad studied James from the rearview mirror, his eyes dark, all pupil.

§

The clouds opened up, drenching the outside world. They passed a man on a country road. Dad waved him over, and James was sure the body at the side of the road was a corpse. Something about him wasn't right. The face? No, more than only that.

The man who wasn't a man stalked over, herky-jerky. He approached the car and James couldn't bring himself to look. From the periphery, he watched the exchange between the living scarecrow and his father, their words a series of clicks and mechanical notes more than language in the understood definition of the word. The scarecrow tipped a look into the backseat, and James was sure he'd wet himself, as he did in the present forty-odd years later while remembering this detail.

"Covered bridge," Dad said, his voice degenerating into a guttural growl.

Dad drove forward through the maelstrom. James stole a look at the scarecrow as it returned to its resting place among the rock wall and caught a note of something rotten in the breeze spilling through the quarter-open window. Death filled his lungs.

Long stretches of farmland followed—pumpkin, corn, apple orchards. Some other crop grew among the trees. Those flora draped branches, grew inelegantly up from the damp forest floor, and coated trunks. Harvesters picked the crop in the rain, but to James the workers resembled badly drawn stick figures—upright, two-legged versions of a Daddy Long Legs spider.

They approached the covered bridge, an assemblage made of silver beams with a dome for a roof.

Saucer, said James' inner voice.

They passed under the saucer, into an overgrown field. A dozen vehicles sat rusting in the grass. Polly giggled, but the sound quickly degenerated into sobs. Lights and music emanated from beyond the ragged wood line.

The family walked through the rain, Polly screaming, pulling against Dad's hand. James saw his sister's favorite doll abandoned in the grass. His instinct was to retrieve it. But pain exploded over his hand, and the mark of the red star was back, the same as on Dad's ring, tattooed and bloody atop his flesh.

More of that medicine got forced in his system. The blue room. A man with enormous dark eyes. And after that, he found himself ascending higher, higher into the storm clouds. When he looked up—

The lights!

James screamed.

And screamed.

§

He jolted awake in the present, on a rainy Saturday night, on the day before his father's funeral. Only there'd been a problem—a missing ring, the one that never left his father's right index finger.

Drool soaked his chin and shirt. James moved to wipe his mouth, only to freeze. The ring—it wasn't on the body at the funeral home because that wasn't his father. His father hadn't died. What was put in that coffin was for viewing purposes only. A ruse.

The temperature in the apartment plummeted. Having forgotten how to blink, James faced the door.

Breathe, his inner voice pleaded. *Breathe and wake up!*

Another moment passed. He noticed the hands of the clock on the wall had traveled past midnight. It was Sunday.

And then a single knock sounded on the door.

Majestic Dawn

Jason J. McCuiston

Major Peter Staff leapt from the truck before it came to a stop. The sun rose above the Mississippi River, turning the April sky to fire and glory—what his missionary parents would have called one of God's great miracles. He might have chuckled at that prosaic notion if not for the chaos swarming over the smoke-shrouded stretch of ground. Vehicles, lit by headlights, flame, and the first crimson rays of dawn, spilled scores of soldiers, policemen, firefighters, and even a few dozen concerned locals onto the frenetic site.

Staff had seen thousands of sunrises in his thirty-six years on Earth, but the thing that had just crashed in the field outside of Cape Girardeau, Missouri—now that was a miracle.

Dressed in his olive-drab field uniform, boots, and leggings, Staff headed to the parked ambulance, guessing that's where his expertise would be most valuable.

A local sheriff's deputy shared a smoke with the two ambulance drivers, standing above three lumps covered in white sheets on the ground. A few feet away, another deputy spoke to a dark-clad man; possibly a country minister. Staff adjusted his glasses and produced his credentials. "Morning, gentlemen. I'm Dr. Peter Staff, United States Army Air Forces. I'd like to see what you've got here."

"You think it's a Nazi spy plane?" One of the ambulance men asked. "I mean, these sure don't look like no Germans I ever seen."

"What are you looking at?" the other driver said. "In case you hadn't noticed, these are bona-fide Martians, just like in *Amazing Stories*. That ain't no Nazi plane." He waved at the shining silvery object burning several hundred yards away.

Staff ignored the speculation. Whatever this event was, the Army had given him specific orders to gather information; not to give it. He knew someone would be dispensing government funds to hush things up once the trucks, the soldiers, the debris, and any other evidence were on their way back to Sikeston Air Field.

"Hope you've got a strong stomach, Doc," the cop said, kneeling to remove the sheets.

Staff smiled, almost felt like crying at what he saw. He'd dreamed of something similar to this moment since he was a boy. He'd grown up not far from Aurora, Texas, and had been fascinated by the tale of the reported Martian Crash of 1897. He'd even run away from home when he was ten, hopped a train, and hitchhiked to get to the town. Though he hadn't found any evidence of the storied encounter or the alleged grave of the alien pilot, it had still been worth the whipping he'd gotten upon his return home. It had been his first adventure into the unknown, just like those pulp stories he loved so much. And now, almost three decades later, the government was funding a brand-new installment.

"You okay, Doc?" the deputy asked with an odd look. "Because I can't for the life of me think of a reason to smile at something like this."

"I'm sure you can't," Staff said, taking a pen and pad from his pocket. "Now, if you'll see that these remains are loaded onto that Army truck over there, I'll need to get your names and statements."

"What?"

"The United States Army is now in charge of this site, officer. And we'll require a sworn statement from everyone here, as well as the confiscation of any and all photographs. I noticed a few camera flashes from the yokels on my way in. Now, if you don't mind…"

§

"Penny for your thoughts, Pete," Captain Edward Miller said. They sat in the back of one of the trucks headed back to Sikeston, with the other ten men assigned to this case. All of them were military officers with scientific specialties ranging from astronomy to zoology.

Staff smiled at his best friend. They'd known each other for years; had attended Baylor at the same time. Ed majored in engineering while Staff doubled in engineering and pre-med. They had bonded over their shared love of aviation; both getting their civilian pilots' licenses before Staff had gone on to Johns Hopkins for his MD. "Can't say my thoughts are worth a penny right now, Ed."

"You had a look at the...crew yet?"

"Yep. Not a pretty sight, I'll say that. But the degree of injury and burns made it difficult to make a definitive call in the field. Won't know anything conclusive until we can get them under the knife..." Staff shook his head. "I just wonder how much the Army had to pay those folks to buy their silence."

"Probably not much. Farmers round here are still hurting from the Depression pretty bad. A little goes a long way these days."

"I guess that New Deal hasn't reached everybody just yet," Staff said. "What about you? Had a look at the hardware?"

"What's left of it. Whatever wasn't junked in the crash was all but toasted by the fire. Then the locals hosed it down pretty good, so there's quite a bit of water damage, as well."

"Well, if it's not a Nazi spy plane and some of the smallest fascists the world has ever known, I can't imagine a little fire and water could completely erase evidence of whatever's out *there*." Staff waved at the truck's canopy.

Commander Bill Hennessey, a Navy linguistics expert and code-breaker, grunted. "You ask me, we got enough problems on this world without looking for more *out there*. You heard Hitler signed a deal with the Japanese, right? While his goose-steppers are marching all over Europe and Africa, Tojo's guys are carving up Asia.

"How long you think it'll be before one or the other of 'em decide to come for us? But instead of getting ready to crack some skulls, we're chasing little green men around in the middle of nowhere."

"All very valid points, Bill," Ed said with a grin. "But my money's still on this being some kind of a hoax. Probably circus performers in costumes and a rigged-up barnstormer."

Staff chuckled. "You're probably right, Ed. And once we prove it, we can get back to preparing 'to crack some skulls.'"

But he had seen those bodies, and his gut told him they weren't dwarfs in Halloween get-ups.

§

His gut was right. Beneath the harsh glow of half a dozen lamps and the watchful eyes of two movie cameras, Staff sweated through his surgical gown and dictated his process for the reel-to-reel recorder. Of the three subjects, only one was suitable for autopsy; the one claimed to have been alive when the first witnesses had arrived at the scene. That's why the minister had been there—to administer last rites.

The first thing Staff noticed was that the subject was considerably greener than when he'd first seen it only a few hours before. At the site, it had been a greenish-grey, almost pearlescent. Now, it looked like it was made of green-dyed India rubber. At least the undamaged parts of the skin did. The wounds appeared to be a soupy mess of black ash and gelatin, as though some accelerated healing or scabbing action had been suddenly arrested.

Those big, unblinking black eyes were just as wide and shiny as before. In better lighting, he could see that they were multi-faceted like those of insects, but the individual lenses were so tiny he couldn't tell if they were hexagons, octagons, or decagons. He'd have to look at a sample under the microscope.

"The reproductive organs appear to be sheathed, similar to those of a dolphin or porpoise," Dr. Wagner said. The Army zoologist was assisting in the post-mortem, which only made sense as Staff was an expert in the anatomy of one species; Wagner was schooled in many. "That fact and the quality of the skin makes me think it might be aquatic."

"Perhaps, but the nostrils, while not pronounced, are located on the anterior of the skull, and the skeletal structure resembles our own." In fact, the situation of limbs and joints, and even the number of fingers and toes were identical to a human's. The only difference was a matter of scale. The body seemed to be roughly half the size of an adult human, while the head was almost half again the size of same.

And yet the muscular structure of the neck and shoulders did not seem augmented to deal with the disparity of weight. If anything, the entire musculature system actually appeared underdeveloped. "Perhaps a different gravitational system," Staff muttered. "That might account for the crash…"

"What?" Wagner asked.

"Nothing. Let's make the Y-incision and take a look at what's inside." He picked up the scalpel.

Nazi… Spy…

Staff looked at Wagner. "What did you say?"

The zoologist raised an eyebrow above his surgical mask. "I didn't say anything. I thought you muttered something. Might want to speak up." He nodded at the microphone hanging above the table. "This is for posterity, you know."

Staff shook his head and made the first cut. Green blood oozed from the incision.

The lights in the room flared bright, almost blinding.

Nazi… spy… looking at… case…

The bloody scalpel fell from Staff's hand. He staggered back a step. A searing white light hit him, but from behind the eyes.

"Are you all right, Pete?" Wagner said before covering his face. "Ah! That smells like ammonia… We'd better get some gas masks if we're going to finish this. And some better electrical equipment."

§

Staff sat alone in his assigned room, smoking a Lucky Strike and wondering exactly what had happened during the autopsy. As soon as he and Wagner had stepped out of the lab, they'd been met by MPs with orders to confine them to quarters until further notice. He'd seen two men in dark suits, darker glasses, and hats enter the surgery as they left. They had carried large leather valises, no doubt to gather up the film and the audio recordings. Probably the test tubes filled with tissue and fluid samples as well.

There was a knock at the door just before an MP entered, followed by General Alexander Morgan. Staff stood to attention and saluted the head of the Army Air Corps Science and Research Division.

"As you were, Major," the older man said. Morgan had been a fighter ace in The Great War, and had come home to rack up three PhDs while climbing the brass ladder during the ensuing years of peace. He was the reason there was an SRD. Turning to the guard, he said, "Wait outside."

When they were alone, the general sat at the small desk, motioned for Staff to take a seat on his bunk. "So, what do you think, Major?"

"I think that this is an actual alien event, sir. Without any information on the craft, itself, I can't say that these beings come from somewhere other than Earth, but I can say that they are an as-yet unidentified species of sentient life. The brain alone—"

Morgan raised a hand. "Easy there, Staff. I know about your… obsession with this sort of thing. In fact, that's one of the reasons you were recruited. In addition to your academic prowess in both medicine and mechanics, I thought this program could use someone who thinks outside the box. I'll admit, I never really put much stock in the whole H.G. Wells idea of beings from another world, but I guess it's a good thing you do."

"Thank you, sir."

"So tell me about the post-mortem."

Staff cleared his throat. He knew that Morgan would have already seen the film, heard the tapes. Maybe even spoken to Wagner. So why would he ask Staff about what he already knew. "Did the tapes pick anything up, sir?"

Morgan pulled a pipe from inside his dress uniform and carefully loaded it. Without looking up from the process, he asked, "Like what, exactly, Major?"

Staff licked his lips and ran a hand through his hair. "Like…the words, 'Nazi spy looking at case?'"

The general lit his pipe, took a long puff on it until the tobacco glowed almost cherry red. "And you didn't say that?"

"No, sir."

"Do you think Wagner did?"

"No, sir."

"Then who did, Major?"

Staff took a deep breath. "I think…I think the subject did. With its mind."

The two men sat in silence, letting the words hang in the smoky air.

"Any idea who it could have meant?" Morgan finally asked.

"Not a clue, sir."

Morgan stood and Staff did likewise. The general picked up his hat and turned for the door. "I've got to get back to Washington, Major. If you want this division to continue as a military entity, I suggest you find out if one of your people really is playing for the other team."

"You mean I'm now in charge of this operation, sir?"

Morgan paused in the doorway. "You've got the rank, Major. And you've got my trust. Now find me that spy, and try to do it quietly. No need to involve the locals."

"Understood, sir."

§

Staff looked at the schematics spread out on Ed's desk in the heavily-guarded hangar, where they were trying to reconstruct the craft. He was having a hard time reconciling his friend's sketches with the lump of twisted and scorched metal occupying the center of the cavernous building. Ed imagined that the silver, disc-like thing had once possessed wings on each side, and a pair of dorsal stabilizers running across the top like twin shark fins.

"What do you think?" Ed asked, lighting a Chesterfield as he stepped to the desk.

"I think you've been watching too many Buster Crabbe serials," Staff said. It came off as short and irritable. "Sorry. Just on edge since Morgan put me in charge of this mess." He hadn't told anyone else about the spy hunt. Not even his best friend.

Ed laughed. "No problem, *Major*. Got to admit I wouldn't want to be in your shoes right now. I got my hands full trying to corral a bunch of enlisted grease monkeys into reverse-engineering a bona fide rocket ship. Can't imagine how many plates you've got spinning at the moment."

"Too damn many," Staff said, lighting a cigarette of his own. He didn't add that one of those plates—the most important one—had a big fat swastika painted on it, and he had to find it before it sent them all crashing to the floor.

"You gonna tell me about the autopsy? I know I woulda lost that bet about the midgets in the biplane, so what's the scoop? Anything you learned might make my job a little easier. I mean, if I understood how they looked and moved, I could understand how they might build their machines."

Staff smiled. "Sorry. That's classified. All I can tell you is that they had hands and feet, and all the rest pretty much like us. Only smaller." Although to be fair, Ed had a point. If an alien species had some kind of mental telepathy, wouldn't they incorporate that into their technology? Machines that ran on mental commands, rather than knobs, pedals, and levers?

"What're you thinking, Pete? I can see the gears turning behind those horn-rims of yours."

Staff shook his head and tossed the butt to the ground. "I'm thinking, I need to get over and see what Flannigan, our resident chemist, has come up with. He's been studying the crew's flight suits." As he headed out of the bay, Staff turned and called to his friend, "And you let me know as soon as you find a Flash-Gordon Death Ray on that thing, huh?"

§

That night, Staff stood in his room, smoking too much and staring at a bulletin board he'd covered in photos and personnel files from his team. Eleven scientists from both branches of the service; all with different backgrounds, specialties, and personalities. One of them was loyal to that madman in Berlin, and it was up to Staff to find out who the traitor was.

Lt. Banks of the Navy was a mousy, little astrophysicist; the quintessential absent-minded professor. If he wasn't a certified genius, he'd have been busted out of the military a long time ago for uniform infractions alone. His mother was Austrian.

Commander Hennessey, the Navy linguist and codebreaker, was loud and outspoken; critical of everyone and everything. But he knew his business, which had not come into play at all on this case as they had absolutely no samples of the aliens' language or communications.

But that didn't stop the man from being at everyone else's workstation at least once a day, telling them how they could better do their jobs.

Captain Wagner, the Army zoologist, was a disciple of Frank Buck of *Bring 'Em Back Alive* fame. And like his idol, he seemed wholly without political interests. In addition to sharing a surname with Hitler's favorite composer, he had traveled the world extensively both before joining the Army and after. Plenty of opportunity to come into contact with Nazi agents in the dark corners of the map.

Lt. Commander Flannigan, the Navy chemist, was Irish-born with a German wife. Her brother was a known member of the Bund, but had subsequently fled to Mexico when his peacetime draft number had come up. This had almost kept Flannigan out of the program; had almost gotten him booted from the Navy, altogether. But General Morgan had vouched for him after Flannigan had promised to shoot his brother-in-law in the face if he ever saw him again.

Captain Bauer, the Army archaeologist, was of German descent and had crossed paths with members of Himmler's Ahnenerbe several times in the past five years. Rumors claimed he had punched or shot his way out of most of those encounters, but still...

Of the six remaining members of the team, there was a Navy astronomer and an Army geologist who had family relations who were either of German descent or German nationals.

And then there was Captain Ed Miller.

Staff was surprised when he looked over the file. He learned that Ed's surname had originally been Müller, changed by his father back in 1916. Ed's family had been some of the first German immigrants into Texas, but had left their ancestral home during the Great War, moving from town to town five times between 1914 and 1918.

Staff knew this was the easiest connection to disprove, and so decided to start there. He'd clear Ed of any suspicion, and then the two of them could work the case together, bringing in the rest of the team as they were vetted.

He crushed out his last Lucky Strike, grabbed his hat and headed for the door. He glanced at his belted sidearm resting on the footlocker. Decided he wouldn't need it.

Opening the door, he didn't notice the envelope which had been slid under it sometime during his ruminations. Primarily because of Captain Wagner's pistol crashing down on the bridge of his nose, shattering his glasses, and toppling him to the floor.

"Don't move, you Nazi bastard," the zoologist said, a watery blur in Staff's vision.

"Wagner? What the hell are you doing?" Staff sputtered through the blood streaming into his mouth from his broken nose. "What are you talking about? *I'm* trying to find the spy!"

Wagner waved the pistol at the bulletin board. "That why you're going over our personnel files? More likely you're putting together a report to send to your buddy Adolf." He raised his voice and touched his chest with the muzzle of the weapon. "I know! I heard that…thing in my head. It said there was a Nazi spy looking at this case!"

Staff cleared his vision, was just about to try and reason with the excited scientist, when an explosion outside shook the room's windows and bathed them in a bright yellow light.

When Wagner glanced in that direction, Staff swept the man's feet out from under him, pounced on him, and punched him three times until he was unconscious. Climbing to his feet, he sprinted from the room. "That came from the direction of the hangar where Ed was rebuilding the craft!"

By the time he reached the exterior of the dormitories, he could see that it was too late. The entire hangar was consumed in towering flames. Soldiers were gathering on the periphery while the emergency teams scrambled into action. Staff turned and looked, but he did not see a single member of his team among the swelling crowd.

§

Five days later, Staff and Wagner sat in General Morgan's office in Washington. Both wore their dress uniforms. Staff also wore new spectacles and a bandage across his nose—for which the battered Wagner had profusely apologized many times in the days following the tragedy at Sikeston Field. They were the only two surviving members of the team sent to investigate the crash.

"As you were, gentlemen," Morgan said as he hurried into the office and settled behind his big mahogany desk. "Let's get down to business, shall we? I presume you've got your reports in order?"

"Yes, sir," Staff said. "After a thorough investigation, we have determined that there was, in fact, no Nazi spy—or any foreign espionage agent—present during our investigation of the Cape Girardeau Incident." He opened the folder in his lap and produced two letters; one which had been slid under his door, and one which had been slid under Wagner's.

As Morgan scanned the handwritten documents, Staff summarized. "They're both from Ed—Captain Edward Miller. The one addressed to Captain Wagner is an invitation to come to the hangar in order to share a remarkable technological discovery. The letter to me describes Captain Miller's plan to lure the Nazi spy to the hangar via his invitations to all the members of the team. Miller believed that the spy would be the first to arrive, and he would be able to apprehend him.

"It goes on to describe an explosive he had rigged to the craft as a last-ditch measure to keep any intelligence from reaching Berlin."

Morgan dropped the two letters to the desk and folded his hands. "Continue."

Staff looked at Wagner, who nodded; content to let him be the spokesperson for their findings. "We believe that the other members of the team thought Miller was the spy, and all went to the hangar with the intent of apprehending him. When confronted by such odds, with all concerned suffering from a sort of paranoia, we think that Miller enacted his fail-safe plan. Killing himself and the rest of the team in the process."

"And destroying the lion's share of evidence," the general said, swiveling his chair to glance at the sunrise. "But why, in the wake of this…catastrophe, Major, do you insist that there was no spy? You two heard something. Apparently, the rest of the team did as well. The audio recordings even picked it up."

"Which is why I thought Major Staff was the spy, sir," Wagner volunteered. "Following the autopsy, he was acting very secretive and asking a lot of questions. I thought Captain Miller's letter was a trap, and so went my own way."

Staff licked his lips. "I have a theory, sir."

Morgan spread his hands. "I'm all ears, Major."

"When we arrived on the scene of the crash, the subject chosen for autopsy had apparently just…passed. However, it is entirely possible that it was merely slipping into a dormant phase similar to a coma. In that case, it may have still been receiving sensory stimuli."

"Yes?"

"I have gone over every detail of this encounter a hundred times, sir. I distinctly recall the two ambulance drivers using the words, *Nazi, spy, looking, at,* and *case*—in that order, while standing above the subject. I believe that those words filtered into the subject's mind, and the trauma of the premature post-mortem caused it to utter a telepathic cry. Just as a delirious person might repeat the last words they heard in a moment of crisis. I believe that the team's proximity to the alien technology might have somehow made us more susceptible to receiving that cry."

Morgan scowled and drummed his fingers on the desk. "So we've been chasing our tails, lost a lot of good men, and the opportunity to study advanced technology all because of a…what? A Martian's insane deathbed rambling?"

Staff grimaced, thinking of his best friend. "Yes, sir. That is what we believe."

After a long silence, General Morgan took a deep breath. "Well, it is clear to me and to the higher-ups that we definitely have a lot to learn about these things. Which is why we've decided to sanction a permanent team, and give it a higher level of autonomy." He opened a drawer and took out a pair of small boxes before stepping around the desk.

Staff and Wagner rose.

"Gentlemen," Morgan said as he opened the boxes, revealing new oak leaves; silver for Staff and brass for Wagner. Handing them their new rank insignia and shaking their hands, he said, "Congratulations on your promotions to lieutenant colonel and major, respectively. You two will be heading up the top-secret department now designated as Code Name: Majestic.

"First order of business is to recruit a new team. And then get out there and find me some more Martian rocket ships. I have a feeling we'll be needing all the advanced technology we can get our hands on very, very soon."

"Yes, sir."

Intrusion

Gordon Grice

*D**ear Sir:*

Per your request, I write to tell you what I know of the discoveries in Chaves County in the fall of 1952 and the following spring. I do not wish to be quoted in connection with these matters, for reasons relating to my professional credibility. I myself have considered writing a paper of the sort you propose, but have decided not to do so because my early inquiries led me to suspect I would be exposing myself to derision. I have in fact kept silent about the entire business, and am only providing you this informal account because your letter makes plain that you have got hold of some preposterously inaccurate information. Let me therefore try to tell the entire thing chronologically and, I hope, plainly.

The incidents began in September, with the sheriff's office receiving several complaints about burglary. The items taken were in all cases different, and no pattern emerged. I cannot detail these for you, since I have no connection with law enforcement; indeed, my original involvement came about only as a favor to Sheriff Drake, who needed the advice of a scientific man and had known my family. I do seem to recall that the missing items included an anvil taken from one farm and a complete set of China from another. Other incidents included the defacing—I might even say defiling—of a car interior, and a peeping Tom report. I should emphasize that my information as to this part of the narrative comes only from Sheriff Drake, who has since died, and that there was, even at the time, only the most tenuous suspicion of any connection to the later events.

The principle incidents which have occasioned your inquiry occurred on the morning of October 10 at the Houck farm. The Houcks were known to me, though only on a casual basis. The man had some sort of literary ambitions and had, as a consequence, scaled back his legal practice to allow him time at home for writing. They had lived on the farm only a few months, having bought it from Mr. Long, a prominent local man who provided no useful information when I questioned him afterward, though he rather illogically blamed the Mexican laborers from the next farm.

It was Houck's dream to live on a farm, and he had reached some sort of personal crisis, some determination to "fulfill himself," as more recent jargon would have it. It was this which caused him to alter his working life, buy the farm, and move his wife and son there. His wife, I gathered, did not prefer this bucolic arrangement, but had eventually agreed to go along with it. This is my impression from talking to others afterward; on the actual day of the incidents, she stated categorically that she never wanted to live on the farm, that something seemed wrong with it from the first, that it was entirely too far from town, and that other incidents reported by their rural neighbors had terrified her before any of this ever happened. These statements seemed to be influenced by the stress of the moment, and are perhaps best viewed as exaggerations.

The weather that Tuesday morning was cool. Despite the early date, snow had fallen the week before, and some of it still lay on the ground in ridges among the shadows. Houck was home, but he had shut himself up in a room he used for an office. His wife was canning. Their tomatoes had done well, and she had harvested what was left of them ahead of the frost. After a week on flats under the beds, the tomatoes had ripened, and something must be done. I am being particular about all this because you asked about climatic conditions, and these bits of information, which Mrs. Houck eventually thought fit to share with me, are the best I can do at this remove in time. You will appreciate, I'm sure, that I had no idea I would eventually want to know such particulars as temperature, solar activity, and the like. In fact, I am not sure now that these matters have any bearing, but I endeavor to provide what you have asked.

Having sent her six-year-old son outside to play, Mrs. Houck set to work blanching the tomatoes. As they came out of the hot water, she arrayed them in glistening rows on newspaper. She had cored and peeled about half of them when she paused to search out a better pair of tongs in the utility room.

As she came back into the kitchen, Mrs. Houck saw someone standing behind the table. The room was slightly steamy, but she knew instantly, before she had more than a hint of this person in her peripheral vision, that something was terribly wrong. She turned to look at the person full on, saying as she did so, "What are you doing here?"

It may be well to say a word about the customs of the country at the time. It would not have been considered especially ill-mannered if, on receiving no answer to a knock, one were to walk a step or two into a house and shout. The fact that Mrs. Houck, who was well mannered and, if anything, rather meek, immediately resorted to a challenge signifies her instant, and perhaps instinctive, discomfort in the presence of this individual. But this, of course, is my own interpretation.

This first impression, and her demand, took only a second, and by now Mrs. Houck was facing the intruder. She claims that at this point she nearly fainted, and in fact did fall, only to be jarred into full awareness as soon as she struck the linoleum floor. Even though she was sure she had not actually lost consciousness for more than a second, she afterward told me more than once that she was worried about what might have happened while she lay insensible in the presence of the stranger. I was never able to sort out these apparently contradictory statements.

What you have heard about the appearance of this stranger is not accurate. He was, she said, "extremely heavy-set." His clothes were khaki, as were the work clothes worn by many men at that time, but his seemed loose and ill-fitting. Her next impression was that he was extremely dirty, nauseatingly so. On a closer look, it seemed as if the dirtiness of his appearance was actually to be explained by a peculiar texture of his skin. She had not, on first glance, noticed that he was doing anything, but now she realized he was eating one of the tomatoes she had peeled, gnawing at it messily and rather ineffectually; from this she deduced that he had no teeth, or at least none in the front. Though he was facing her, he did not seem actually to be looking at her, until she screamed. At this point his eyes seemed to shift and, with great effort, to focus on her. She had the impression he was a man who normally wore glasses and now, being without them, could not properly manage his eyes. He neither moved toward her nor said anything, nor indeed did he at that point react in any of the obvious ways. After she had screamed a second time, he stuck out his tongue, which she perceived as abnormally long. She felt that he was trying to imitate her scream, but couldn't make any sound. He could only manage to open his mouth into a sort of yawning posture and whip his tongue around ineffectually. The tomato he was eating fell out of his mouth and onto the floor. What followed seemed to be a spell of silent vomiting, perhaps even a seizure.

She then bolted from the room. Halfway through the living room, which was adjacent, she collided with her husband, who had heard her screams. She blurted a few words of explanation. He went into the kitchen and found no one. He told her she must have experienced some sort of hallucination, perhaps a symptom of her faint, which she had by this time told him about. She countered by pointing out the mess on the floor. An unpleasant odor like burned rubber rose from this substance.

Before the discussion could go further, she screamed "Kerrick!" She was suddenly seized with the idea that the boy was alone and might be harmed by the intruder. He might have gone in any of a dozen directions to play, and they might not find him before the intruder did. Both parents rushed to the kitchen window and, to their relief, saw the boy carving roads for his toy cars in the sand box twenty feet from the kitchen door.

As they looked, another figure entered their view. As Mr. Houck described it, it was the figure of a fat man, grossly corpulent, in fact, and his ill-fitting khaki clothes were buttoned off-kilter, as if he were too incompetent to dress himself. His walk was at the same time clumsy and stealthy, and he was moving directly toward the boy. "Stay here," Mr. Houck ordered, but both parents then rushed into the yard.

Mr. Houck demanded, in language it is unnecessary to repeat here, that the man stop. The man did not stop, and in fact appeared not to have heard Mr. Houck or even to be aware of his presence. As he lumbered forward, he intensified his gaze at the child, lowered his head between his shoulders, and raised his hands before his chest in an attitude Mr. Houck described as resembling that of a praying mantis. The boy, startled by his father's shouting, saw the stranger and began to scream. Mr. Houck interposed himself between the boy and the intruder, but, incredibly, the intruder continued to behave as if he were unaware of Mr. Houck's presence. You will doubtless notice how well this peculiar lack of sensory function comports with your own idea that the intruder had somehow taken on a form unfamiliar to it. He moved forward in a sort of crouch.

Mrs. Houck darted forward and snatched up her son and ran toward the house. The intruder altered his course to intercept them, still ignoring Mr. Houck. He continued to seem oblivious as Mr. Houck picked up a garden hoe and threatened him with it. Mr. Houck held the hoe like a baseball bat and promised to slash the intruder, but this too produced no effect. Mr. Houck found himself unable to follow through on his threat. He was deterred by a kind of disgust, or horror, at the corpulence of the intruder. The latter smacked his lips in a way that suggested a mental illness or disability, and this seemed an argument against harming him. At the same time, the intruder continued to advance toward Mrs. Houck and the boy. She had carried him to the door, but seemed unwilling to go back into the house, even in the face of this danger.

Mr. Houck took the only course he could think of: He jabbed the intruder with the handle of the hoe. It was at this point that the intruder finally took notice of Houck's existence. He opened his mouth in the sort of frozen yawn Mrs. Houck had seen earlier and looked at Houck as if he could not focus his eyes on him. By his own admission, Houck went into a frenzy, cursing at the intruder and belaboring him with the hoe handle. The intruder seized the handle and began to inch toward Houck, shifting his grip up the handle as he went. All the while his open mouth was pointed toward Houck, his tongue lashing around with moist noises and flinging saliva. His eyes still did not appear to see Houck; it was as if he could determine the location of his enemy only by feeling his way along the hoe handle. Houck became even more desperate and wrenched the hoe away from the intruder. He needed several attempts to manage this feat, for the grip of the intruder was strong. Now Houck struck him with the blade of the hoe.

The intruder received this blow with what seemed to Houck an expression of surprise. Houck said he must have chopped with the blade three or four times; Mrs. Houck said it was more like ten or twelve blows. In any event, both of them saw blood. Mr. Houck, who was of course closer, described this for me in detail—I might say gory detail. I will spare you the unscientific terms of his description. It will be useful to say, however, that this description established to my mind that Mr. Houck had seen a very great quantity of arterial blood, indicating serious wounds that one could expect to prove fatal. Also of possible interest, though frustratingly vague, is Mr. Houck's claim that the blood, though red, was not of precisely the expected color. I could not get Houck to be clear about this.

His injuries did not much alter the intruder's behavior. He tried repeatedly to seize the hoe. Mrs. Houck reported hearing a hissing noise, possibly that of stertorous breathing, but Mr. Houck claimed to have heard no such thing. Eventually the intruder did grasp the hoe, and this time Mr. Houck couldn't wrench it free. He abandoned the battle and ran toward his wife and son. He was furious that she had not already taken the boy inside and locked the door. As he tried to push her inside, she resisted, screaming something at him. But he succeeded in getting both wife and son inside and bolting the door. Then he finally heard what she had been trying to tell him: the intruder in the yard was not the same one she had seen in the kitchen.

Mr. and Mrs. Houck spent some time impressing upon me the state of confusion in which they found themselves. To Mrs. Houck, the most important thing seemed to be that all three of them stay together. To Mr. Houck, it seemed necessary first to determine whether the other intruder remained in the house. He had the impression that more than two intruders might exist, though he admitted that no firm evidence to this effect existed.

While the couple talked over their options—and that way of putting it probably gives the proceedings a greater clothing of reason than they in fact possessed—the boy, who was perched on the counter looking out the window, said something that threw them into even greater panic: "He's going around to the front door." Mr. Houck threw open the back door through which they had just entered, seized up the boy, and ran for his car, his wife beside him. They drove away without further incident. Both refused to return to the house, even in the company of Sheriff Drake. My impression is that they abandoned their belongings.

Late that afternoon, at Sheriff Drake's insistence, I visited the house.

We pulled into the graded dirt driveway. I saw nothing unusual. Once out of the pickup, we approached to within two yards of the sand box. It was at that point that the blood became visible, abundantly so. It lay in smears on the grass and up to hip level on an elm tree. The sand box was puddled with it to a surprising depth. I stuck a pencil into the puddle; it went in up to the eraser before it hit sand. The substance was certainly blood, as the boiled-eggs-and-liver smell of it proved, but even in this cool air none of it seemed to have clotted, and its red was so rich as to seem purple from an angle. "Good God," Sheriff Drake said. He hung back, running his hand along one side of his red mustache and then the other.

"We should take a sample of this," I said. "I didn't bring the proper gear—" —I hadn't because the sheriff had dragged me into the matter unprepared— "but perhaps we can scrounge some jars from Mrs. Houck's kitchen."

I actually thought giving the sheriff something to do might help steady him, but he replied with shocking hostility, "No samples!" I hardly knew how to answer.

I looked for footprints. They were easily found in the bloody soil. I saw plausible matches for each of the Houcks, and also the marks of two dogs—the thumb-sized tracks of a puppy and the wide, four-toed trapezoids of a bigger dog. It struck me as odd that no dogs had barked at us when we drove up. They were nowhere in sight. It was this absence, oddly enough, that made me suddenly feel afraid. Up to this point my curiosity had kept me from thinking much about danger.

I looked to the Sheriff. He, too, was looking at signs on the ground. He moved his lips like a poor reader sounding out words. I joined him there beside the tomato patch, where the half a dozen plants lay scattered and the earth seemed disturbed. I could make nothing of what I saw in the soil, no pattern at all, but it seemed to me Drake had. I knew he was an experienced hunter. I was on the verge of asking him what he saw, but I refrained—a moment of cowardice I've regretted ever since. "In any event, we can see what's to see in the kitchen," I said instead. I bustled in without waiting for him to approve.

Inside the kitchen we found the tomatoes arrayed on damp newspapers, the unmolested ones still firm, some of them even beaded with water, the skinned ones dull and losing their shapes. Brownish moths had gotten at them and were crawling in and out of the holes where Mrs. Houck had cored them. The same sort of moths crawled on the considerable quantity of red vomitus on the floor. Burning rubber, indeed, with perhaps a hint of rancid milk. I observed that several moths stood with their proboscides deep in this matter, and that these individuals were visibly gorged, their abdomens so tight as to appear translucent. They were reluctant to move, even when I prodded them with my bloody pencil.

Drake must have left to survey the other rooms while I was making these observations, for I suddenly heard his boots click on the linoleum as he re-entered. "No sign of the burglars," he said. "I thought they might come back when I cleared out before."

"One of them is surely dead, or close to it," I said. "That's a lot of blood out there." The kitchen was growing dim. In this lesser light, the substance on the floor began to seem much darker and heavier.

"They might come back at any minute," Drake said. He actually put one hand on the holster at his hip. We left, taking no samples. I felt grateful when the pickup growled to life. Somehow, I'd feared it wouldn't.

There is little more to tell. The months passed. I heard that looters had been at the Houck's farm, and then I heard that the sheriff had boarded it up. I asked a few questions when occasion arose; no one else seemed to have seen anything. The Houcks moved away. Their dogs were never seen again, or at least never reported.

The final piece of evidence, and the one which put rather a different spin on everything that came before it, occurred on March 10 of the following year. When Drake called me this time, I was somewhat more reluctant to participate, my advice having been so thoroughly ignored in the first place. Then Drake informed me I would not be examining a crime scene, but rather something of scientific interest, though he refused to prejudice my view by being specific. I believe I had the impression that a meteorite was involved, though obviously I was either mistaken or mislead in this.

What I observed, when I got out of Drake's pickup truck in a pasture eleven miles south of town, was an organism of considerable size, obviously long dead. In its gross aspect, this organism seemed nothing but a long silky patch of wind-blown hair, a billowing parachute of skin, and a foamy expanse of tissue revealed by a gash.

"Pretty much proves that was a hoax at the Houck place, don't you think?" Drake said, smoothing his mustache both ways. I suppose, to his untrained eye, the organism appeared fake.

I paced it off at something over ten feet; I was never allowed the opportunity for more precise measurement. The organism was roughly human in shape, being bilaterally symmetrical and possessing four limbs, each terminating in five digits. Its corpulence caused me some difficulty in viewing its face and genitalia, though both were present. In other ways its humanity appeared doubtful. In girth as well as length, it was out of all human bounds. I had no method for weighing it, but its mass must have far exceeded even the most pathologically obese human specimens. There was, moreover, some question in my mind as to whether this organism even belonged to the kingdom Animalia. Its skin showed the evidence of considerable postmortem exposure to weather, and had broken through at the abdomen. The substance within did not appear consistent with human viscera. It might conceivably have been fatty tissue, but I considered this conclusion unlikely for two reasons. First, fat is a high-energy tissue, and thus among the first to be taken by scavengers; even if not scavenged, it is highly susceptible to biochemical conversion. Second, the substance did not, when I poked my hand into it, feel like fatty tissue. It was creamy and interlaced with some sort of tough, fibrous material.

I'm aware that my description is too vague to be of scientific use. The reason for this is that, once I had pronounced the thing organic, I was abruptly ushered away from the scene, under threat of force.

"Get the hell out of here!" Drake said. "How do I know you didn't rig the whole thing up?"

So, I retreated—to Drake's own pickup. He had forgotten that I had come with him. During the ride back to town, he kept puffing angrily and tugging at his mustache.

Since I was never allowed to take samples or make a proper examination, I cannot speak to your suggestions about the origin of these phenomena. I returned some weeks later, only to find that the pasture had been cleared by a controlled burn.

Sincerely yours,

Wm. Gardner, PhD
Prof. Emeritus
Dept. of Biology
Eastern New Mexico University

A Different Path

Laura Kostur

G*inger's walk home got longer every day.*
"Never take the same path twice."
Her Mama's directive kept her safe, until it didn't.

It was easy at first to step to the left or right when all the straight lines had been used; hopscotch without the chalk, following, then avoiding, contraction points and the cracks where they'd failed. Then, when she'd walked every path, the road had to change.

"They're waiting for you to make a mistake. If they can't follow you, they can't see you, and you won't see them."

Mama liked Ginger to ask why and how. Questions were how you learned, even when the answers weren't clear.

Ginger never knew how she knew the sky people followed them. Her Mama knew, that was enough of a reason for her to teach Ginger how to walk. It was enough of a reason for her Mama to stay inside once she'd forgotten which paths she'd followed and which were new. Without the memory of her paths, going outside was too big of a risk. Ginger could still go outside, she had a good memory.

Side roads were the best. They had room to navigate new paths. You could cross and re-cross the road; impossible to predict. Then, a new road, a new path, and a longer walk. She didn't mind the long walks. She used them to collect information about the world to share with her Mama; sharing the world obscured by the silver foil sheets protecting their inside spaces.

Ginger did all the walking to and from. To and from school. To and from the shops where Mama had accounts she could pay by the phone. To and from all of the places that it was no longer safe for Mama to go.

Inside was safe. Mama worked hard to make it safe. She sculpted safety from hangers and bits of metal Ginger found on her walks; twisting and changing the lines to protect their inside places so the sky people couldn't find them and take them away. On the days her Mama couldn't work, they stayed in bed, careful not to draw too much attention.

Sometimes people asked questions about Mama, and Ginger gave them the answers her Mama had given to her in turn. Questions were how you learned, even when the answers weren't clear.

The night they came, Mama had been in bed all day. Ginger knew she should have stayed still and waited for Mama to fix the wires; twist in the washers she'd found in the alley behind the house with the loud, black dog. She knew when they came that it was because of her mistake. It was her fault, but the night was hot and she went out into the air. In the dark of the night it was harder to tell if a path was new or a shadow was a path you'd taken before, one they may notice you taking again. The wrong type of patterns were dangerous. It took Ginger years to realize the dark had been the problem.

They came in a van.

"You shouldn't be out here alone."

Her Mama had never said how they were following, just that they were.

"We'll take you home."

The van smelled like Mama's kitchen cleaner. The one you never mix with bleach.

"Stop crying, honey. Dammit, Jim, she's crying."

They didn't look different than other people. Ginger'd always thought sky people would look different, but when they watched TV Mama had always been quick to point out when sky people hid in plain sight. It was a lesson in how to be careful.

Ginger sat in the back seat of the car, her bottom providing insufficient cushion. The seat was hard but she liked the mesh between her and the sky people. It was like Mama's mesh.

"Is your Mother in there?"

The man pointed at their house as they approached. Ginger pressed her lips closed. Maybe Mama was still safe, if she was still in bed. The men knocked. No one answered. Ginger let herself hope they would leave her Mama alone. She let herself hope that her Mama's work would hide their safe place for one more day, even if the safe place was for Mama alone now.

"Who should we call?"

The men went to the neighbor's house. Ginger hoped they wouldn't take her, too. She gave out raisin cookies at Halloween, even when Ginger came to the back door instead of the front and even when she didn't wear a costume.

Another van came, met the first, and took Ginger away. They scrubbed her down and measured her, just like the TV said the sky people would. They poked her with needles and *tsked* and lisped words in a language that she couldn't follow.

If they got Mama, they must have brought her to another place.

Ginger didn't believe the words she could understand. The words that said she was safe, that Mama was being taken to another safe place to help her get better. Mama didn't need to get better, she needed to get away. She knew it was too late to worry, she'd taken a path twice, and they'd been found.

They didn't take Ginger home again. They took her to another place that was like a home with windows that were dangerously clear. Ginger wondered why no one was hiding, why no one there hung a mesh, until she realized that once the sky people had you there was no need to hide. There was food and television and a little room with a pink comforter in full bloom with poppies and purple anemones.

"You don't have to talk to me. It's okay."

The woman who made the bed up and stirred the oatmeal insisted that everything would be fine. She was one of them, Ginger could tell by her eyes, they didn't flash with life like Mama's. The woman was wrong in so many ways. She wasn't a thing like Mama. She went out every day, and she sang with the radio. Ginger remembered the day her Mama had thrown the radio into the yard.

"It has metal in all the wrong patterns! They'll know us by it!"

Her Mama had let her collect the bits of metal from the yard later to add to their mesh protection but no more radios were allowed in the house after that.

The woman was nice. She didn't care if Ginger wanted to be quiet. The nice almost won out over her own careful nature, but the woman's strange behavior reinforced that this place was wrong and stopped Ginger from making a second mistake.

I will stay quiet.

She watched the woman, and watched the world move by, waiting for the chance to run away, to get back to somewhere that was real safe, not like this place of pretend.

There were new shoes for her feet. She kept the shoebox under the bed in the little room with the pink comforter; her room until she could get away. Into the box went the scraps of foil discarded from the woman's kitchen. Into the box went a screw worried from the wooden desk in the corner of Ginger's pink room.

The woman learned to trust Ginger in measures through her silence.

Could she could go in the backyard and pick a zucchini for the salad? Into the shoebox went a clip that had once supported climbing beans.

Could she run next door with a note to borrow milk? Into the shoebox went a copper butterfly the wind used to push in circles.

It was time to start going to school again. Into the shoebox went the plastic wrapped coil from an old phone in the classroom closet. Ginger's Mama had taught her how to find metal to keep them safe. Bits of metal were everywhere, if you knew where to look.

It took Ginger three years to collect enough metal to be ready to run. It took those same three years to plan an escape. And on the day she felt ready, she finally spoke.

"I'm going to the park."

The woman stammered an approval and was on her phone calling another sky person with words like *breakthrough* and *appointment* before the door closed behind Ginger and the shoebox in her backpack.

On the way out, Ginger walked slowly, tracing her steps along a path she'd left carefully unused in all her years at this house with these sky people. They would not be able to follow.

Only move when you're sure it's safe.

Ginger stepped into the world with a plan, carrying a bit of her safety with her in the shoebox. It was time for her to find Mama and build a new safe place.

The walk back home took longer than she'd planned. She had to stop in yards twice for the night. She set up her own little mesh each night before curling up under a table or in a shed, draped in the safety of wires strung in a pattern to hide her from the sky people.

The two nights were wasted time. She arrived at her home and her Mama wasn't there; everything was gone, different. The windows were clear of foil, covered instead with a layer of filmy fabric that showed different furniture and a different family. She'd hoped the sky people were lying when they said they took Mama to the hospital. She'd hoped they were just trying to get her to tell them some of her secrets.

She spent that night in the neighbor's yard in the company of ceramic gnomes that guarded the carrots she pulled up and ate, dirt and all. The next part of her plan would be harder.

It was three buses to the hospital. Three chances to be seen and three chances that couldn't be avoided. Mama had taken Ginger there once when she was little and broke her arm on some toy with wheels. Ginger remembered the cast, and the long talk on the bus explaining what she could and couldn't say at the hospital to make sure they could get out of there quickly before any sky people thought to pay attention. It was a long way to the hospital, too far to walk.

Ginger knew the front door wasn't an option, there were too many people who wanted to be helpful and ask the wrong questions, so she waited, almost until dark until a side door burped open and she could slide in behind two men in a hurry to smoke or drive or just leave. She walked with purpose.

"Look like you know where you're going and people won't bother trying to help you." Her Mama's words guided Ginger, reminding her not to draw attention.

Her Mama was behind three more doors. Two that opened when she walked near and one that only opened when a nurse buzzed, but it was visiting time and no one asked who she was when she swept in behind a couple looking sheepish to be let into the ward. They said a name and Ginger waited. When the nurse went to find the couple's son Ginger walked the other way, peeking her head into door after door until she found her Mama, prone and small on a single bed thrust up against a wall and bolted in place.

Ginger knew at once that they sky people had drugged her Mama. She wasn't asleep but there was nothing awake about her face. She stared into the corner watching an old stain on the wall.

Ginger closed the door behind herself and moved to her Mama's side, shaking her, not daring to use words that could be overheard in this place. She didn't respond. Ginger pulled at her arm, trying to force her Mama to stand.

Her Mama looked at her for a moment, then rolled her head back to stare at the stain.

A tear ran down Ginger's cheek and she rubbed it away in frustration. There was no time for weakness. Mama had worked hard to protect her and now it was Ginger's turn.

She pulled the shoebox from her backpack and began to build a mesh around her Mama's head. There wasn't enough metal to cover her whole body, just the head. It would have to do. She wasn't strong enough to try any of the other ideas her Mama's training suggested might break the sky people's control. She couldn't hurt her own mother.

Ginger twisted wire and bits of metal into a cage for her Mama's head, leaving it ornamented with girlish bracelets discarded, she was told, by other girls who'd lived in the little room with the pink bedspread. Ginger looked up from her work as the sound of footsteps approached.

"Why is that door closed?"

Ginger's hands shook as she guided the last line of wire around her Mama's neck sealing her inside its protection. The door opened and Ginger dove into the bathroom, pulling her backpack, the only other evidence of her presence, in behind her.

"What the hell?"

The voice belonged to a nurse, dressed in violet scrubs head-to-toe. Ginger wondered for a moment if the woman wore violet every day or if she had a personal rainbow at home in a closet somewhere.

The nurse rushed to the bed and fluttered her hands over the mesh sculpture. Ginger flushed with pride at the woman's confusion as she examined her work and her Mama's head. Ginger willed the nurse to go away and let her work take effect. She knew her Mama would need longer than this to throw off whatever the sky people had done to take away her personality and make her lie there staring at the stain.

"Ruth, get help."

The bed creaked as the nurse set her weight on it, leaning in to examine Ginger's work.

It would take time to get it off. I've done a good job. Ginger congratulated herself on the years of preparation she'd made and the years of listening to her Mama that had made it all possible.

More footsteps, running now. The PA system announced a code Red.

"Dr. Galliger, to room 214."

Two nurses blew into the room and Ginger held her breath trying to stay hidden and hoping her pounding heart wouldn't give her position away. She knew her Mama needed longer; she could tell by her eyes still empty and staring at the stain.

"Can you get it off?"

"I think we'll need tools."

"Who the hell—"

"Do you think her daughter?"

"Poor kid just went missing."

"Why would anyone—"

Ginger smiled again at their confusion. They didn't know about the mesh. They didn't know she was there. They were leaving it on her Mama. Every moment they were confused was one more moment Mama had to recover. A man followed the nurses into Mama's room.

"What are you all just standing there for?"

"Dr. Galliger, we—"

"Can't do anything right? Get out of here, I'll handle this."

The nurses filed out of the room. Dr. Galliger closed the door.

"Let's get that thing off, shall we?"

Ginger felt and then saw her Mama come awake on the bed in the corner and then heard the voice she'd missed for three years.

"Ginger."

"Your daughter's not here. I'm going to help you."

Her Mama began to thrash and Ginger dragged a deep breath in, covering the noise with her Mama's movements.

"No, Ginger!"

Her Mama was fighting now, pushing the doctor away.

"I won't let you do this to me anymore."

The doctor stopped talking. He tilted his head to look deeply into Mama's eyes, straight through the mesh. He stopped looking like a doctor.

"You think you have a choice?"

The doctor grabbed a section of the protective mesh in his fist and lifted the fighting woman's head from the bed then let it fall back.

"You think this will do you any good?"

Ginger watched her Mama's eyes clear and knew the moment when her Mama saw her hiding in the bathroom. She knew when her Mama's words started to be for her and not for the sky person doctor.

"Ginger, my girl."

"Gone. I told them not to tell you, but she's gone and she's not likely to come back to you, is she? Why would she after what you put her through?"

What Mama had put her through?

Ginger fought back the urge to argue, strengthened by years of practice at silence.

The doctor yanked at the edges of the mesh over her Mama's head.

"I don't matter anymore."

Ginger's Mama fought Dr. Galliger's hands, clinging to the mesh.

"I taught my Ginger."

Ginger locked eyes with her Mama, feeling her mother's knowledge that the mesh was her daughter's gift; that she hadn't abandoned her.

The doctor's frustration at the resistance won the day, and he used the emotional strength to yank at the mesh again, tearing the skin on Mama's neck. Red bubbled from her throat where the wires cut deeply. The doctor grunted in his own pain and Ginger watched a new fluid drip down onto her Mama's face, green and thick. She tore her eyes away from her Mama's wound to watch the doctor cradle his damaged hand; ripped by the same wire that cut her Mama's throat. Deep green blood flowed from his wound.

"Krull! You trouble making beast, this is going to take forever to explain."

"We will all make trouble." Ginger's mother was fully aware now, staring down the sky person in front of her. Before the day they had come for Ginger, she'd never seen one in person, only seen the online reports; little bits of truth on message boards flooded by crackpots trying to warn the world about the wrong invasion, the wrong conspiracy.

The doctor wrapped his hand and swabbed the green blood, doing nothing to stop the flow of blood from the defiant woman's neck.

"I'm done with you."

The sky person doctor shoved his hand in his pocket and walked out the door.

Ginger darted out of the bathroom and pressed her hands to her mother's neck.

"Mama we have to go."

Her mother's hands came up to the mesh then to her daughter's temples.

"It's too late."

The words bubbled from her lips with true red blood.

Tears streaked down Ginger's face.

"Mama, we have to go."

Ginger watched the light dimming in her mother's eyes.

"Do you remember everything I taught you?"

The question was a challenge.

"Never take the same path twice."

Ginger's reply was an epitaph.

Flyover World

Jarod Anderson and Evan Dicken

*R*ay *was plucking chickens and thinking of Cheryl when* the saucer flew overhead. He just stood there, covered in blood, sweat, and bird feathers, squinting up at the thing while pinfeathers swirled around him like falling snow.

On TV, flying saucers always stopped and started beaming stuff up, but this one came on like an eastbound flight, whipping by in a flash of unrolled tinfoil, blue and white lil lights bright as the neons outside the Variety Lounge. There was a puff of silence, the saucer's booming chatter trailing behind it like a kid brother.

Ray wouldn't have even looked up except the thing damn near took the top off the feed silo. He thought about popping off a warning shot—the flare gun from last Fourth of July was probably still in the barn somewhere. Instead, Ray just pulled his ball cap down low and pressed his lips together. Last time, the saucer caught him with his mouth hanging open and he'd been picking grit out of his teeth for the rest of the day. When the last of the dust and feathers settled, Ray glanced at the clock on the barn wall.

5:04 pm.

Just like yesterday, and the day before that.

The saucer had come crosswise to Route 70, and Ray's farm was a good half-hour from town. Still, he'd talked it up enough yesterday that if any of them idiots stopped laughing long enough to look up,

Ray might be drinking for free tonight. He considered tossing the last of the chickens into the freezer and driving to the Variety Lounge, but thought better of it. Any regulars thirsty enough to sidle in soon as the sign flipped weren't liable to make for a good audience. Besides, Cheryl's shift didn't start until eight.

Above, a 747 spun silken contrails across the sky, the distant roar familiar to Ray as the whisper of breeze through a cornfield. He wondered if anyone in the plane had seen the saucer. Probably not. With a snort, he tossed another headless chicken into the pot of water boiling on the camp stove.

Ain't nobody ever looked down over New Mexico.

§

A blast of warm, sweaty air washed over Ray as he pushed into the Variety Lounge and squelched across a floor sticky from rivers of spilled beer. Familiar shadows looked up from where they hunched in booths and on bar stools. Ray's name flashed like minnows in the murky babble of conversation and Sugarland singles, but he pretended not to hear.

Cheryl had her back to him, but he caught her eye as she glanced into the cloudy mirror behind the ranks of liquor bottles. Ray nodded, trying his damnedest not to let his gaze creep down to where her Pearl Jam T-shirt had slipped to reveal the light dusting of freckles on her shoulder. A few strands of graying auburn hair had pulled free of her ponytail to hang across her forehead. The hazy reflection smoothed the spreading hardpan of wrinkles around her eyes and mouth so that, for a moment, Cheryl looked just like she had back in high school.

Air hissed through cracks in the bar stool's vinyl-covered cushion as Ray settled into his customary place by the cooler. Cheryl hammered the cap off a Bud Light and slid it over. He started to fish a crumpled bill out of his pocket but she held up a hand.

"On the house."

That was new.

Ray opened his mouth, but Cheryl turned and marched toward the other end of the bar. Chuck Gonzalez was banging his upside-down glass on the bar with one hand and playing a video game with the other, poking the greasy screen to highlight inconsistencies between two almost identical pictures of a topless woman on a dirt bike. Ray had heard that Chuck managed to get on disability after he fell during a roofing job. Ray didn't know what disability paid, but Chuck always had the time and money for Old Thompson Whiskey and for feeding dollar bills into that video game machine. Chuck's expression of concentration made Ray think he oughta be doing something a little more complicated, like performing brain surgery or changing the belts on a running tractor.

Cheryl must have seen the saucer. Yesterday, she had snickered along with the rest when Ray told everybody what he saw. Today, it was free beer. She'd seen it.

Ray threw a smug glance over his shoulder. There were plenty of kooks in Roswell, but most regular folk didn't have time for aliens or government conspiracies.

That was all about to change.

Ray turned a conspiratorial smirk toward Cheryl. She was smiling at Chuck. Ray saw her hand linger on Chuck's for a moment as she switched out his empty glass for a full one. Chuck never looked up from his game, but his jaw had fallen open as if he couldn't spare enough attention to keep control of his face.

Ray's throat tightened. He raised his chin to Cheryl to call her over.

She picked up Ray's beer and looked a little annoyed when she found it wasn't empty.

"Whaddya need,?" She sounded tired.

"You saw it didn't you? Today. Just after 5:00."

"Saw what?"

Ray leaned in and lowered his voice.

"The saucer. You believe me now, right?"

Cheryl's eyebrows went up. "Not today, Ray."

Ray swallowed. "But, the beer…I thought…"

"I *knew* you were gonna do this." She shook her head. "Ray, you tip so goddam much it feels like I'm half robbing you. It ain't Christian. Figured I owed you one. Don't make a thing out of it, okay?"

Ray took a deep breath and wiped the sweat from his face. His hand still stank of chickens.

"Somebody musta seen it," Ray searched Cheryl's face for some connection.

"Is Ray talking UFOs again?" Chuck said as he walked past them. "Houston, we have a moron."

Cheryl brought her hands to her mouth, but if she was trying to hide her smile, she didn't do a very good job.

"I gotta take a leak, Ray," said Chuck. "If any aliens come in here, distract them so the rest of us can run. Seems like it's you they wanna probe."

Chuck smiled at Cheryl and walked off to the bathroom.

Ray finished his beer and Cheryl brought him another before he asked. She didn't make eye contact. He finished the second beer and left enough cash on the bar for both. Somebody in one of the back booths whistled the *X-Files* theme as Ray walked out the door. He didn't look to see who it was.

§

By late afternoon, the ladder leading up to the top of the feed silo was hot as a frying pan. Some of the fancier farms in the county had silos with enclosed staircases, but nobody had ever accused Ray's farm of being *fancy*.

The weight of his mom's Polaroid camera had more to do with age than quality, and the frayed strap cut into the back of his neck. A breeze plucked at his work shirt as he climbed, making the whole thing balloon like some sort of fat suit. Not that Ray needed any help— too much beer and barbecue had gone straight to his gut. Probably would've taken piles of crap about it from Chuck and the rest down at Scooters if they hadn't all been drilling new holes in their belts, too. Honestly, Ray was probably cruising for a heart attack, just like his dad.

The wind kicked up a notch and he turned, half-expecting the saucer to be hovering right behind him like the killer in one of those slasher movies Cheryl loved. The sky was empty, but Ray gave a shout all the same as his boot slipped on one of the rungs. There were a couple dicey seconds, knuckles white, boots squeaking on metal as the Polaroid swung back, strap tight across Ray's throat. Although he got his feet back under him and the camera sorted out, the tight, fluttery feeling in his chest lingered long after he'd made it to the top of the silo.

Ray had to squint against the glare of the concrete, bright as old bone in the late afternoon sun. Streaks of red-brown rust bled from the rails and casing of the feed elevator, the last coat of paint his mother put on long since flaked to nothing.

He hunkered down in the shadow of the elevator and lit a menthol. Beer cans lined the wall, half-full of rainwater and cigarette butts, their labels long since bleached a uniform silver. Ray frowned down at them through a cloud of smoke. He'd done all of his drinking on the ground for a long time. Had to be some kids, sneaking up late at night to get a stupid, scary buzz on just like Ray and his buddies back in the day. God, how long had it been—twenty, twenty-five years?

Ray snorted at the memory of nights spent high in the breeze, laughing over the schoolyard gossip that had been their world. Dave Kennedy, Miguel and Anna Loredo, and Chuck, still a solid decade from whatever bullshit injury glued him to that stool at Variety. Back then, he'd seemed so cool. Ray should've known better—who comes home from community college to hang out with high-school kids? Cheryl had been there, too. Not often, but enough so Ray could still picture her hanging over the rail like she was daring the wind to take her. He remembered standing beside her, wincing into every gust, legs tingling like he was about to pee himself.

It was a wonder they hadn't broken their necks. Come to think of it, he probably *should* pull the ladder up. Last thing he needed was a dead kid or two.

Ray's watch beeped 5:00.

He dragged on his menthol then stubbed it out, the smoke cool and hot at the same time. Doing dumb stuff was kind of the point of being young. It hadn't hurt Ray any. He didn't mind kids on his silo. Hell, he might even leave a six-pack up here for them.

The lens of the Polaroid was gummy with grime and old dust, so he wiped it with his shirtsleeve. He went over to the rail, then thought better of it and lay down on the warm concrete.

Tempting the wind was one thing, but that saucer came on mighty fast, and Ray's dumbass days were far behind him.

§

"What the hell am I looking at?" Chuck leaned in close enough Ray could smell the Old Thompson on his breath.

"Careful, careful." Ray held out an arm to shield the pictures as whiskey slopped from Chuck's glass. "That's it. The thing. The saucer."

"Buuuuuullshit." Chuck made the word last.

"I dunno." Cheryl chewed her lip, head tilted to regard the pictures Ray had fanned out in front of him like a winning hand. "They're pretty blurry."

"I told you, goddamit. It's *fast*," Ray said.

"That's what she said." The only thing worse than Chuck's grin was Cheryl's snort of laughter.

"Ray," said Cheryl. "Listen, I know Roswell trades on aliens, but nobody's gonna respect you less for *not* seeing a flying saucer."

"It's real. I'll show you. Come to my place tomorrow."

"You know I work afternoons at King's," Cheryl said. "I can't just take off in the middle of the day."

"You think I'm bullshitting you?" Ray swallowed. "Alright, alright. If there's no aliens, I'll give you a hundred bucks."

"Ray, I—"

Cheryl flicked her towel over her shoulder and turned away.

"A *hundred* bucks, c'mon." The words came out in a half-whine. Hearing the desperation in his voice made Ray feel all queasy like up on the silo.

"I'll take that hundred bucks, if you wanna get rid of it so bad." Chuck set his tumbler down, settling onto the stool like he planned to move in.

At the other end of the bar, Cheryl poured a double shot of Jack Daniels over ice and slid it to someone. She didn't come back.

Ray finished his beer.

"Don't know how you can drink that." Chuck smiled, tapping the neck of Ray's bottle with his glass. Ray had the sudden urge to sweep both the drinks off the bar. Instead, he ordered another Bud. The crowd was starting to fill in, and Cheryl was out at a table, laughing with a couple of girls from the co-op while she cleared empties.

Ray's beer didn't taste so good, so he had Bucky set him up with a few shots of Jack, then shifted around so he could watch Cheryl in the mirror. Chuck was talking about how his aunt once went to a presentation by one of the scientists from that show *Ancient Aliens*, and how he'd said the pyramids were actually nuclear reactors or something. Chuck's voice chipped away at Ray's composure. He wanted to go home, but dreaded the muffled roar of laughter that would chase him into the parking lot. Eventually, Chuck petered out, and they drank quietly through a half-dozen songs.

"It's okay—forget the money," Chuck said into the babbling silence.

Ray looked up from his glass. The liquor had given him a warm, distant feeling, like he was underwater.

"If you're just gonna sit there sulking, there's no fun in it," Chuck said.

"What?"

"You're just screwing with us, right? Like, I know we all pretend for the tourists, but this is locals you're tryin' to fool. What you got out there—an old tractor with Christmas lights? Bucky in a rubber mask?" He nodded at the grizzled bartender.

"S'real." The words slipped between Ray's buzzing lips. He paused, then took a breath. "It's *real*."

"C'mon, Ray, this is—"

"I don't care what you think!" He pushed himself up, glaring around the bar. The music was back on, and the night in full swing. No one even glanced his way.

Chuck grabbed his arm. "Maybe we should get you home."

"I'm fine." He shook off Chuck's hand.

"Christ, okay. I'll see you tomorrow." Chuck gave a little wince as he turned to leave, like *Ray* was out of line.

"Don't bother." Ray called after him, but wasn't sure he heard him over the noise.

§

"Dammit, Ray."

If Cheryl had moved just a few inches to the right, the full moon would've made a perfect halo around her head.

Ray squinted up at her from the dirt beside his truck. The night had only gotten worse after Chuck left—every hoarse cackle scraped across his nerves, the sweaty heat of the bar seeming to bleed through his skin. The outside had been blessedly cool, and Ray had sat down to watch the stars and sober up.

"I was just relaxin'. Nice night for it." He stood, brushing the gravel from his shirt and pants. His legs still felt a bit wobbly, so he settled for leaning against the side of his truck, nice and casual.

"It's three in the morning."

"Is it?"

Silence pressed in between them.

Cheryl glanced around, crossing her arms over her stomach. "Well, I should go."

"Yeah, okay." Ray fished out his keys and dropped them.

"You okay to drive?"

"Sure, just tired s'all." He brought a hand to his mouth has if to stifle a yawn.

Cheryl gave him a strange look, then shook her head. "C'mon, I'll drive you home."

"No, I'll just..."

"Shut up, Ray," Cheryl said without heat. She stooped and picked up Ray's keys and headed for her old green Buick before Ray could respond. He shuffled after her, the crunch of his footsteps on the gravel piling on to the sound of angry bees buzzing in his head. His stomach was doing cartwheels, but he managed to keep his jaw locked and slide into the stale cigarette and hairspray smell of Cheryl's car.

The streetlights shone sulfur yellow on Ray's pale, damp hands, and he made an involuntary noise like a burp mixed with a swallow as Cheryl backed out of the parking lot.

"I swear to God, Ray, if you puke in my car, I'm gonna drive you straight to Constable Jack and you can sweat it out in the drunk tank. I mean it."

Cheryl kept her eyes on the road, but Ray could see the cords of her jaw muscles.

Ray pressed a hand to his mouth and did his best to think sober thoughts. When he spoke, it was through fingers that still smelled like chicken.

"You remember back in high school... The night after we beat Artesia and...drinking up on the silo at my parents' place?"

"Yeah, I guess," Cheryl said.

"That was good, right? Good times? That was... How's come you hate me now, Cheryl? You didn't used to hate me."

"What? Ray, I don't hate you. I barely even know you. You're just annoying everybody the last couple nights."

"Chuck's not a good guy, Cheryl. He's a..."

"Just shut up, Ray. I'm doing you a favor right now, so just shut up. Okay?"

"Okay. Okay, I'll be quiet."

Cheryl sighed and relaxed her grip on the steering wheel.

"But you are going to come see the saucer tomorrow, right?"

"Jeezzus."

"I know, but just come…okay?"

"I have to work, Ray."

"If you come, I'll never talk about it again. I swear. If you don't see nothing, I'll give you a hundred bucks. A hundred bucks!"

"Ray, you're probably not even going to remember sayin' that when you wake up."

"I'll remember. I mean it. A hundred bucks. Be there by 5:00."

Cheryl pinched the bridge of her nose and shook her head.

"Maybe. Only if you don't say another goddamn word for the rest of the ride and I can get somebody to take my shift at King's. Maybe. And if Chuck can come. Maybe."

"Okay, just…"

"Not another word or the answer is no."

Ray stared at Cheryl for a moment. In profile, Cheryl looked like a woman Ray had seen on an old coin or in some painting on TV. Somebody important. Royalty, maybe.

It wasn't easy, but Ray managed to keep his mouth shut for the rest of the drive. When Cheryl pulled up next to Ray's place, she dropped the keys in his hand.

"Go to bed, Ray."

Ray thought about answering, but he wasn't sure if the no-talking rule was still in effect, so he just gave a shaky thumbs-up as he groped for the door handle in the dark. Once he was out of the car, Cheryl drove off so quickly her tires spun on the gravel driveway. Ray stood in the watched Cheryl's taillights speeding towards town. When the Buick was out of sight, he fell to his knees, puking like he was a teenager again.

§

4:50 p.m.

Ray checked his watch and looked out at Route 70. Nothing.

He hopped up on the silo ladder, scrambling up a dozen rungs to squint into the distance. The late-afternoon sun was in his eyes, still too bright no matter how he turned. Was that a plume of dust? A flash of tarnished chrome and peeling paint out beyond the cornfield? Definitely a car, and definitely coming this way. Had to be them.

The drop wasn't far, but Ray still managed to roll his ankle. He limped over to the barn, wincing up at the clock.

4:58, and the car was still a good ten minutes away. Ray could picture the Buick pulling up after the dust had settled. Chuck would crack some joke about probes, like always. Ray couldn't even take a swing at him without seeming like a jerk. Even worse, Cheryl would laugh, then look at Ray like last night—not angry, not sad, not anything.

He felt drunk, head far away and stomach queasy. He'd cashed in his chips. Cheryl had almost dumped him out on the roadside last night, she wouldn't come back.

There were guns in the house—old hunting rifles from his father and a couple AK's Ray had picked up at the Albuquerque gun show. A few seconds of full-auto might be enough to get the saucer's attention, maybe even slow it down. Ray snorted—even desperate, he wasn't stupid enough to think shooting at aliens was a good idea.

He looked around the barn: camp stove, feedbags, chicken cages, rusty tools on the wall, his old Honda hatchback. Maybe if he set a fire on top of the silo, or threw a chicken at the—

The flare gun sat on his workbench, glinting in the lattice of dusty sunlight that slanted through gaps in the barn slats. Ray snatched it up, grabbed a pocketful of flares, then glanced at the sky. He might be able to get a shot off from the barnyard, but the saucer came by so fast the passengers might not notice. Only way to be sure would be from the top of the silo, that way he could put it right alongside the aliens' path.

Ray hobbled over to the silo, wincing as he leapt to catch the bottom rung. It was slow going, the flicker of pain every time he put weight on his ankle like someone poking it with a lit cigarette. He gritted his teeth and kept climbing. Everything was going to be different after this. Ray would be on the news—local, for sure, probably national. This was a big thing, the biggest thing. He'd get to meet the president, there'd be a dinner reception. An R.S.V.P. for Mr. Raymond Woodford, plus one. He liked the sound of that.

The air at the top of the silo felt cold and thin like on a mountaintop. Ray couldn't seem to get enough into his lungs. He flopped onto the roof, concrete hot against his sweaty cheek. Must've taken four, five minutes to climb up, wouldn't be long, now. He pushed to his feet, mouth dry, chest tight and prickly as a bale of barbwire. There was already a flare in the pistol's breach, but he let it drop and thumbed in a fresh one, just in case.

Silence.

The sky seemed fuzzy, clouds like pale smears on some kid's finger painting. Ray raised the flare gun, pressed his back against the rail, then flicked a hopeful glance down at Route 70. The road was empty. Panicked, Ray squinted down at the blurry driveway, straining to hear the familiar pop of gravel beneath tires.

He was so intent on listening, he almost missed the saucer.

It didn't come like a cross-country airliner, slowly growing from a single, glittering point, but just sort of popped into view, careening through the air like a skipped stone.

Ray shouted as the thing bore down on him, lights semi-truck bright even against the late-afternoon sun. There were shadows behind the blue-glass windows, maybe heads pressed against pillows, maybe staring at alien smartphones. The flare gun didn't have a sight, so Ray just pointed it to the right of the saucer's path and pulled the trigger.

It wasn't as bright as he hoped, just a little sputtering arc, quickly lost against the reddish sky. Ray's legs gave out, which was good because the saucer damn near took his head off. He caught himself on the rail, rusty metal digging hard into the crook of his arm.

The saucer stopped. No brakes, no slowdown, it just hung in the sky like it had never been moving. One of the beams pinioned Ray, bright as a cop's searchlight.

Ray felt hot all over. For a second, he thought they really were beaming him up, but after a moment, the saucer just whipped away, skipping out of view fast as it had appeared. He tried to stand, and found he couldn't. The pain came on then, sharp and electric, running from his chest down to his fingertips. What had those bastards done to him?

Tasting metal, he looked down at the yard, smiling at the battered green Buick parked next to the barn, and the two slack-jawed faces staring up at him, one bearded, one beautiful. Ray grinned as he slipped back onto the concrete. This was it: national news, fame, fortune, presidential dinners.

And Ray knew exactly who his plus-one would be.

§

"Welcome back, buddy." Chuck's face bobbed into blurry focus. "Had yourself a goddam heart attack."

Ray's eyes felt like they'd been glued half shut and his mouth tasted like a garbage fire. He pawed at his face with shaking fingers until he rubbed and blinked his vision back into working order. Everything was very bright and very white.

"You're in Lovelace Regional." Chuck bopped Ray on the shoulder with the rolled-up magazine he'd been clutching. "They moved you out of critical care this morning."

"Is Cheryl here?" Ray asked.

"Thanks for calling the squad and saving my life, Chuck. Thanks for helping the EMTs track down a cherry picker to get me down from that silo, Chuck. Thanks for sitting in that hard hospital chair until I woke up, Chuck. You're a helluva guy, Chuck."

Ray tried to sit up, but it felt like there was a cinder block strapped to his chest.

Chuck shook his head and scratched at his greasy black beard.

"No, Ray, Cheryl ain't here. She's at work. She did stop by earlier to bring me a sandwich, if that matters to you."

"She saw it, right?"

"Saw what?"

"The ship, dammit!" The effort of shouting sent a spark of pain behind Ray's eyes.

Chuck leaned in and found the bed control. The motor hummed as it pushed Ray into a sitting position.

"Yeah, we saw it, Ray. Calm down, man."

Ray blew out a long breath and nodded. A bubble of spittle clung to the corner of his dry lips.

"Are the news crews here yet?" Ray asked.

"News crews?"

Ray flushed, cheeks hot as cooked ham. For a second, he wondered how much of Chuck's beard he could rip off before the orderlies came.

"Okay, pal, don't blow another gasket," Chuck said. "I just can't help pullin' your leg. No, nobody called the news."

"Why not?"

"Well, for one thing, you were dying on top of a grain silo and also…why would we?"

Ray's mouth moved, but he only muttered sounds of disbelief.

"The saucer didn't come back." Chuck gave a little shrug. "You been out for two days. Cheryl and I went over, though. Drove out plenty early and waited around for hours. There was nothing, man. No aliens. No saucer. Probably didn't like having flares shot at them."

"They'll come back."

"And what if they do? Buddy, I seen enough rednecks on TV talking about aliens to know I don't wanna be one of 'em. Hell, what makes you think you could even get a news crew out there? You barely got Cheryl and me to show up."

"I'll get it on video next time," Ray said.

"Yeah? You gonna outsmart them aliens, huh? Then what? They'll stop and start given' out interviews?"

Ray pressed his lips together.

"Buddy, why would aliens care about you? About any of us? Do you stop and pay attention to the ants out front of the Variety Lounge? Hell no."

"They'll stop," Ray said.

"Yeah? Okay, they'll stop. They'll stop and make you their king. Then what?"

"You just keep laughing, Chuck. You keep laughing. I'm going to make history."

"Ray, I hope you do. I really do. That would be something."

Chuck slumped back in his chair with a wince. "What are you gonna do with all that fame and fortune, bud?"

Ray stared at Chuck and said nothing.

"Oh, right," Chuck said. "Cheryl."

"She ain't your girlfriend," Ray said. It sounded more like a question than a statement.

Chuck snorted.

"No, I guess she ain't. She actually likes me, Ray, and she ain't my girlfriend. She ain't interested in being nobody's girlfriend. That's what she says. So, what do you think that means for your chances with her?"

"Well, when I'm famous, she—"

"Still won't owe you nothing, Ray. Just like the news crews don't owe you. Just like them aliens don't owe you. People ain't gonna pay attention to you just because you really want them to. That's not how it works."

Ray scowled down at the shapeless bulge of his body beneath the beige hospital blanket and said nothing.

Chuck stood with a groan and stretched.

"Hell, I don't owe you nothing either, but I walked to the Speedway a few hours ago and picked this up for you anyway. You're welcome."

He tossed the rolled-up magazine onto Ray's lap.

"You take 'er easy, pal," Chuck said over his shoulder as he walked from the room.

Ray unrolled the magazine. It was a copy of *Ancient Encounters*. The cover was a crude drawing of three willowy, gray aliens flanked by a field of corn and the gold disk of a full moon.

The pain in Ray's head had increased from a dull ache to a steady throb. There was a call button attached to a thin wire resting on the bedside table. Ray picked it up and pressed the button. Nothing happened. He tugged on the wire, coiling loop after loop onto his lap. The end of the wire wasn't connecting to anything.

Out in the hall, two nurses walked by the open door to Ray's room chatting.

"Excuse me," Ray said in the loudest voice he could muster.

The nurses didn't slow. Ray pressed his throbbing head back against his pillow and listened to the fading echo of their footsteps, the murmur of their conversation like the hum of a distant engine.

Heirloom

Paul R. McNamee

*B*ud *Merrill could remember when the dried lake bed* would be half-filled with RVs and tents, and a hundred or more telescopes of all sizes would be pointed at the night sky. Hot dogs, hamburgers, and chicken wings would be cooking over fires or sizzling on camp stoves.

All the people had looked to the sky—searching, waiting, hoping.

Passage of time had dwindled the number of attendees. More than that, though, Bud knew most had moved on, both physically and with respect to their beliefs. Each year the gathering was smaller than the year before. Then, it had died out during his early high school years.

Bud and his father sat alone on the dry lake bed. Bud hadn't been out there for a number of years. College, career, marriage—a failed one. His father had been out there consistently, though, holding a lonely vigil where once there had been a gathering and a celebration. When Bud did the math, he was shocked to realize those years had passed into decades. Even his father had finally needed to let the last few years pass without his annual visit.

Father and son, the last believers.

That was not entirely true, either. Bud let his father think he still believed. But Bud hadn't thought about those nights of long ago any more than he pondered those Christmas Eves he'd spent in anxious anticipation of Santa Claus's arrival.

He never did hear reindeer hooves clattering on the roof.

He had seen an odd light in the sky once, out here in desolate wilderness. But in hindsight, that could have been explained away.

He had believed.

Oh, how he'd believed. He'd been raised as a child to believe and he'd held on to those beliefs for a long, long time.

But beliefs can change, fall away with time and experience. He'd held onto the UFOs and the alien visitors until the last. Until that day had come.

The day when his father had said there was an implant in his head, behind his right ear, Bud finally understood. Aliens, abductions, UFOs—those were tinged with the fantasy and thrill of science fiction. But an implant? Bud had substituted *government* for *aliens* and then he had seen it all. How many interviews, news stories, online statuses had he read that sounded just like that? Conspiracy theories. F.B.I. bugs in the lamps of a motel room—as if the F.B.I. had any reason to bug and shadow the people who thought they were being bugged and shadowed.

And there it was.

There were no aliens. No UFOs. There never had been. And they had certainly never implanted a device in Bud's father's brain.

Bud's father was mentally ill.

He always had been. Bud had never seen the forest for the trees of almond-eyed, gray and little, green men from outer-space.

It was that simple, profound—disillusioning, and sad, too.

Bud shifted his lawn chair. His butt was getting numb. He sat back down, put the shotgun back across his lap. He wouldn't let his father hold the gun anymore. His father had bristled. Bud had pointed out the gun had never stopped the aliens from abducting his father before. They had some means of mesmerizing their victims. That had seemed the only plausible explanation, according to Bud's father. Bud and his father had reached a compromise. Bud had promised to stay armed and vigilant.

"I think you picked a good time to come back here, son."

His father's words startled Bud out of his reverie.

"You think we'll see a UFO?"

"I think they'll come tonight." His father nodded. "I think they'll come looking for me."

"You do?"

'Uh huh."

"Why?"

His father shrugged, lapsed back into silence. The Alzheimer's. He'd have trouble getting on track, keeping on track, and getting back on track. It was weird how icebergs of life experiences had drifted away and yet the alien stuff had held on. It was too late to attempt to bring the old man to his senses concerning the nonsense of alien visitations. And because Bud's father could still engage via the subject of UFOs and aliens, it was the one thing that kept his failing mind from completely seizing up.

He remembered Bud, too—most of the time. Bud wasn't sure there was anything else in his father's mind, though. He hadn't mentioned his wife—Bud's mother—in months.

"Pa?"

"What?"

"Why do you think they'll be here tonight?"

His father pointed a finger behind his right ear. "I'm an experiment. I don't know if this thing can broadcast over interstellar distances. I'm guessing it can't. I figure it's a recorder. Makes sense doesn't it? All those nights I can't remember anything that happened. I bet it's them. Checking up on me, and downloading my data. Been a while since they came last. I figure I'm due."

Before the dementia had started there had been a time when Bud wanted to force the truth on his father. He'd come short of challenging his father to get an X-ray to prove he'd had something inserted in his brain. In the end, Bud had merely made a pointed suggestion.

"Ah, bullshit," his father had said. "You think they're stupid? It's made outta some material we don't know about. Some weird metal or plastic or something that just looks like metal or plastic but isn't. It won't show up on some X-ray."

Bud tossed another log into the stone-encircled fire pit. The orange flame lit up the night. If anyone else were out here, they'd see the fire from miles away. The dry air would carry their voices far, too. Bud wasn't concerned, though. He was certain they were alone, and would be for the rest of the night. It was far too late for anyone to trek out onto the lake bed in the dead of night.

Bud studied his father's face. Bud had inherited the hawk nose, but the roundness of Bud's face came from his mother. His father looked so old. Age had come on rapidly. Bud father's shock of thick hair had changed from gray to white overnight. Bud sometimes thought each white hair represented a memory lost.

When had it started? When had it been paranoia and when had it been dementia? Bud couldn't say. He did remember his father had always been enthusiastic about seeing UFOs. But the alien abduction claims hadn't started until those years when his father had camped out alone—conveniently lacking corroborating witnesses to his tales.

His father nodded off and snored softly.

Bud clenched his fingers around the gun until his knuckles went white. His guts roiled.

This was the night. This was the moment. There would be no other.

Nervous sweat slicked Bud's palm as he ran his hand along the stock of the shotgun.

No witnesses. His father doing what he loved—camping out and searching for flying saucers. The only memories the old man had left.

His vision blurring with welling tears, Bud stood up quietly. He wiped his nose with his sleeve, felt the dampness of the snot seeping to his skin.

He walked around behind his father's chair.

"Remember, Pa? Can you?" Bud whispered. It was hard to say anything at any volume around the constricting lump swelling in his throat. "You said it enough times. I knew it was true. I knew it was what you always wanted. Mom and everyone else thought you were making a joke but I know better.

'Son, if I go senile, don't you ever let them put me in a home. If it comes to that, you take me out in a field and shoot me in the head.'"

Bud had kept his father out of the home. He'd packed him off in the RV and they'd kept moving. There was no point in putting his father under some kind of care. They had no money and his condition couldn't be cured. His father had drifted away chunk by chunk. That would have happened whether or not he'd stayed put in a home or had hit the road with his son.

On the road, Bud and his father had called their own shots.

At least, they had, until all the decisions needed to fall to Bud. He'd had one last decision to make. And he'd made it.

He had kept his father out of the home. Now it was time to take him into that field. To put him out to pasture.

He leveled the shotgun behind his father's head.

Bud couldn't do it.

He needed to do it.

His father wanted this.

Bud did not want this. *You can't wait until he's a vegetable. You can't wait until he has nothing left to remember. This is the end of his road. You'll bury him here, where he always wanted to be. Help him go. Now,* he thought. The thought was a plea. A plea for strength and cold, clinical analysis and acceptance of what needed to happen. What must happen.

Bud stood frozen. His arms were rubber. He could hardly hold up the gun. He felt indecision gathering, trying to push the gun away.

He squeezed shut his eyes, and then he squeezed the trigger.

The gun bucked in his hands. The shot blasted louder than thunder at the heart of a lightning strike. The sound rolled away across the lake bed.

He opened his eyes.

The fire still burned bright. Bud could see it all.

His father had been knocked forward; the lawn chair sprawled on its side. There was a spray of red mist under his father's body.

Bud took a shaky step forward. The left top half of his father's head was gone. Gray and blood red goop oozed out onto the dry, hard-packed thirsty ground.

Bud dropped the shotgun, dropped to his knees, and vomited.

He kept retching until there was nothing left to come up.

He reared back up to his knees, hitched three breaths, and let out a wailing scream against the night.

Then Bud cried, and sobbed, and hollered, and beat the ground with his fists, and cried again until he didn't know if minutes or hours had passed. He collapsed to the ground, and fell into a fitful sleep of utter emotional exhaustion.

§

The light touched his face and he groaned. An odd whirring sound buzzed into his unconscious, burrowing and digging until it raised Bud up out of slumber.

He blinked and needed to put a hand in front of his face to block the brightness. The light shone down like a sun in the night sky

He panicked. His first thought was a police helicopter. Someone had been out there. Someone had heard the shot and called the police. He'd shot his father. He'd killed his father! He'd get prison, if not the death penalty. What would he get if they found him guilty of euthanasia? Would they make any distinction at all? If not, he'd be guilty of murder in the first degree.

No!

He scrambled to his feet. Looked up, gazed at the light as much as he could. There was a halo of multi-colored lights spinning around the corona.

They weren't blue police lights.

The whirring sound was high-pitched and musical. It was not the sound of chopping rotor blades.

His mouth hung open. He tried to say something, anything, even a cuss-word but he was too dumbfounded.

He stared up at the UFO and believed again.

The saucer-shaped craft descended. Desert topsoil clouded the light issuing from the underside of the saucer. The craft used a cushion of air or something to soften its landing, though Bud heard no air expelling from the UFO.

Bud ran. He dove under the RV, crawled, and came up on the other side.

The whirring noise of the spaceship receded into a mild hum.

Bud dared to poke is head around the front of the RV, where he could see what was happening.

A gangway emerged from the smooth surface of the underside of the UFO. Just like in every movie and faux documentary Bud had ever seen about flying saucers. Shapes moved down the ramp, toward the fire and the body of Bud's father.

They were—honest to God and spite the Devil—green men. They were not little, green men. They were tall, skinny, and humanoid. They wore silvery jumpsuits and had large, black, bulbous, insect eyes.

One knelt beside the corpse of Bud's father. It shoved its three-fingered hand into the mush that had once been his father's diseased brain. Bud heard—or imagined he heard—the squelching sound as the alien probed into the skull. Hot bile crawled up the back of Bud's throat, but he fought it down. He couldn't afford to wretch and draw the aliens' attention.

The probing alien chattered excitedly. The others gazed down with interest. The alien pulled. Its fingers came out, clutching something. The alien held it up close to its over-sized eyes and turned the object about with its fingers. Its other hand wiped away the blood and slimy gore to reveal a small device, the color of white porcelain.

"Holy shit," Bud whispered. "It was real. It was in his head. It was in his head behind his goddamn ear for real!"

He caught himself gnawing at the heel of his hand and forced himself to stop. He had to think this through. He thought of all his father's claims of abductions and strange visits in the night. The fact these aliens had landed right on top of them could not be coincidence. The thing they had pulled from his father's skull. They had been tracking his father, all these years.

What the hell did they want with a doddering old man? A man mentally ill and sliding into the dementia of Alzheimer's disease?

Just because his father was ill, didn't mean he couldn't have had extraterrestrial alien experiences. The two weren't mutually exclusive.

His father had thought the aliens were gathering data.

Experimentation.

Why not?

Human doctors and scientists were interested in test subjects. They studied unhealthy subjects and healthy ones. Why should alien scientists be any different?

They stood around chattering and gesticulating with their bony fingers. One pointed at the RV. Bud worried but they seemed to be looking at the door and the windows on the side of the camper, not at the front where he stood. They had such big eyes—like owls. Did they have night vision? Did they see better in the dark? If they did, why the bright lights from the ship? Bud didn't know—couldn't know. They were alien. They didn't need to have counterparts and comparisons to the creatures on Earth. Hell, he'd read some articles that theorized that because of interstellar distances, aliens could never reach Earth. They might have come from a different dimension, or a different universe.

The one holding the bug they'd implanted in his father's head nodded and shrugged. What did the motion mean? Were nods and shrugs universal? Bud didn't know.

They all turned now. Heads turning and unmoving eyes searching.

Bud couldn't understand any of their body language, or chatter. But he had a hunch. And his hunch filled him with dread.

They'd lost their test subject.

They needed to find another one.

Bud father's death had thrown them off. They hadn't expected it. He felt sure.

If they didn't come this way often, they'd need to improvise acquiring a new test subject.

Immediately.

Bud was the only human being for miles around.

He withdrew his head—slowly, so the sudden movement of wouldn't give him away—and leaned against the RV. The door was on the other side. In full view of the aliens. Could he risk it? Could he get in the door, start the engine, and start driving before they grabbed him?

He doubted it.

If he could, how far would he get? The RV was no race car. He felt sure they could track him from the sky in their saucer. Did the ship have weapons? Laser beams? Rockets? A few well-placed shots at the tires and his jaunt would end real quick.

Should he run?

He considered those lanky, scrawny bodies. Were they as weak as they looked? Or were they marathon runners? Was gravity a factor? Was it different from their home world? Would the difference help or hinder them?

Bud thought he heard a whisper. He turned his head to the right.

And looked into the pair of giant almond eyes regarding him from inches away.

Fight or flight instinct decided for him.

Bud ran.

The aliens swarmed over him like locusts.

They pinned his arms and legs to the hard ground. He struggled briefly but with all he'd been through, his strength ebbed away. They were unnaturally strong.

He heard a strange humming. One of the aliens held a metal stick which flashed, and pulsed, and vibrated. He felt the pressure come off his arms and legs. He could not look away from the pulsing device. He wanted to get up and flee but his legs and arms would not respond. He tried to look around, and his neck wouldn't move, either.

Bud rose from the ground. He could only stare up at the stars and the alien's upper torsos as they carried him past the RV and into their waiting vessel.

§

Bud awoke. He was in his little bed in the RV. He let out a relaxed sigh. He furrowed his face. It was like every morning on the road. For some reason, it shouldn't have been. He bolted upright. He couldn't remember how he'd gotten there. He'd been outside last night. They'd laid him on the ground and...

The aliens!

The UFO!

It was true! They were real!

He had to tell his...

Father.

Bud slumped off the bed to the floor. He rubbed his hand up and down his face.

God! His father. His father was dead. He'd killed his father.

He forced himself to his feet, staggered out the RV door into the blinding morning sun.

The fire had burned to ash.

His father's body was gone. The shifting sandy topsoil covered where there had been blood and gore. There was no sign of bloody murder.

The nights events all streamed back. He remembered everything, except the gap between the aliens holding him down and waking up. But there were flashes—images from those lost minutes.

That thing—that white device. The thing that had been inside his father's head. They'd had it. He'd seen it pass over his face, headed toward the side of his head.

Hand shaking near to palsy, Bud reached up and felt behind his right ear.

He could feel no bump, no raised scar. But he winced.

Oh, how the skin was tender to the touch in that spot.

Laika's Fractured Eden

James Edward O'Brien

On November 3, 1957, the Soviet Union launched a stray dog named Laika into space aboard Sputnik 2. She was thought to have died from the stress and heat associated with her flight several hours into the journey. A hundred years later Laika returned, having discovered the key to immortality and an urgent desire to try and set things right.

The millennia-old bond between species turned out rather one-sided. All it bought me was a one-way ticket into space. I was no stranger to fear—a stray sprung from the midnight squares of hungry, wintry Moscow—but I did not know real terror until they fitted me with electrodes and a harness, and sealed me in that cabin.

My well-being was never a consideration; the rudimentary spacecraft was unequipped for reentry. The Progenitors pried open the ship like a tin can and vacuumed me right up as the ship left the atmosphere. Salvation.

They felt culpable in some roundabout way, this solar system just one of the many Petri dishes the Progenitors have stashed around the multiverse. For eons they had their lenses trained on more interesting developments when they realized too late that the pot they called Earth was boiling over.

All that primordial ooze had been left unattended too long. They intended to cut their losses and run.

The Progenitors did not want to intervene themselves, out of the concern that they'd make a bigger mess of things should they be misconstrued as gods by the facile minds of the naked bipeds who were causing all the trouble.

I became the linchpin in their exit strategy. Admittedly, I was no rocket scientist myself until they administered a few tweaks to my physiology and brain capacity. They threw in a few bells and whistles. Still, I'm no rocket scientist—only a pilot. And this vessel's no rocket to be exact; it's an ark.

I'm tasked with salvaging what's left worth salvaging. Before the Progenitors cut their losses. Before they call it a day and let the lid boil over.

§

The ark handles well for a craft the size of Vatican City. I hit the pounds and zoos, the factory farms and laboratories—the institutions where the costumed bipeds have imposed the worst of their natures over their neighbors.

Before sending me back home, the Progenitors showed me the different ways sentience manifested on over a half dozen of their other test worlds. After seeing that, it's hard to deny there are more than a few screws loose in the terrestrial machinery down here.

My game plan—and I'm not sure it's a valid one—is to salvage as many creatures as I can that have been put through the ringer. Build a better, more compassionate world on the shoulders of those who've been on the receiving end of mankind's oversight.

When I bring the ark down, a tractor beam tears the roof right off whatever structure needs breaking into and then zeros in on the organisms in need of springing. It's bullish, but effective.

Tractors vacuum the liberated right into the belly of the ark the same way the Progenitors extricated me from Sputnik 2. Transit is seamless for all but the most high-strung—rabbits, voles, veal calves,

Chihuahuas—the prey animals and the developmentally stunted, the beasts prone to bolt at the sight of their own shadows.

There are hideaways for each of them onboard, the ark's winding halls riddled with impossible chambers—cubbyholes carved into the time-space continuum. It's the only way to fit them all—even on a ship this size.

There are seven in-flight oceans—one hostile to any but the orca, otter, and polar bear, another like equatorial bathwater to house the marlins, green turtles, and tropical fish. Five in between.

There are excavators and DNA-extracting drones for the beasts I've come too late for: the dodo, the mammoth, the Tasmanian tiger. My philosophy is that once you're out of the game, there's no point in being resurrected and thrown back on the bench; the extinction bank is a precautionary measure. A historical record.

I steady the ark over Bayonne, New Jersey. The bridge toward Staten Island is awhirl with the lights from the roofs of cop cars. There's an entire unit of national guardsmen with all their popguns trained on me.

There are so many of them that their fear is tangible. Fear hangs over the city like smog does out west. They're so cramped down there and have nothing left to conquer—nowhere to turn their hate anymore but inward.

They've devoured an entire planet, livid over the fact that they're still psychologically—and dare I say, spiritually—famished. The ark's abrupt appearance gives them something to rail against for the first time in a long while.

The military industrial complex is bent on selling the idea that the ark is full of little green men here to take what's theirs. On the opposite end of the seesaw, there's a whole new-age sect devoted to my worship. A bunch of crackpots convinced I'm Anubis, the jackal-headed god of the dead.

Some conspiracy theorist snagged my picture on a drop over Uzbekistan. I don't have the heart to tell them I'm just a mongrel no one bothered to name until they shot me off into space to die.

They want to put you on a pedestal and prostrate themselves before you one minute, and then throw you in a meat grinder to extract every last bit of marrow from your bits-and-pieces the next. Textbook Madonna-whore stuff, if you ask me.

§

The ark closes in on a three-family dwelling down near the port. Projectiles from the soldiers' popguns skim the fuselage like water across a hot pan.

The tractor beam gnaws right through the roof: a hailstorm of splinter and shingle. The bipeds bark orders through megaphones. They'd have better luck staving off a blizzard with a Zippo lighter.

The beam zeroes in on psychic distress. Some jerk had been keeping a tiger chained up in his guest bedroom. There are so many degrees of stupid that all the mercury in all the world's thermometers would fail to measure it all. Three hundred pounds of striped, thrashing muscle, tail, and fang is sucked up the tractor beam's flume.

The third floor gives out, its rotted planks warped and mealy from months—years, maybe—of urine soak. Frozen months, years, of the terrified cub trying to claw its way through the floorboards. Toward the mewling downstairs.

There's a misfire. A miscalculation. The tractor reels in a six-toed calico. A tabby next. Then a Turkish Van and a flailing scarecrow of a dripping wet biped in a hairnet, bathrobe, and faux bear paw slippers. The beam must have dredged up some old plumbing with the fauna, prompting the specimen's hose down.

Slack-jawed and trembling, the biped whirls like a palsied dreidel, ogling the frenzied police car lights through the ark's glass-bottomed hull. Knock-kneed with vertigo, he shifts his gaze to the myriad gaping passageways that flank him.

Eyes dart to the crisscrossing web of light that leads to-and-from each portal: concentrated kinetic waves that usher passengers to their appropriate chambers. Sizzling vanilla blue.

The biped screams—the projected response from *Homo sapiens* under the erroneous impression that it's just been abducted by an extraterrestrial entity. It's a nightmare I'd have thought they'd given up on by now, even with the modest knowledge they've gained regarding space travel—but I suppose *abduction by immortal dog* is even less comprehensible.

Judging from the scream, I posit it's a male of its species. Being that this is the first time I inadvertently vacuumed one up, and the fact that my memories of humankind from my time in the Soviet space program are hazy at best—there is a substantial margin of error. After all, I'm 700 and change in dog years. I'll have to get a whiff to be sure.

When the biped spots me, he drops into a crouch. A smidgen of tension melts from his frame. He pats his thighs, calling, "Here, boy!" in a clumsy falsetto.

Boy. Clearly, he's no student of canine dimorphism.

"How'd you get up here?" he asks. He rubs his eyes in disbelief. "Crap," he mumbles. "How'd I get up here? And where is here?"

I don't understand a lick of English, but the cerebral upgrade the Progenitors provided me with grants me heightened empathic, as well as telepathic, abilities. I'm a dyed-in-the-wool mind reader.

While most sounds excreted from *Homo sapiens* voice boxes are gibberish, I can cull the intent of their babbling—the *meaning* behind it. *The ark.* I project the words straight into his gourd. He flinches. His eyes comb the rafters for the source of the voice in his head.

"You have no right!" he shouts into the uninhabited empty above us.

You don't need to shout, I explain. *You need only think.*

'You have no right to keep me here!' the biped thought.

I don't intend to. You're not supposed to be here in the first place.

'What have you done to my cats?' he seethes.

Your cats? So quick to claim dominion over anything not fast enough to evade your greedy paws, you Homo sapiens.

'What are you? Aliens?' He scans the rafters for signs of life.

I'm right in front of you, I explain, staring right at him.

He lowers his gaze and looks around, looking right past me.

'I just see a dog.'

Exactly.

'Piloting a flying saucer.'

It's an ark, I correct him. *Otherwise, you're quick on the uptake.*

It takes most people a while to wrap their heads around the concept. In all of humanity's self-published funny books, one of theirs is always at the helm of these sorts of endeavors: Noah, et al.

§

You're not scared, I observe.

"Scared?" he says, "I've gone hoarse talking to cats, dogs, parakeets, guinea pigs, my entire life. You've all just looked at me cross-eyed. Until now."

A smile creeps across his face.

"It's a revelation. That bastard upstairs—now he was something to be frightened of—threatened to feed my cats to whatever it was he kept up there. I called the police. I called animal control. But they all thought I was crazy."

Are you injured? I ask.

"No," he says.

Those labored facial contortions...those growls...the whining...

"The talking?"

Yes, talking. I'd forgotten how gutturally singsong it all sounds. *You need only think and I'll think back.*

He scrunches his nose. Digs his pointers into his temples. 'My cats...the cats...they're okay?'

They're fine, I tell him. *And those gestures...that pained expression...there's no call for them either. It's telepathy, not a magic show.*

He tightens the knot on his dripping bathrobe. His eyes reassess every inch of the massive hangar. 'This some kind of ship?' he asks.

This is a mistake. You're here because of a tractor beam's imprecision.

He chews on his lip as he weighs his situation. 'Abducted, then.'

No. You're going straight back.

The ark has no chambers for humanity. There's simply nowhere to stow humankind where they won't cause trouble. They're too caustic a species—every rung of their evolution forged out of genocide, ecocide, extinction.

'But my cats—' he begins.

Consider them liberated. En route to a world much gentler than yours.

"But you can't!" He adopts the baseless bravado of a species that has suffered under the misconception that they are the center of the universe. "I'm all they've got."

Please, I remind him, *thoughts, not grunts.*

He shudders. 'They're all *I've* got.'

I should just port him back down right now, but I must have some residual Stockholm syndrome ingrained in me from my days in the Soviet space program. *Such narcissism from you bipeds—the hairless ones, at least. What makes you so special?*

'Nothing,' he frowns. 'I'm what, in less enlightened times, might be called a cat lady.'

I sniff him out, confused. He smells male. Pheromones don't lie.

'It's just a label,' he clarifies. 'For those who...who...I don't know...shut-ins, loners, square pegs, people who reject—or have been rejected by—'

I sniff at his robe. *Like a monk? A leper?*

'No,' shrugs the cat lady, 'I just prefer the company of animals over people.'

I'm listening.

'Dogs...cats...there's a simplicity there—no offense. Maybe simplicity's the wrong word—an honesty, maybe.'

The natural world has a brutality all its own—an ambivalence sewn into the very fabric of its order. I'm afraid it might be you who's oversimplifying us.

'But you don't *lie,* do you?' the cat lady insists. 'Nature doesn't lie. Humanity's the only species that *lies* as far as I can tell.'

Well, no other species has honed it quite like you have. You're masters at wounding, I posit, *no matter which way you cut it—whether your tongues...your technology...the wounds you've inflicted—the factory farms and puppy mills, the laboratories and razed forests. You've left us nowhere to run. You've transformed our world into your world. Made it a hell.*

I direct him toward the tractor beam hatch. *Please, step onto the platform.*

§

"Not yet," howls the cat lady. He buckles, clawing at the see-through floor. "I'm afraid...afraid—of heights—of falling. Of...so...so much."

His protestations conjure memories long buried inside me. They were not gentle, the men in lab coats, when they harnessed me into the molded stand in that suffocating metal chamber. They scolded me when I urinated on myself, strapped me in so tight the leather dug into my ribs and belly. After what they've done, how is it that I still see so much of myself in these bald, trembling primates?

Perhaps this cat lady's right. Perhaps we quadrupeds are simple things. Punished for our compliance. Our trust. Our inability to lie.

Shrapnel careens off the ark's see-through bottom. Its affect inconsequential as lightning bugs flitting against a rhino's hide.

"They...they're shooting at us," frets the cat lady.

I send a mental prompt that engages the sleek steel barrels encased in the belly of the ship. Snubbed nozzles earthbound.

'You've come to destroy us?' he asks.

I sense a faint hint of relief buried in his question. I must be mistaken. *No,* I inform him. *As history illustrates, you're doing a fine enough job of that on your own. I'm here for something much more elusive: salvation.*

I still haven't figured out *whose,* though. The barrels spew forth dense skeins of cloud. They twist and twine like imagined dragons against the ark's belly until the entire vessel is enshrouded in cloud cover.

Camouflage. A close approximation to lying in the animal kingdom. But it's not just lying that sets humans apart from other animals; it's their ability to institutionalize pain. Commodify cruelty. *I need to put you back now,* I warn him. *You don't belong here.*

'I don't belong down there, either,' he insists.

§

There was a woman who fed me, all those years ago: she wore a tattered woolen coat that stank of tobacco smoke. She'd bring me gristle and pork fat in a folded napkin, boiled bones salvaged from soup stock. Empathy as rare a bounty then as it is today.

This stowaway reminds me of her: that same palatable loneliness. The police chased that woman off eventually, scolding her for drawing the feral packs that scoured Moscow's squares after nightfall.

Weeks later, when another man in a drab, state uniform found me rooting through trash in some January alley, I thought I'd found my own sort of salvation. Or it had found me. It seems like yesterday, all those decades ago—this keen memory and intellect the Progenitors granted me a curse.

I've always been a docile whelp. It granted me a blanket in a wire cage and clean water in a brightly lit room.

They fattened me up. Prodded me with this. Poked me with that. There was a cold economy to my treatment, seemingly preferable at the time to freezing to death or having my throat torn out over the leavings in trashcans.

There were other cages in that room, other dogs baying and whimpering through the night. It was only when we joined our voices and howled that a bleary-eyed lab attendant would burst through the door and threaten us with the spray bottle they used to spritz down our kennels.

But a confined, comfortable life stripped of self-determination is only comfortable so long. I yearned for the dizzying freedom that once seemed so frightening. Maybe I'd forgotten the freeze of the Moscow streets. Maybe it's because a slim chance holds more promise than no chance at all.

§

'I raised those cats from kittens,' he tells me. 'Schwartz, Drusilla, and Mephistopheles. Same litter. Found them kneading at the belly of the carcass of their mother. Had to bottle-feed them. Can I see them?' he asks. 'Just one last time?'

The spot on the ark where the cats are housed is a place of eternal summer. Warm sun and sweet, uncut grass: a frolicsome chamber abuzz with dragonflies and timid dormice. I don't know why I've showed him here—as an assurance maybe, in a world devoid of assurances, that my word is good.

The tabby and the Turkish Van bound through the snout-high grass. The six-toed calico sharpens her claws against the bark of a crooked maple. This pocket of time-space stretches on for miles. Here, the felines are legion. I'd have lifted every last one if it had been up to me. But I do my best. This place is not like the world I have rescued them from, nor is it like the place they'll be going.

'A tiger,' the cat lady marvels, the cats unconcerned by the man and the dog encroaching upon their kingdom. 'Still hard to believe. In an apartment. In Bayonne, New Jersey. He was a cruel man.'

The last time I counted, there are more cruel men than tigers down there, I note.

"Guns," grunts the cat lady aloud, his bathrobe drying in the simulated sun of the chamber, "a gunrunner or something like that. Shady dealings. There's no punishment too great for what that man did to that poor animal."

But there is, I correct him. *A world without tigers.*

When my reconnaissance is complete and I set forth in the ark, humanity will be condemned to look into a mirror that holds no reflection save their own. They will look in that mirror and realize that, after all this time, they are still strangers to themselves.

'The tiger,' he asks, 'could I see it?'

The nanotech afire in my brain carves a door in the time-space of the cats' summer room. The cat lady whispers his goodbyes. We step through the door, and return to the sleek, winding halls that maze through the ark's belly.

§

The tigers here are skeletons banded in fire. Captives sprung from zoos and circuses and canned hunting ranches. Stripes enmeshed with scars from whips. Fur pocked with buckshot. Robbed of most instinct. Suspicious of all the space this liberation affords them.

There is a separate chamber aboard for the tigers I've plucked from the wild. You could traverse that jungle chamber—with its thick, waxy leaves and suffocating heat—for an entire afternoon without a single glimpse of a tiger.

Here there are concrete alcoves and tires set against a creaking forest, synthesized protein flanks set out each day for the captives to feast upon, sparing the goats and boar a protracted exit at the jaws of creatures that have never been trained to hunt—refugees denied the place from whence they came, misaligned with where they've found themselves now.

The jaw of the gunrunner's prize goes slack when he picks up our scents. He freezes. Locks us in the gaze of his amber eyes— an unbroken, magnificent, threatening thing. The cat lady and I tense upon our perch beside the door.

I suppress the growl that rises in my throat. Fur prickles along my spine. A shadow of the instinct that's been bred right out of me.

The cat lady trembles, but I smell no fear off him. He shudders as a devotee might in the presence of a deity that's eluded him his whole life. We are caught between two worlds. All three of us.

The tiger soon loses interest and returns to his tire. He bats it clear across the yard with one vibrant, golden swipe, effortlessly as a tomcat would a felt mouse stuffed with catnip.

We should go now, I prod him. We've both been here too long.

§

The cat lady traipses toward the platform as if he's walking the plank. I paw a lever to disperse the cloud cover that swaddles the ark. His legs go rubber once they disperse. The tractor beam swathes him in honey-yellow light. He becomes weightless, swimming in air.

It's a cinch, I assure him.

'I once puked sliding down a log flume,' he informs me.

You made the trip up, I tell him. *Down's the easy part. You won't feel a thing.*

'I don't have a roof anymore. I don't have my cats anymore. Are you sure there's no room—?'

It's not a question of having the room, I remind him. *There's a whole planet of strays down there—entire continents speckled with rooftops. You'll find your way.*

They'll all find their way. Or they won't.

He struggles to extract himself from the beam. He loses one of his faux bear paw slippers. He lashes around like a drowning man: a person who might pull the entire world down around him.

'What am I supposed to do?' he asks.

Peddle your story on the talk show circuit, I tell him. *There'll be no shortage of footage of you being spit out of a flying saucer come morning.*

'And just what do I tell them?'

I'd embellish things a little. Make something up. Humans don't have much appetite for the truth. Give them bug-eyed aliens. Evasive probes. Nothing too outside their comfort zone. The parts they don't like they'll just disregard anyway. You could make a killing and open a cat sanctuary somewhere.

'But *my* cats,' he insists. 'Schwartz, Drusilla, Mephistopheles...'

I pause for a moment and try to understand. For all the hyper-evolved circuitry in my brain, attachment is a concept alien to me. From the day I was weaned off my mother, I was never afforded the luxury of *missing.* No pack, no pride, no nothing. An empty belly. Teeth bared against a cold, cold world.

Live as long as I have and you begin to understand that everything is adrift, always.

§

The cat lady folds and begins to weep, knees drawn into his belly. Embryonic. I am sending him off. One of the greatest tragedies of the time we spend breathing is that we seldom get to go out on our own terms.

It's hard to be reminded that this man is not so unlike me, tied down to the same spinning world—clutching at me as he drowns.

I could never have fathomed what an affliction intellect truly can be until the Progenitors cursed me with my own—how the specters of tomorrow's worries, of yesterday's missteps, constantly encroach upon the here-and-now.

Perhaps it's this steady diet of uncertainty that tempered these hairless bipeds into such callous, cruel things—erecting fictions about their own grandeur for so long that they started believing their own PR. Lies that made victims of us all.

This frightened little man hovering in the stasis of the tractor beam is one cell in a malignancy devouring a dwindling planet. My decision should be easy, but there are chinks in every armor—no matter how slight. Even my own.

Bearing witness to such vulnerability is crippling. My paw lingers over the tractor beam lever when I should just spit him back out where I found him.

But in cleaning shop down here, I've stumbled upon a world replete with clipped-winged angels. Noticeable only if you take the time to dig deep enough: a soup stock bone out the pocket of a woolen coat reeking of tobacco smoke, a man in bear claw slippers opening tins in a mewling alley.

In turning my back on humanity's worst, perhaps I'm blinding myself to the best. At this very moment, on an ark full of things no one else thought worth saving, the cat lady suddenly does not seem to be the odd man out I first thought he was.

§

I kill the beam. The cat lady drops across the sealed hatch. I pad toward him. Sniff at the worn seat of his robe. Night has fallen over Bayonne, New Jersey.

What do they call you? I ask. Names are given, seldom chosen—even among their own kind.

'Sal,' he replies. 'You?'

Once upon a time they called me Laika, I tell him.

'Russian?' he asks.

Human, I tell him.

'So, can I—?'

There's only so much harm just one of you can do, I suppose. It will be a lonely life, just you in a whole, wide world. You need to understand that.

He nods. 'The cats will be there, won't they? Schwartz, Drusilla, Mephistopheles?'

And the tigers and black bears and lab mice and veal calves. Still, nature's no less ambivalent up there than down here.

His thoughts spew forth like the contents of an upset stomach. 'W- why the sudden change of heart?'

Speaking from one failed experiment to the next, I confess, *I'm not entirely sure. Temporary blindness, maybe.*

But there is something there—some bond frayed threadbare, some lapsed promise unfulfilled. The chalky light from tenement windows—blue and red and seismic from the roofs of police vehicles— sets the world afire; they are legion down there with their fractured hearts and studio apartments.

Perhaps this is where it started, I think to myself, the bond between our species: one predator weaseling its way beside the other's fire.

Sal the Cat Lady breaks the psychic silence. 'Look how far we've come,' he marvels.

And how much further we need to go. By sheer force of will I point the ark skyward, away from the blinding lights, the musk of death and asphalt.

The Dark Defines Us

TJ Perkins

The car chugged to a halt on the back road west of Fallstaff Drive.

"Crap!" Jesse pounded the steering wheel. "I just had a tune up!" In his mind there was no reason for his car to act up. It was practically new, give or take a few years. But still—

"I can't be late." Tonight's meeting was important. He finally had proof there was something in the Canis Major Constellation and could show the skeptics exactly where it was coming from. The sound waves and signals; they were real. This was his one chance to prove his theory, and as an up and coming astronomer he didn't want to blow it.

"Come on. Come on." He turned the key in the ignition and gently tapped the gas. Nothing.

His cell phone buzzed next to him.

"Abby? Yeah, my car stalled." He paused and looked around. "I don't know. But I'm not far away. It's gotten really foggy all of a sudden. Weird. It's hard to see. Wait, I think I see the sign for Munster Hill Road." He turned the key again. The car sputtered as if coming to life, but stopped short. Jesse blew out a miserable sigh and rolled his eyes as Abby rambled on. "O-okay, okay. Tell them to stall the panels for as long as they can. Make sure my notes are in order and the projector is set up and ready to go. Yeah...yeah...okay...bye."

Jesse regretted the decision to take the back road to Stephen's Observatory, but it was the shortest way. The Science Committee had gathered; big wigs from all parts of the government and even small facilities, including the SETI program, were in attendance. It had taken him years to get an audience with these people. He couldn't let this opportunity slip by.

Maybe Aaron could fill in for him until he got there? He started to punch in Aaron's number and stopped; his muscles tensed up. Jesse stared at his hands. Confusion rose as they began to uncontrollably tremble. His heart pounded in his chest like a thousand running horses, as his breath quickened and his mouth went dry. He didn't understand it, couldn't explain it, but something was happening. A God-awful feeling of absolute dread came over him.

Movement from his peripheral caught Jesse's eye. Two boys stood there in the thick swirling fog and stared at him…just stared. He sucked in his breath. There was something wrong about these kids.

Dressed in plain faded black jeans and tattered black hoodies, the boys couldn't have been any more than twelve and fifteen years old. They kept their hoods up, didn't smile, didn't wave, and didn't act the way young teens normally would if they saw a stranger in trouble. Jesse was on edge at the sight of them. *And why were they wearing hoodies for as hot as it was?* he wondered. But his curiosity piqued when they started to quietly talk to each other. Though they spoke in soft tones their voices rang out loudly in his mind. *How were they doing this?*

"This is the one," the younger boy said to the other; his voice monotone, emotionless. He never took his eyes off Jesse. "The one we must take." It wasn't a question.

"Yes. Father wants this one," the older boy replied in the same lifeless tone. "He *knows*."

"Yes. Father will say we are good."

"Agreed. Father will say we are successful."

Jesse stared with mouth agape. He regained a bit of control, shook the jitters from his hands and tried to start his car again. The slow whine and grind made him a bit hopeful, but the engine refused to turn over. The lights were on, all the other accessories appeared to be working, but the blasted auto just wouldn't start. He put his window down a crack.

"Hey, what're you kids doing out here? Do you live nearby?" Perhaps their parents were less creepy and could give him a jump.

The boys didn't respond. They didn't have to. To him their plan was clear and their target, Jesse, was within their grasp.

"You should give us a ride," said the older boy.

Jesse was dumb struck. "Well, my car won't start. So, I can't give you a ride."

"We need to use your phone," the younger one said stepping closer to the car door.

The kids' overly-pale, lifeless faces sent chills up Jesse's spine. He noticed the boys walked stiffly, with no sort of swag, taking small, determined steps closer to the driver's side door. They regarded him with black eyes—all black, the entire thing—like a shark's!

Jesse gasped. Black-eyed children! He had heard of the urban legend, read accounts of their association with abduction and aliens and death, but he never thought they were actually true.

Fear gripped him in the chest with a squeezing force and he couldn't tear his gaze away from the boy's dead eyes. He tried to move his hand to the car keys, but it wouldn't respond. His arms felt heavy, so very heavy.

"Yes. We need to use your phone. You have to invite us in so we may use your phone," said the older boy.

Jesse couldn't stop staring at their eyes—black as a deep abyss, unblinking. *No*, he wanted to say, but couldn't. His muscles refused to cooperate and the sensation of being paralyzed took over his entire upper body. Sweat trickled down his face and his chest hurt from taking nervous, shallow panting breaths. He had to move. He had to get away.

"Will you invite us in?" the younger one said, a bit more forcefully. His hand reached for the slight opening of the window.

They're here to take me away! Jesse was screaming in his head for them to get away, shouting deep inside for his hands to move. His body wasn't responding and his logical scientific mind couldn't comprehend what was happening. *Or maybe, it doesn't want to comprehend,* he thought. *The black-eyed children can make you do their bidding!*

The younger boy's hand touched the window.

Eyes wild, terror overtaking every aspect of this body, Jesse gasped for breath as the small fingers reached through the opening, wiggling slightly, trying to worm their way inside, reaching for him.

Move, damn it, move! Jesse thought. He willed his muscles to obey, his hand to reach for the key, and turn it.

He couldn't look at them. He assumed their eerie power would loosen its grip if he could break eye contact. He focused on his hand; telling his rational mind to look away from the boys. His hand obeyed, and he was finally able to turn the key in the ignition. Jesse's car roared to life. He welcomed the rush of cool evening air filling his lungs as he threw the vehicle into gear and stomped on the accelerator.

Dirt flew into the air as the tires spun on lose gravel. He sped down the dark road, ignoring the fog and danger, and swiped at the sweat on his brow. Jesse gasped and panted; half crying, half moaning as the terror that had gripped his body slowly released its hold. He cast a glance at the partially opened window, almost expecting to see the boy's hand ripped off and lodged in the tight space, flapping in the wind as the car sped along, but it wasn't there.

Almost immediately, Munster Hill Road came up on his left. His tires screeched and the car's rear end fishtailed as he made the sharp turn, pushed down on the gas and sped up the hill to the observatory.

The conference was in full swing as Jesse skidded to a halt in the first parking space he saw. In a flurry of panic he grabbed his charts, maps and briefcase and dashed through the large wide-open double doors. Abby met him just inside; a look of relief on her face.

"What's going on," she asked. "You look terrible."

With breath taxed and hands shaking, Jesse reached for his paperwork, dropping pens and his glasses.

"Seriously," Abby said, retrieving the items. "What happened to you?"

"Why, do I look…strange?"

"You're pale and breathing hard and, well—out of sorts. I'll ask again: What's going on?"

"N– nothing," he stammered. "Nothing. I just needed to get here." He looked at the doors, eyes wild with fear. "Why are the doors open?"

"It's hot and the air conditioning isn't working very well. Seriously—are you all right?"

"Fine."

"You're all sweaty—"

"My presentation. I– I have t– to—"

"Go. You're all set," Abby quietly urged.

Aaron was on stage, stammering through an explanation of Jesse's findings and losing the attention of everyone present. *Hopefully, I still have time to save my reputation, Jesse thought.*

After several minutes of apologies, and back tracking through the mess that Aaron had made, Jesse finally had the full attention of all those present. He walked them through his data, pointing at maps and star charts and stepped through the collection timeline.

"And due to these findings, I have pin-pointed the location from which the signals are coming." He tapped his map with a long, slender wooden pointer. "Directly in the Canis Major Constellation and, more precisely, from behind Sirius."

This comment created a stirring of mumbled conversations that rolled through the crowd. Some scholars sat up, looked at each other and started taking notes while others smiled, shook their heads and quietly laughed.

Now, he had their attention. "I know this area has been a target of interest in the past and nothing has come of the research. However, we've taken a slightly different approach, which I'm not at liberty to discuss at this time." Though his confidence had improved Jesse remained nervous as he pulled up another one of his maps and pointed. "Alnilam, Mintaka and Alnitak, which form Orion's Belt, are also involved with the signals. These stars are directly lined up with the pyramids in Egypt. My research has proven, because of this," he tapped the map and smiled, "we're able to detect the signals. They're a giant receptor, like an ear for the Earth.

Jesse paused, letting the importance of what he'd said sink in then resumed speaking. Some people think the Egyptians had been taught by the Sky People, the Gods, or more precisely—ancient alien visitors, who are the real reason the pyramids exist. Now you don't have to believe that, and I'm not asking you to, but I want to share with you the signals that we've been monitoring for the past four months."

Abby took her cue and began playing the recording. A combination of static associated with high- and low-pitched squeals filled the room. Then the recording shifted to a flow of dots and dashes, followed by more static, before ending in what was reminiscent of radio gibber.

"Now, see here, Doctor Palmer," said a heavyset, balding man. He regarded Jesse from over a pair of small, round glasses perched on the end of his nose. "Those signals almost sound like ones from our military during World War I."

"That's exactly what we thought when we first heard them." Jesse was ready for the backlash. "Could this be sound waves from years past, right from our own planet? Perhaps they traveled away from Earth then came back? But it's not. Our calculations have tracked these sounds coming from behind Sirius. And one of the stars which make up Orion's Belt is receiving this signal and so are we."

"It's coming from a planet?" someone called out.

"Not a planet. It's an area of dark space…a Stargate, if you will. *Nibiru.*" Jesse motioned for Aaron to join him on stage and assist with holding a large star chart.

Again, speculation was verbally thrown about the room. Jesse puffed out his chest and scanned the audience, anxious to see if the SETI group were regarding him with interest. They were. *Mission accomplished.*

Jesse continued. "Nibiru isn't a planet, as many people believe. It's an area that allows extraterrestrial visitors to come and go like a wormhole, only it's not a wormhole. Think of it as a door opening and closing. And when the door is open the signals come through." Aaron stepped away and rolled up the chart.

He looked up at Abby to motion for her to stop the recording, and froze. His voice caught in his throat as he spotted the black-eyed boys standing just outside the double doors, The boys looked at him—waiting. Abby didn't seem to notice them. She just kept tabs on his speech, turning pages, waiting for cues and periodically digging in her purse.

Jesse blew out a nervous breath. The fear that had enveloped him on his first encounter with the strange teens crept into his chest once again. Cold sweat broke out on his forehead.

I've got to hold it together, he thought. *I can't let this audience see me come unglued. I'm was surrounded by all these people—protected. At the moment, these kids can't touch me.*

"Doctor Palmer? Doctor Palmer?" said Aaron.

Aaron was suddenly next to him holding a small piece of folded paper. Jesse didn't see or hear him approach. His vision skewed to the left, and then to the right. A slight ringing echoed in his ears.

What is happening to me?

Jesse gazed at the audience, half expecting to see people staring blankly at him as if he were acting weird. But they weren't. Nothing had changed. He looked back at Abby again, and noticed the black-eyed children were gone from the doorway. Immediately, his vision and hearing cleared.

Jesse exhaled slowly and took the note from Aaron. His hands shook slightly as he opened it and looked at the scrawl.

Time to go, it read.

Jesse sucked in his breath and tried to still his thumping heart. He wasn't going to obey the message. He didn't have to go anywhere he didn't want to go.

"Who gave this to you?" he asked Aaron.

"It was passed up through the audience and given to me by that man," Aaron pointed to an old man in the front row, leaning on a wooden cane, sporting facial stubble, thick-rimmed glasses and a hearing aid.

Jesse blew off the idea that the man would have anything to do with the black-eyed boys. He looked like he could hardly walk on his own, let alone be part of an abduction.

The floor was thrown open for discussion and Jesse was drawn into a tailspin of explanations, hypotheses and fact-checking. A few people present seemed determined to embarrass or discredit him. But he handled it all with polite professionalism. Thirty minutes later he left the stage and attention was turned to the final speaker of the evening.

Abby collected his maps and charts as Jesse joined her at the back of the room.

"Whew, that was something, huh?" Abby smiled.

"Yeah. Glad it's over," Jesse laughed. "I think we may be getting grants or a little bit of funding from a few of these guys to help continue our research."

Feeling accomplished and confident, black-eyed kids forgotten, Jesse nonchalantly headed out the double doors and stood on the wide, long concrete steps.

The night was hot and muggy. His clothes clung to him and he tried to find a bit of comfort in the sounds of the crickets and frogs serenading each other in the surrounding trees. He scanned the grounds. No creepy emo kids lurking nearby. *Good.* He'd wait around until after the last presentation was over, mingle over coffee and snacks, then make his getaway.

Low thrumming from beyond the parking lot, across a grassy opening and through the surrounding forest caught Jesse's attention. He turned and strained his eyes as he peered into the night. Off in the distance and partially blocked by the trees, flashing lights of red, white and light blue pulsed, slowly flickering, running horizontally from side to side. Then the flickering lights paused before repeating the pattern in the opposite direction. The light show continued as thin spotlights scanned the ground and treetops.

"Wow," Jesse breathed.

"Beautiful, isn't it."

Jesse started at the voice coming from his left side. He looked down to see the older man who'd passed up the note standing there, hunched over and leaning heavily on his cane.

"Should I know you?" Jesse asked.

"You should. But you won't remember." The man sighed and looked around. "Few believe. Some do, but most don't. You can't force people to believe. Sometimes I think people want that mystery of *what if* to keep lingering on so they can have something to keep them occupied." He shrugged his hunched-over shoulders and started walking across the parking lot and towards the flashing lights.

Jesse stared after him. He wondered, *was the man talking about aliens? He had to be, but wait, where was he going?*

The old man stopped. He looked over his shoulder. "You coming, or not?"

All rational thinking left his mind as Jesse walked down the steps and joined the man.

"Where are you going?"

"There," he pointed with his cane. "The lights beckon."

Jesse froze. "If that's an alien ship, do you mean to board it?"

The old gent slowed, but didn't stop. He cast an amused smile over his shoulder.

"Are you crazy?" Jesse said.

"Do you want to live the rest of your life, here, trying to get people to believe you, when you could venture out, right now, and see for yourself? The truth is right there, my boy, right in front of you. All you gotta do is grab it!"

Jesse swallowed, rubbed his chin, then ran his fingers through his hair. Wild thoughts flashed through his mind. Should he go? Maybe he should run back inside and try to get everyone else to come with him? If he did the craft, if that's what it was, would most likely take off before he got back outside. Then, he'd look like a complete idiot. No. He should go investigate first, and then come back with the evidence.

He checked his pocket. Cell phone charged and ready for pictures or videos. This was going to make him famous.

"Hey! Hold up," Jesse called, running to catch up.

The old man could move pretty fast when he wanted to and disappeared into the dark. Branches rustled, twigs snapped as the old man pushed through the thick growth and trees. Jesse gathered his courage and ventured in.

The lights blinded Jesse the closer he got to them, but he pressed on. He reached for his phone. The low whirling sound pulsed with the beating of a heart as the lights flickered and changed direction. *Do they know I'm here?* Jesse wondered.

The spot lights turned off, the forest darkened and Jesse got the video mode on his phone ready then froze in mid-motion. Undeniable fear overtook him. He couldn't breathe. He couldn't react.

"We need to use your phone."

Jesse sucked in his breath and the hair on his arms stood on end. Prickles of energy swirled over his exposed skin and he shook and trembled as if standing naked in the dead of winter.

"Yes, we need to call our father."

Jesse slowly turned his head. A small gasp escaped his trembling lips and his knees felt weak as he realized the two black-eyed boys were right next to him, reaching out for him.

"N– no! Why are you here?" Jesse backed away, bumped into a tree and felt his way backward in the dark. "What do you want with me?" his voice wavered as he continued backing up, never taking his eyes away from the two boys.

"Don't you want to come with us?"

"Yes. Come with us."

Throat tight, mind whirling, Jesse could only get out a few words. "What do you want with me?"

The black-eyed teens advanced with slow, steady steps, seeming to steer Jesse where they wanted him to go. They each reached out a hand, their eyes boring into his, penetrating his mind, staring unblinking, picking apart his panicky thoughts.

"Don't be afraid," the younger boy said, and forced a small smile.

"Father is waiting," the older boy said. "It's not polite to keep him waiting.

Jesse backed into the dark trees and foliage; his cell phone held tightly in his hand ready to record. He wanted to run, but couldn't get his legs to obey. He just stared into those black eyes and kept backing up.

The whirling became louder at his back as he broke through the dense foliage. He turned, shielded his eyes, and gawked at the craft and the three creatures standing next to the old man he'd followed earlier. He dropped his phone to the ground. The kids could have it; he didn't care.

"Doctor Jesse Palmer," he heard in his mind. "So good to finally meet you."

The voice was clear as day, but none of the creatures' mouths moved. Jesse's scientific mind went into over drive.

"You really are here," he gasped. "You're using telepathy. I knew it. A– and this is your craft." He glanced at the old gent. "Are you their ambassador?"

The elderly man tossed down his cane and pressed a small devise in his hand. His image wavered, blurred and transmuted; in a matter of seconds the he was one of the aliens: Tall, thin and gray. The aliens were shaped like the extraterrestrial beings he had heard about his entire adult life.

"No, Doctor Palmer. We do not have such a thing. I am the mission leader. We've been watching you for a long time. Your intelligence is above other Earth Beings, and we sought you out for assistance."

The other aliens flanked him and ushered him towards a ramp that slowly lowered from beneath the craft.

"You've done well, boys. Father is pleased. You may go."

The black-eyed children had been forgotten in all the excitement, and when Jesse turned his head to look he saw their shadows melt into the darkness.

"Come Doctor Palmer. We have much to discuss," the leader said, his voice soothing and calm. He placed a large four-fingered hand on Jesse's shoulder and guided him towards the ramp.

Jesse stopped, dug his feet into the ground and resisted the gentle push forward. "Wait. In there?" All of the encounter stories he had heard of flooded his mind.

"Doctor Palmer, we really shouldn't conduct business out in the open like this; and so close to the observatory. It could draw unneeded attention. Don't you agree?"

Before Jesse could agree or disagree, he felt an invisible grip on his body. His arms fell to his sides, his body stiffened, his jaws tightened and his feet lifted slightly off the ground. Unable to protest, he was levitated over the grass, up the ramp and into the brightly-lit craft.

The hatch sealed with a snap-hiss, the lighting dimmed slightly, and Jesse was finally able to move of his own accord.

"This is much better, don't you think?" the alien thought to him. "You always did want to see inside of our ship. Yes?"

Jesse relaxed and allowed his gaze to sweep the large, open area. Void of furniture or trappings, the inside of the ship was white, stark and sterile. It smelled that way, too.

"Your mind is very intriguing to us. You are much more intelligent that your fellow Beings." The leader gracefully moved in a floating fashion from the entrance ramp down a short hall.

Jesse smiled and nodded sheepishly. The flattery filled his heart with admiration for these creatures. He dropped his guard. It wasn't needed. They liked him, and made him feel comfortable.

"They don't deserve your theories. They will never appreciate what you can offer. They don't deserve all the knowledge you possess." The leader stopped as they entered a small room, just as white and sterile as the rest of the ship, and gracefully gestured for Jesse to proceed ahead.

Jesse walked over to a table and happily undressed and lay down. He wasn't sure why he did that; he just knew—felt, really—it was what his new alien friends required of him.

"But *we* have need of your intelligence, Jesse." Bright lights came on above him as another alien wheeled a table lined with instruments within arms' reach.

"We will appreciate your intelligence. We will appreciate all you can offer us." Two more aliens appeared at his side and picked up the scalpels.

"Wait!" Eyes wild with sudden panic, Jesse went to move off the table, but his body didn't respond. "What're you doing?"

The leader waved his overly large hand just above Jesse's face. A feeling of peace and calm enveloped him.

"This won't hurt. We're just going to do a few…tests. Lie still," the second alien said.

"It won't take long," the third alien assured him, moving closer to the table.

Jesse smiled and closed his eyes. "I want to learn all I can from you. Take me to your world, show me the cosmos, help me understand where the signals I've been tracking are coming from."

"Of course. As soon as we complete our tests."

Jesse drifted off; a smile on his face. Moments later he awoke to the feeling of his head floating.

Bubbles flitted up from around his eyes, tickling his brain. He went to speak, but nothing came out. He went to move but nothing responded. Though moving, he was not walking of his own accord.

This is puzzling, he thought, gazing around the room. He realized he was at waist height, looking through a fluid-filled tank. Looking more closely, he saw large fingers gripping the tank on either side.

What the hell?

"There is no need for alarm, Doctor Palmer. You're all right." The alien that held him turned and waited for the leader to catch up, wheeling a table with a body laid out upon it.

Prone and still the body wore familiar clothing and the shape was familiar, but the eyes were missing and the skull was split down the center, laid open like a peach. It was familiar…too familiar. Wait—

Jesse wanted to scream and shout a thousand curse words. That was *his* body!

He accompanied the aliens as they wheeled his body to a laboratory and parked it next to several others.

"You see Jesse, it's true, we are creating hybrid humans—ones we can control, and plant among the masses until we're ready for, how do you humans put it? *The big reveal.* The signals you picked up are from our planet. We get instructions the same as you humans do from our boss."

"We're ready for the transplant sir."

"At your leisure," the leader said.

Jesse's eyes watched as the aliens brought a large bubbling tube of a brain, just a brain, floating in off-blue liquid.

"Yes, a new brain, that we programmed, will be inserted into your body and it will be released back into your life. It was necessary, you see. We couldn't have you convincing your kind to do more research on our signals. But we are not without compassion. We allowed you to keep your eyes attached to your brain, so you may witness that which you researched all of your life. We are quite pleased with your brain. It will be very useful to us."

Trapped in a watery tank with only his brain and eyes, Jesse wanted to scream, to cry, and beg to be released. But he couldn't.

"Don't worry Doctor Palmer, you will be connected to our computer. Your mind *is* actually most unusual, so full of knowledge and the mysteries of human thoughts and emotions."

What was left of Jesse was placed on a table. Long thin wires touched him, tingling with a pulse like a heartbeat. He didn't feel fear. He didn't feel panic. He didn't feel, well, anything. His mind worked overtime, no rest, no peace, only the continuous nudge of the computer system begging for knowledge. And he had no choice but to obey.

The flashing lights of the spacecraft darkened just as it rose quietly from the earth, gaining in distance and speed, before it shot beyond the earth's stratosphere and into the darkness of space.

Jesse's cell phone, left where he dropped it, finished recording.

Invisible Spheres

W. T. Paterson

There was a sixty-inch flat screen television mounted to the wall. A Bluetooth surround sound system hung behind the overstuffed cushions of a tan sectional couch. The windows were each lined with light blocking curtains, which, for a farmhouse in Orfordville, Wisconsin, seemed out of place.

"It doesn't make sense," Mrs. Montgomery told the detectives. In her dark purple sweater, mascara running like dark veins beneath her eyes, she blew her nose into a tissue and kept scrolling through the home's security footage. Eight different camera angles showed the outside perimeter.

They rewound and played the clip over and over again. The footage showed little Jessi Montgomery running through the yard in her pink jeans and Disney princess T-shirt, exiting frame, and never reappearing inside of any camera. Detectives Burgos and Innason had watched the clip, and then gone outside to measure the distance between the outdoor cameras. A foot and a half blind spot, hardly anything to lose sleep over. Yet, if the little girl were running along that route, she would have, *should have* been spotted.

"Who else has access to this feed?" Burgos asked. His thinning hair slicked back, sagging cheeks after years of hard drinking, he still found a way to look compassionate.

"Just my husband. But he's out in LA talking to some financiers," Mrs. Montgomery said.

"Have you made any enemies?" Innason asked. She knew it was a bad question the moment she asked it. Always looking years younger than she was with dark brown hair and thick dark eyebrows, Innason had a way of unintentionally making people actively dislike her.

"Is she serious?" Mrs. Montgomery asked Burgos, shocked. She turned back towards the young detective. "The whole town hates us! You were here two weeks ago when our porch was vandalized! Obviously, we have enemies!"

Innason knew she had to stand down. Burgos had taught her that to back step during an intake leads to a lack of trust. She remembered the scene, too—bright orange dollar signs spray-painted across the newly finished porch, the manure dumped through the sunroof of their brand new Chevy Silverado, the tire tracks cutting through the green lawn in brown designs like crop circles, it was both a warning and retaliation.

"I know the town is unhappy that you sold off your farmland to developers," Burgos said. His voice was calm and steady. "What we need to know is if anyone lost out, if anyone might take Jessi for ransom so that they can recoup."

"No," Mrs. Montgomery said. "It was family land. We didn't even sell all of it either. These developers offered us triple the market value and…how could we say *no?* We could send Jessi to whatever college she wanted."

It was two o'clock in the afternoon, but the pale sun was already hanging low in the January sky. The day had never lifted beyond a dull gray and light snow kept sweeping through and dusting the frozen hills like powdered sugar across a half-eaten strudel.

Innason excused herself and stepped into the hallway. Jessi's framed pictures lined the wall. From the looks, the fourth-grader always wore her hair in pigtails. She had thick glasses with purple, plastic rims. Her body was a short, stout frame, looking as though she had come from a long line of farmers. One of her eyes pointed more inward than the other.

"Who's this with Jessi?" Innason called out. She was staring at a picture of a grown man in a casual green button-down shirt tucked into his khakis, kneeling and smiling with an arm around the little girl. Burgos and Mrs. Montgomery stepped into the hallways.

"That was Mr. Betts, her guidance counselor," the woman said.

Innason started to scribble notes onto her pocket-sized notepad. She was nearing the end. The name *Betts* rang a bell.

"How would you describe their relationship?" Burgos asked.

"Wonderful. Sincerely lovely. Bullies at school kept making Jessi cry. They called her *Blubby*, and Mr. Betts was the only one who cared to take action. The boys got suspended and he talked our little girl through all of those complicated emotions."

"Do you think we could talk to him?" Innason asked.

"What? No..." Mrs. Montgomery said, looking at Burgos. She was deeply confused by the question.

"I understand you think highly of him, and he's not in any trouble, we just..."

"He's dead, you idiot! He was beaten to death by some homophobic jerks! It has not been an easy year for any of us and, you know what? Can I get a different detective, please? I don't trust her to find my baby girl!"

"Mrs. Montgomery," Burgos said, taking the trembling woman's hand inside of his callused palms. "I assure you that we'll do everything in our power to find your little Jessi. I promise."

"Are you familiar with your neighbor Carson Braddock?" Innason asked. Burgos immediately and audibly sighed with disappointment. Mrs. Montgomery pointed to the door and told them both to get out.

§

The temperatures were dropping as fast as the sun. Burgos and Innason sat in the idling car until warm air began to blow through the vents of their state issued navy blue Crown Victoria.

"I'm not losing my career and pension over this," Burgos said. He was looking across the frozen, desolate farmlands where single trees stood shivering in the wind like abandoned martyrs.

"You don't find it odd that Carson Braddock has *never* been wrong?" Innason asked. She, too, was scanning the horizon wondering how many patches of land there were in the country, let alone the state. Wide expanses that grew corn and wheat, the dairy farms that stretched farther than any one person could reasonably maintain. She wondered how much of that land held buried secrets.

"He's a lunatic! Okay? End of discussion. And I'm reporting this to the Captain."

"March eighteenth of last year, Carson Braddock was beaten to within an inch of his life outside of the Ryan Gallway and Maggie Schweitzer wedding reception. Why? Because he told Maggie that she would have a baby boy born with six fingers, which would please the alien overlords that surround us all."

"Stop…"

"On November nineteenth of that same year, Maggie gave birth to Benjamin, an eight-pound, four-ounce boy with six fingers on his right hand. Shortly after, Ryan gets a massive promotion. Maggie receives a big inheritance. They live in luxury inside of a community that's almost entirely blue collar. How did he know?"

"He's a kook. That's enough," Burgos said, only it felt less like an order and more like a plea.

"We need to go talk to him," Innason said. "Follow all leads, right?"

"He's not a lead, he's a…"

"If the end result leads us to Jessi, what does it matter?"

Burgos put the car into reverse and shook his head. The tires crunched the gravel of the driveway like amplified static shocks.

"There are no alien overlords," he said. The detective closed his eyes and laid his forehead against the steering wheel. "I need you to be grounded. A little girl is missing. We do this by the book."

"No one from the town will talk because they're all a suspect. Even to clear their name means implicating someone else, which makes them subject for retaliation. If a crazy person gives us real intel, who cares?"

Burgos pointed the hood of the car down the road towards Braddock's farm hardly able to believe he was caving.

"You're taking the fall if this goes sideways," he said.

"Fine by me," Innason said, knowing that she was already one foot out the door anyway after being found wandering in a field half-naked, acting drunk and having no idea how she got there. She only remembered flashes of light and a long droning sound, like a thousand voices all singing the same low note at the opposite end of a hallway.

"What if he *is* right?" Burgos said distantly. Innason looked at her partner and for the first time since knowing him, felt concerned.

§

He was outside when they found him. Chopping wood in swift, powerful strokes that sent vibrations through the cold like buckshot, Carson Braddock stood on the dead lawn next to his house like a Grecian statue. It smelled like the static of impending snow and cold, wet mud.

Burgos grunted as he got out of his car. He slammed the door loud enough to let his distant presence be known. Innason got out and closed her door realizing that as she approached, her hand hovered just above the gun clipped to her belt.

Braddock bent over and put a piece of wood on the chopping block. He measured once and paused, letting the blade shave the tip of the log.

"I know why you've come," he said, without turning around. Even with the vast openness of the sparse fields behind him, his voice echoed.

"Why's that?" Innason said. It was spoken confidently, but around the edges of both words was the slightest of tremors. Braddock came down with the blade and splintered the log.

"The girl," he said, and looked at the wood he had just split. "Can't start a fire without kindling."

"What can you tell us?" Burgos asked. He tried to play it cool, but he could feel sweat break out against the back of his collar.

"I warned her," Braddock said. "I warned them all. But none would have it. I know little Jessi Montgomery is gone. That's a fact."

"Can you put down the axe and talk with us for a moment?" Innason asked. They were close enough for the conversation to feel personal, but distant enough to know that if he were to charge, they'd still be able to draw their firearms.

"Let me guess," the man started. "It was like she disappeared into thin air. Wait, no, that's the wrong word. It was like she was *absorbed* into nothing."

Burgos shot Innason a look.

"Is that what your alien overlords told you?" Burgos said.

Braddock looked at them with contempt. He tossed the axe down at his feet and looked up into the sky.

"I used to think that one day, they'd come down and block out the sun like an eclipse. We'd fall to our knees at the sight of these new gods and beg for mercy. Our planet would either be purged of the cancerous human, or we'd become their slaves in some galactic conquest. But that's not what happened. Not exactly. Turns out they've always been here. And we're not slaves, oh no, we're just toys."

"Tell us about Jessi," Innason said.

"You won't find her, but she will show up," he said, almost laughing. "It's part of their storyline."

"The alien overlords?" Burgos asked. There was clear venom in the question. Braddock scowled and started looking over his shoulder.

"They travel inside invisible spheres. They watch us, track us, manipulate us for their own entertainment. Fat, hairless creatures. Hideous, really, like shaved raccoons with the heads of toddlers. They smell like the folds of a homeless man's skin."

He punched into the air and Innason felt her fingertips brush the cold metal of her gun. Braddock wrestled for a moment with something. It looked like he was miming a soccer ball between his hands until he started punching into it and bright neon sparks started to appear. A silver orb manifested and Braddock peeled back a layer of top metal revealing a squirming, crying creature.

Burgos was stunned into silence. Innason couldn't breathe.

"Is that…" Burgos said. Braddock had the creature by the nape of the neck and fully pried it free of its vessel.

"Ask it whatever you want. It'll respond in English, and it has no honor. None of them do. They are cowardly creatures so self-absorbed that they are nearly unable to deal with confrontation."

The creature was screaming and clawing. Its raw pinkish skin began steaming in the cold as it flailed its two pudgy arms, each with six fingers, and two pudgy feet, each with six toes. It kept blinking and looking away, the eyelids covering large black orbs for eyes.

Burgos fell to his knees.

"The…the girl…" Innason asked. She was drawing her service weapon slowly.

"She will be found dead," the creature squealed. "In the basement of her own home. We will manifest her body there and place an anonymous call to the police for investigation. We will watch as mother and father are tried and convicted for the murder of their daughter—a murder that they did not commit, think about committing, or have any part in. We will watch."

"Why?" Burgos asked. Tears had come to his eyes.

"Humans are so fragile. They make for great entertainment in their quest to feel important," the creature said. It sounded like it was choking on water with every painful word. "But they do not know that they are not important. That they are part of a greater system. That what they call God and Free Will are the decisions of an audience looking to stay entertained."

"But if you're all knowing, how did you get caught?" Innason asked.

"I chose suicide. Death is not for us what it is for you, and knowing we exist will have far reaching consequences. It will create for better entertainment."

The creature started coughing and hacking up a rancid brown liquid. Braddock had to shuffle to not get hit by the spittle. In the next moment, the creature became stiff and lifeless, its raw pink skin turning ashen gray.

"And y'all thought I was crazy," Braddock said. He dropped the body to the frozen mud near his feet and watched as it began to blow away like dust. "What else you want to know?"

§

Braddock sat handcuffed in the backseat. He didn't protest and mostly stayed silent. Burgos sat in the front with his head pressed against the steering wheel. Innason was in the passenger seat staring over the empty fields, service weapon in her lap.

"I'm not well," Burgos said.

"How do we even call this in?" Innason asked. She stared out against the blackened sky as the porch lights of Braddock's farmhouse illuminated the chipped and pale blue paint.

"We don't," Burgos said, pulling his head off of the steering wheel and sucking in an alarmingly large breath. "We do nothing, because the rules don't apply anymore."

In the backseat, Braddock started laughing.

"Liberating, isn't it? Once you get past the horrifying truth that our world is cheap entertainment, it's a lot easier to swallow," he said.

"Shut your mouth!" Burgos said, turning around with clenched fists. His face had turned so red that it was starting to look purple in the dark of the car. He snatched the gun from Innason's lap. "How do we fix this?!"

"Only one way out," Braddock smiled. Then, as if washed away by a spring rain, he vanished from the backseat and reappeared on the front lawn outside of the car. When he spoke, it was partly muted by the cold windshield and the winds that had begun to pick up. "But I'm too much of a coward to follow through."

He turned and casually walked to his front porch opening the screen door easily and using his shoulder to push open the wooden door to inside.

Innason was shaking in the passenger seat.

"This is my fault," she said. Saying it out loud brought tears to her eyes. "I pushed for this."

"It doesn't matter," Burgos said, looking at the gun the same way a mother looks at her newborn child. "My life has been dedicated to righting the wrongs of humanity. I've lost marriages over it. Lost sleep. My kids don't talk to me. I thought my quest for a higher truth was noble. Now, I see it as a game. The unbearable pain, the torment, the agony of telling a family that we found their missing child, but to start making arrangements for the body... I wasn't actually doing anything. I wasn't making the world a better place. I was feeding storylines. There's no god, no love, no destiny. There's only fat creatures swarming around us in invisible spheres playing with us like toys."

"I know it's hard to take in," Innason said. "Maybe it's all a hoax."

"No hoax," Burgos said, turning the barrel of the gun towards his face. "I've seen things that no human should ever see. People, bodies, acts, but this...I'll never recover from this."

He closed his eyes and pulled the trigger.

From inside, Braddock watched through the translucent yellow curtains as the cab of the state issued Crown Victoria flashed with white light and Innason barreled out of the passenger door screaming. It only lasted a moment before she was absorbed into the air and disappeared. She would later be found half naked and wandering a field complaining about low, droning voices talking like they were at the end of a hallway.

Then, as if nothing had happened, Burgos manifested in front of the car on his knees. He was sobbing. It started to snow again. He held the gun to his head and pulled the trigger, but it only clicked through empty chambers. For a moment inside of his mind, he saw the rest of his life flash. Every day, he tried to kill himself, and every day his attempts failed.

Above him, the stars shone brightly, twinkling as though part of a happy swarm forever content to watch and rarely, if ever, expose their true nature.

The Cud Brigade

Robert E. Waters

Hagerman, New Mexico, just outside of Roswell, 1991

"Papi, why are the cows floating in the sky?"

Little Rodrigo directed his father's gaze through the open window and out toward the bright lights of the sky machine that hovered above their hundred head of cattle.

Eduardo Diaz shot up from his office desk and stumbled through his son's Legos to get a better look out the window. Rodrigo was sad as Papi cursed with each biting step through his mountain of hard plastic blocks. Not because Papi hurt his feet with each step, but because it would be the last Legos he would ever get. The family had no money.

"No, no, no!" Papi said, visibly shaking as his dirty, calloused hands gripped the window sill. "*Son nuestras ultimas.* Our last!" Papi was out the door before Little Rodrigo could scramble after him.

The wind blowing off the sky machine's mighty turbine engines nearly blew Little Rodrigo back into the house. He leaned into the wind, struggled to keep his footing, and found Papi underneath the sky machine, near their toppled swing set.

Rodrigo fell beside Papi. They hugged each other. They were bathed in bright light, almost too bright to see through, but Rodrigo looked up into the light anyway and recognized some of the cattle as they ascended. There was Rosie; there Hilda. Over there were Brute and Mikey, the smallest but perhaps bravest of the Angus bulls. And there was King, the largest bull that Papi had ever raised. *He'll go for a pretty penny*, Papi had said. Perhaps King would have earned enough alone to bail them out of debt. Rodrigo did not know what *debt* meant, but it must be bad, for every time Papi and Mama spoke of it, Mama would cry and Papi would sulk.

Papi took his pistol out of his holster. Rodrigo tried to grab his hand, but Papi was too strong. He pointed the pistol into the light and fired once, twice, six times until all his bullets were spent. "Don't take them, you sons of bitches! Don't take them all!"

Little Rodrigo had heard of other cows being taken like this, but those stories seemed silly and impossible to believe. Yet, here was proof. Robbie Brooks, from a few miles away, had spoken about three of their cows "sucked up" into the sky machine, but folks around these parts never talked about it. It was something that happened, and losing one or two was no big deal. But an entire herd?

One after the other, the cows disappeared into the little round butthole that opened on the bottom of the sky machine. Rosie went first, then Brute, then Mikey. One after the other, until Papi screamed out and sounded like one of their heifers calling for a bull.

King was the last to disappear into the sky machine. Then the lights went out, the wind stopped, and the herd was gone. The machine drifted away quietly like a balloon released at a birthday party.

Papi fell to the ground and sobbed. "It's over. It's over. We're ruined."

Rodrigo had never seen Papi so shaken, so sad. And he, in turn, began to feel the same way, like all good boys feel when one of their parents hurt as bad as Papi now felt. Rodrigo let his tears come. "Don't worry, Papi," he said, "don't worry. We'll get them back. I promise, we'll get them back."

He did not know how he was going to keep his promise, but he would. If it took forever, he'd get Papi's herd back. And the family would be proud of him, and the family would be happy and prosperous once again, and he, Rodrigo Diaz, would finally get more Legos.

Artesia, New Mexico, near the Esperanza Meat Processing Facility, 2019

Hilda adjusted her high-powered binocs to zoom in on the cattle truck arriving at the gate of the slaughterhouse. A light, cold rain was falling, despite the fact that they were in the so-called *desert* region of this miserable little planet. A planet that held memories for Hilda. Memories she could not quite understand. But King knew their purpose for being here. King would make it right, and if all went well, she would, in time, bear his calf. The thought of it made her steel-enforced spine tingle, her modified face and features flush red. She couldn't wait.

"What do you see?" King asked as he and his commandos waited behind rusty, discarded hook-and-gambrel line equipment. He held out his massive, modified hand for the binocs, the fat stubs of his human-like fingers reaching out from underneath the hood of his blasted hoof. Hilda handed them over.

"Fresh arrivals," Hilda said, snorting away the dew falling into her nostrils. She sniffed the air, her enhanced olfactory senses picking up traces of blood and fear. "Heifers, mostly. One cow. One bull. All Reds."

"Praise The Benevolent," King said, letting a joyous coo escape his broad, black lips. He spit green cud juice and let it drip down his chin. "He will be pleased."

"Or angry," Speckle said behind them.

Speckle was a cow with a black-and-white spotted hide and had already been bred by the previous brigade commander. Now, she was second in command. She wanted King as much as Hilda. She was capable, but arrogant and headstrong. Hilda hated her.

"Say what you mean, Second," King ordered.

Speckle lowered her ears in respect. "My commander, our orders are to locate and identify herds for uplift, and then relay those orders to The Benevolent."

"We will do that," King replied.

"Yes, but you intend on attacking and destroying this facility and all the humans therein. That is beyond our mandate, and our duty is to follow orders. That is the imperative that The Shetai, they of The Benevolent, gave us. The Cud Brigades follow orders. It is our duty."

The Cud follow orders, or the Shetai die.

Hilda knew the imperative, uttered it to herself each morning as she rose from sleep with the herd. She screamed it aloud as she charged into battle against Shetai foe—the Byrg, the Morthos, the Iridanis. But humans were not Shetai foe. They were too valuable. Their bovine herds too valuable. It was forbidden to kill humans, but King's genetic memory, his traumatic connection with this planet, his stories of seeing his mother and father boarded up on trucks and sent to slaughter, compelled him to bring this action to a head, and he would do it despite Speckle's warnings. King both adored and hated The Benevolent, and Hilda admired in him that steel resolve for independence. It was rare among the Cud Brigades. Some of the bulls had it, but The Benevolent had bred most of those desires, those memories, out of their uplifted minds. King was special, and Hilda loved him. It was inappropriate to confess her feelings before King had declared her a mate, but it was hard to keep it secret.

"King is your commander, Speckle," Hilda snapped. "Remember our creed: Commander, Herd, Benevolent."

"That is heresy, Hilda," Speckle shot back, "and I order you to—"

"Enough," King said, "both of you. I have made the decision. We will go in and do what needs to be done. And in the end, when we present to The Benevolent enough cattle to restore all losses from our last engagement with the Iridanis, he will forget the heresy of this engagement and praise our names, and he will understand why we did what we will do here. We will repair the Cud Brigades, and we will ensure that this facility, and its human agents, will never slaughter our brothers and sisters, our fathers and mothers, again. For the Brigade!"

"The Brigade!"

King moved first, for it was required that he lead the attack. He bow-slung his rifle. The others did the same. Hilda admired him even more now, for he was going in with Closed Fists. This would be a shock attack and not an exchange of fire. It was rare for the Cud to engage hand-to-hand among the stars, for their foes were heavily weaponized. But not humans. Here, the Cud could fight, could attack, naturally, as their true nature intended.

Hilda lined up with King and Speckle as they squared their shoulders and put their heads down. They comprised nearly two tons of muscle, bone, and steel. The others followed and spread out in a tight V so that when the truck was struck, those on the ends of the formation could corral the terrified Reds and keep them from bolting. It was all part of the plan, King's plan, and it was going so well.

The shocked human drivers were barely out of their truck when the Cud struck its right side. In these times, Hilda was glad that she and the rest of their brigade were polled Angus and not Texas Longhorn or Ankole-Watusi, those brigades with long, obtrusive horns that would stick in the punctured steel of the vehicle and prevent easy withdrawal. Their strong, hornless heads dented the truck from cab to rear and lifted it off its wheels. The truck teetered, and the red brothers and sisters inside wailed their discontent.

"Push!" King shouted up the line.

They pushed. Hilda put her massive, re-formed leg muscles into it, allowing her human-like toes—tipped with remnants of thick hoof—to grip the dirt and give her the right leverage and angle. She pushed. King pushed. Speckle pushed. The others pushed. And the truck finally tipped.

One of the human drivers fell away from the truck in terror and tried using his small pistol. He aimed it at King. Hilda was on him instantly, ripping the gun from his hand, ripping his hand off completely. He screamed, that shrill, annoying scream that humans possessed. She ended his suffering with a quick jab to his throat. He fell dead instantly. Hilda pushed him aside.

I am now a traitor, Hilda said to herself. *I have betrayed the absolute law of The Benevolent.*

But everyone in the brigade was doing so. Even King. Even Speckle, who had expressed apprehension before the assault, but now was leading a group into the meat packing facility. She and her fire team had their rifles in hand and were popping high explosive rounds into the soft bodies of the human staff who were trying to flee. Lots of screaming, shouting, and a few scatterings of small arms fire deep inside the building.

"Do not hit our brothers and sisters," King shouted to Speckle as he tore the sides of the truck off with his bare hands. "Kill the humans. Save the rest."

What a splendid beast King was. Hilda could hardly concentrate on their mission as she watched him work. He was so powerful, so self-assured. She wanted to reach out and touch him, but his eyes glared with an urgency that she could not ignore. "Get these Reds to safety," King ordered as he pulled one out by the scruff. A small one. A heifer. "Organize a collection spot about half a klick down the road. I'm going to aid Speckle."

"Yes, sir."

He ordered two others to follow him as he took his rifle in hand, ran his thick fingers up the barrel to recharge it, and then disappeared through the large entry doors of the complex.

The Angus Reds were terrified. They tried to flee, but Hilda did as she was ordered and corralled them into a small, tight herd with the help of the rest of the brigade. As they began pushing the herd down the road away from the facility, she rubbed the tough hide of one of the smallest Reds.

"Hush, now, sweetie," she cooed into its soft, round ear. "Just a little further, and then you will be uplifted into the glory of The Benevolent. You will see and hear and do things that you never imagined, and you will one day be led by a strong, powerful bull like King. One day, you will—"

All the lights of the facility winked out. Hilda stopped the herd and turned. There was silence, then more silence. She pulled her rifle, took a step toward the dark facility. What was going on? Why were the lights out? It was difficult to see anything with her normal eyes. They were what they were. She pulled out her binocs and tried focusing them toward the complex. "King?" She shouted. "My Commander... what is wrong? King?"

Then the meat packing facility erupted in small arms and energy weapon fire.

An ambush!

Hilda dropped her binocs and ran at full speed toward the facility, leaving the Reds behind. Her team followed.

She reached the door, and the gunfire inside died. There was silence again as she paused at the edge of the door and peeked her head in to see what was happening. Her team sidled up alongside her, weapons drawn. Then she heard a groan, a soul-wrenching moo, hoofed fingers scratching concrete. She backed away...and King crawled into view.

His body was riddled with explosive rounds and scorch marks from Cud energy weapons. Hilda's instinct, her imperative, was to raise her weapon and fire into the darkness to avenge her fallen commander. But the sight of his bloody, beaten, shattered body made her drop her weapon and simply stare.

"King," she sobbed, "my poor King."

In agony, King reached out for her. "Hilda...Hilda..."

A bullet entered the back of King's head and he pitched forward, dead.

Over his limp body stepped another Cud, a high-powered coil rifle in its hands.

Hilda's eyes grew wide. "Darkcutter," she said, and that was the last word she ever spoke.

§

The lights of the factory came on, and Rodrigo Diaz stepped over the writhing body of Hilda, paused, looked at her lovingly, and then finished her off with a shot to her forehead. Even a small 22 could finish the job at this distance, and it was best to end their suffering. Some of his employees were working through the mangled dead and dying as well, finishing the job so that night shift prep work went smoothly. God, what a haul! The finest beef in all the galaxy was lying at Rodrigo's feet, and he couldn't be happier.

"I always liked you best, Frankie," Rodrigo said, stepping carefully through the bodies, taking counts. "I thank you."

"I'm not Frankie anymore," the Cud bull said. "I'm Darkcutter, head of The Benevolent Inquisition."

Darkcutter held out his arms and turned them over so that Rodrigo could see how his hide had been ripped away to reveal the stressed dark muscle within, meat that would not bring a good profit on the American market, but apparently, was held in high regard among the Cud Brigades. Tiny wires and sensors and metal spokes were interlaced with the fibers of his tendons so that the exposed flesh could work properly in a high-gravity environment like Earth. "I earned this black muscle, Little Rodrigo, from years of suffering and reconditioning. I would ask that you honor it and me by using my official title."

"As you wish, Darkcutter," Rodrigo said, "but I must confess. I'm confused. You and King and Hilda and all the rest used to belong to one big happy herd. What happened?"

"The Benevolent happened," Darkcutter said, going through the dead himself and scanning them with some device he held in his hand. "The politics of the Shetai and of the Cud Brigades are as complicated as any on Earth. These...Cud lying here at your feet, were traitors to the Great Truth, and it is my job, my *privilege*, to serve The Benevolent in ferreting out treacherous beef like this. So, I thank you, Little Rodrigo, for giving me the opportunity to bring glory and justice to The Benevolent. I, and mine, will take our leave of you now."

Rodrigo put up his hand, and the bay doors of the factory began to close. "Yeah, well, you see, I'm no longer *Little* Rodrigo, as you remember me. I'm all grown up now, and I'm in charge of this facility and three others just like it. Do you remember that night when you and your buddies here were *uplifted* as you call it? Three days later, my Papi committed suicide. He killed himself because your precious Benevolent. Your Shetai, are too exulted, too evolved, to fight their own battles. You became an inquisitor among the stars, and my Papi died. Do you remember what I vowed that night as you were whisked away? How could you? I told my father that if it took me a lifetime, that I would get *all* of the herd back. All of it!"

Rodrigo dropped as if he had been struck by gunfire, but the fire didn't begin until he was using King's bleeding body as a shield against men who came out of the shadows and poured round after round into Darkcutter and his inquisitorial staff. The bullets didn't stop flying until Darkcutter and nine other Cud were dead.

Rodrigo pushed Darkcutter away and stood. He wiped Cud gore from his face, breathed deeply, and shook his head. He marveled at all the choice beef at his feet. *What a haul!*

"Okay, men," he said, stepping carefully out of the pile, "you know what to do. Get these carcasses processed. Discard anything that's not choice, and gather up those Reds they let loose."

Rodrigo winced at the cost of having to buy a new cow truck. But it was worth it. Every penny. Tonight was a good night. And if his actions created an intergalactic war between Earth and the Cud Brigades and their Benevolent, so be it. Tonight had been most profitable, and Rodrigo smiled. He had kept his promise to Papi. He had bolstered the financial security of his company. And finally, *finally*, he'd be able to buy that Lego set his daughter Esperanza had always wanted.

Yes, indeed. A great, great night.

Rodrigo Diaz stepped out of the pile of dead cows, smiling and whistling.

Possum

Robert Borski

*P*ossum, *Possum. My (almost) baby boy. How you could* say what you did after all this time is beyond me. And hurtful. To the quick. But Mommy still loves you, just as she has from the very moment you first came to us.

Unlike him.

Jordy, who never has, despite all his complaints about sons over the years.

Him, who you—no, I refuse to say it.

§

A fireball. That's what the men from Lawrence said, as they walked about the ruined grove of cottonwoods in their rolled-up shirt sleeves, taking measurements and picking up odd bits of stone or slag with their gloves, conferring in low voices. Not a plane. No, no, no, Mr. and Mrs. Elwood. Nor a bolt from the blue, despite what you thought you heard as thunder. What we call a meteorite. A bit of space rock. As it enters our atmosphere, friction causes it to burn up. Surely, as children, working the fields at dusk, you've seen *shooting stars?*

But for all their prattle about heavenly debris, none of these men were here when it came booming down out of the night sky. Hammering us with the noise of it. The poor timbers of our house shaking and rattling as if the very earth had opened beneath us, rousting us from exhaustion.

My God, said my husband, sitting up in bed. We have been struck by lightning, woman. Quick, we must check to see nothing is ablaze.

Already, through the screen window, we could hear the animals stirring out in the yard, bleating and lowing in terror. But the house, apart from still ticking with heat from the day's sun, was quiet. Nor, as we stepped outside in our bed clothes, could we see anything amiss with the barn or silo. At the time we did not think to wonder about the moon-rent sky or lack of rain, our brains were still that cloudy with sleep. And on summer eves, when you could see heat lightning all the way to the mountains of Colorado, we both knew the odd bolt could travel far.

Wait, said Jordy, looking from the chicken coop. Out there, beyond the corn field, where the windbreak and woods begin. Is that a light?

Flickering now, as the darkness shifted, what first looked like a will-o'-the-wisp began to flare up, and we could see tendrils of smoke rising.

Best go check this out, Laraine. Hate to think that might have been an airplane come down, with people aboard.

And you found nothing else when you first came out here? asked the military man, looking from the eager faces of his colleagues to us.

No, I lied. Just what you see here now. Busted and burnt trees. And that giant furrow where evidently your shooting star or what was left of it buried itself.

But keeping to myself: *not no almost baby boy.*

§

Come, Possum. It is time for your lesson again. Mommy is going to read you a story from the Good Book. See if you can follow along.

"Now Abraham and Sarah were old and well stricken in age; and it ceased to be with Sarah after the manner of women..."

§

But of course, Possum, you were also there, although it took us a while to find you as we wandered about, stunned to see all that had been brought down by whatever had come out of the sky. To be sure, given how difficult it was to see in the smoke-thickened woods—most of the earlier fires had been reduced to a few random smolders and even these were dying, inundated by bits of leaf and clods of dirt falling from above, as if our farm itself had been lifted up and inverted—we were never quite sure what we were looking at or for. On one hand, it looked almost as if a twister had touched down, the path of destruction was so huge, with blown over and killed trees strewn about like matchsticks, and clumps of flattened grass, and stripped-off bark and stuff. But on the other, by following the half-leveled trees to where they were completely mowed down, we could see where the ground had been torn up, gouged as if by some giant plough, and from which heat rose in waves from the buried object within.

Peering into the furrow as best he could, Jordy said, Don't see nothing that might have been a crop duster or passenger plane, Laraine. Hole's too small and I can see a rounded glowing mass. Just the same: think how lucky we are all this happened here and not a quarter mile back. Or worse, out in the cornfield. Us already in arrears from last year's dismal yield and the bank still threatening. Thank Providence we were passed over tonight.

More walking about, breathing thickly of the curdled air, shaking our heads as we sought to make sense of the altered terrain, with the murk leavened only a bit by our kerosene lamps.

And that's when I heard the tiniest of peeps.

Jordy, wait. There's something down there. In the hackberry bush.

And that's when, by the light of my lantern, I saw you for the first time, my son. A small pinkish-black thing, writhing about, your snout and tiny limbs moving back and forth. Aw, look, Jordy. Poor thing. And encompassing you with my hands, I drew you forth from the thicket.

Must have been a possum nest in one of the trees or something, Jordy ventured, scratching his beard. Or a coon. Hard to tell, all the fur singed off like that. Tail clipped right off too, by the looks of it.

Held closer, with your warmth infusing me, I found it impossible not to nuzzle you, to marvel at how frail your little body seemed.

Lord almighty, Laraine. You and your blasted critters. Best put it out of its misery now. Why prolong its suffering?

But as I held it to my breast, feeling the foundling shiver, I stood firm. You say the same thing each time the barn cats bring forth a new litter. And yet when was the last time you saw a mouse or rat anywhere on the Elwood farm? For some reason God saw fit to let this little guy survive and far be it from me to overrule His decision.

Knowing I would not relent, Jordy grunted. Not much point in us standing around out here losing more sleep then. Not with dawn and chores just around the corner. You coming?

§

When we got back to the house, I put you in a cardboard box with a blanket and a ticking alarm clock, Possum. Your first cradle. And while I hoped you'd still be alive in the morning, I'd also seen enough lambs, calves, and colts come out into this world from their mama's bloody haunches that looked healthy and spry and filled with life that never lasted a single night.

§

But you survived, Possum, didn't you? And then some. So much so that even Mr, Elwood, looking in on us after he'd finished his breakfast, felt compelled to say, That the same critter you brung home last night, Laraine? Looks like he's already growed some. Then again, I was pretty much half-asleep when I first saw him, so maybe I never really got that good a look. Thinking maybe now it's a squirrel or prairie dog, huh? Head's a whole lot rounder than a possum's or a coon's.

Which it was. And where the fur had burnt away, it looked as if new skin was filling in. Perhaps that's why you felt heavier, Possum. Your new parts were taking on weight even as my own, especially my heart, felt lighter.

Not that Mr. Elwood seemed to feel an ounce different. Or said anything about your eyes, which reminded me of a cat's, except they were bluish.

Time's a-wasting, woman. So maybe you should save the dawdling for later. Cows ain't gonna milk themselves, you know.

§

I found Dolly's plastic baby bottle in my hope chest, along with all the other things I'd held on to from my girlhood and thought wouldn't have to pay good money for if ever the Lord blessed us with a daughter. *Back before that dream died.*

Filled it with milk fresh from the cowshed, waving once again to the morning arrival of the men from Lawrence, who continued to mine the crash site of what they called their *bolide*. At least they've finally stopped asking us about the night it thundered down from the sky.

Put the bottle to your mouth, Possum. And heard the gratifying sucking noises.

You a hungry, boy, aren't you? Don't you worry now. Mama's got plenty more where that came from.

Me, clucking like a brood hen.

§

Evidently, something had gone wrong with the ploughing under, because when I finally caught up to Jordy, enveloped in thick clouds of dust, he still had half a field to go.'Spected you some time ago, Laraine, he said, idling the engine. I'm famished.'Spected you'd have finished turning the beets under by now, I said, handing him his sandwich.

Between mouthfuls of chewed bread and meat: Yeah? Well, me too. But then every time I give Betsy more throttle, she starts to cough and backfire. Idles fine, so it's probably carburetor related. Won't know for sure till I pull the engine later. Taking a glurg of water: You manage to finish tossing that hay?

Most of it, I told him, watching as crows hopped in vain from row to row of crumbling dirt, looking for grubs or worms. But then after the baby woke up—

Baby? said Jordy, wiping his mouth. Laraine, no. Are you mad? I swear to God, if this is more of your crazy times—

Feeling myself redden, I held my words in for all of two seconds. You mean like naming your tractor *Betsy* and calling it a *she*? Or trying to grow a second crop of beets when the first crop was so dry and stunted not even the hogs will eat the culls? That kind of crazy?

Tarnation, woman. We ain't got troubles enough you gotta run your mouth like that? Jiminy Christmas. Hurling the remains of his sandwich toward the crows, then wiping his hands on his overalls. There's a Grange meeting tonight, Laraine. Word is, the bank's foreclosing on the Mortensons. See to it supper is on the table by the time I get back if you know what's good for you. Muttering as two crows fought over his sandwich, he climbed back onto the International. Damn beets anyway.

§

Farm life is nothing but hard work, Possum, toiling from the time the sun comes up till long after it goes down, barely able to escape the drudgery and demands in the few hours of sleep we did allow ourselves to get (*at least when the sky was not falling*). Plus, at least tonight, with Jordy gone to his meeting at the town hall, I had to pick up on his share of the chores. Thus, I did not have time to sew those trousers I promised you, Possum. Forgive me, my son? I was so plum tuckered out, I barely even woke up when Jordy climbed not only into bed, but on top of me, smelling of whiskey, and determined once again to have his way with me. Can't really say for sure, although I do seem to remember hearing him make the same sorts of grunting noises he made in the privy like he always did. Or maybe I was just too busy in my dreams candling eggs or slopping the hogs or milling flour to ever take proper notice.

Not that it ever made a difference before.

§

Looking haggard and tired, my husband spooned more sugar into his coffee. According to Jack Leland, Government's been shooting stuff up in the sky, he said, taking a sip, testing for sweetness. From Nevada or Utah. Some kind of rocket ships or something, hoping to beat the Russians into outer space.

Jack Leland, huh? (Jack, who'd come back from Korea wounded. Farm Bureau chieftain now, hard to imagine him tipping up a jug of corn squeezins with those iron hooks he has for hands.) Well, he'd be the one to know.

Jordy turned in his chair toward the big front window, beyond which we could see the university vehicle trailing a plume of dust along the access road to the cornfield.

What? You think that's what this is all about?

Ain't saying nothing of the sort. Just curious, is all.

Possum-noises then, as my baby boy stands upright in his cradlebox: half squeak, half trilled coo.

See you taught your little fellow to walk on his hind legs. Cute. Like Jip when we had him.'Cepting he taught himself, I said, beaming proudly.

Still ain't sure what kind of animal he is, though. And every time I have half a clue, next time I look, he appears completely different. Maybe when Old Doc Simpson comes to check out Goliath next month, we can ask him. Walking his fingers along the table's checkered oilcloth like a spider. That being said, I hope you remember what we talked about last night, darling.

I do, I do, I lied. Startled by the endearment. Almost scared even. *This must be some hangover.*

Cuz I'd hate to have to do anything, you know?

Right. Right. Struggling to remember anything at all from last night, but feeling only a slight stab in my bladder. Well, you won't have any problems on my end.

Jordy drained his coffee cup. Fair enough. Like I said, time and a place for everything. You just need to prioritize.

Possum agreeing, chittering and nearly falling out of his box, on the edge of pre-speech.

§

I'll be the first to admit my hearing's not the best. Growing up and living on farms, you're exposed to all sorts of mechanical noise from tractors, combines, harvesters, hay-bailers, sump pumps, diesel engines, winches, and what-not. No big surprise. Even Doc Bradley was wise to this, telling me the one time I underwent an examination to see if maybe he could determine why I remained childless, saying, 'Bout the only thing physically wrong with you, Laraine Elwood, is your ears. And so, as I continued to hang laundry on the line, hearing it up close luft and flap like sails in the wind, I blame only myself for not discerning the prairie rattler's telltale warning. Certainly, I had no reason to believe Possum was in any sort of danger. Last time I looked, he was darting in and around my feet, chasing a baby chick, looking ever so cute I could hardly wait to tell Jordy about it.

And that's when starting to come back the other way, on the next clothesline over, I saw the big rattler coiled not two feet away from Possum, and my heart froze. Reaching for the long wooden pole that held up the laundry line in the middle, saying *Jesus, Mary, and Joseph, please God, don't let anything happen to my baby*. But apparently in my motherly concern, in the rush of adrenalin through my limbs, I hadn't quite assessed the situation as it really was. For when I turned with the upraised pole, ready to rain down a series of blows to the serpent's spade head, I saw that it was already dead, or at least lying inert, just beyond where Possum sat scratching himself.

Carefully, for I'd been told all my life a viper could still bite you even after it was long dead, I prodded the reptile, at the same time, saying, Come by Mama, baby, stay away from that mean ol' nasty snake.

But there was something wrong with the snake, its head dangled from the rest of it like a broken flower. Best I can figure, it must have been mortally injured in some battle with a hawk or eagle and crawled under the henhouse to die. Possum—or maybe Scratch, the yard rooster—had fetched it out, and I'd just not noticed it, these things are colored so they blend right in with the landscape.

Whew, I said as a new flurry of heartbeats thumped anyway in my chest. Dodged one there, didn't we, son?

And then resolved at once to find time to sew my child some trousers: Possum, baby? If you must groom yourself down there, at least have the decency to do it in private.

§

Words count, Possum. Although you will be hard pressed to get Mr. Elwood to admit anything like this. In fact, I can still remember way back to our one-day honeymoon when lying in his arms with the motel sheets twisted up beneath us, I was foolish enough to ask him if he loved me.

Married you, didn't I? Married you darn good, I'd say.

Guess he never did learn that women sometimes need a little more on the comforting end. So maybe as you're growing up you could keep that in mind, son. Or even start now by honoring the first woman in your life, as the Fourth Commandment obliges.

Say, Mama, baby. Come on. You can do it.

§

Us lying in motel sheets, him asking, So, you think we made a baby? I'm betting a son, huh? A big strong boy, the first of many, who'll help us with the farming.

§

The same question, repeated endlessly, in our home bed, until only the echo of it remained like an afterthought.

§

In your new trousers, Possum, you could almost pass for a real boy. Which makes me think we should maybe have a proper christening for you. Because as beautiful as you look to me, others may not always find you so, especially children, who contain both devil and angel within them. No sense reminding them of your backwoods origins by introducing you as Possum, although that name at home will always be dear to me. But what name then? Back when your grandmother was carrying me within her and thought maybe I'd be a boy, she wanted to name me after President Coolidge. So that's one possibility. Yet others are gleaned from the Good Book. Moses, say. Making me Pharaoh's daughter, who rescues you from the river of night and the burning rushes. Or Sarah, whose magical only child comes to her after years of desperation at the age of ninety. Perhaps I like that one best, son. Meaning you'd be Isaac, then. Maybe even 'Ike' for short, just like our current President, who grew up only sixty miles away in Abilene. How'd you like that, Possum? To be named after a President, just like your Mommy almost was?

Isaac 'Ike' Elwood, born in the year of our Lord 1957, died - ???

You babbling away now, almost as much as your hopeful mother.

§

Mama, baby. Just those same two simple sounds, repeated one right after the other.

§

Like this, sweetheart: *Ma-ma. Ma-ma.*

§

C'mon, Isaac. Pretty please? Say Mama. I know you can do it, child.

§

Feeding him leftover scraps from the table every day as the summer lengthened (although I could feel my breasts swelling, my milk had yet to come in). Growing in fact so much faster than our corn ("Knee high by the Fourth of July—pah!" despaired Jordy, "I'd like to shoot the son of a gun who came up with that one") that I'd already had to expand his trousers and little shirt two times, and although he had yet to speak any words of English in his utterances, there was a lilt and heft to what he did say, you'd almost swear he was talking, like a Pentecostal, in some cryptic tongue known only to him and the

Almighty. But even more impressive, with lots of patience and small treats, I'd taught him to respond to over twenty commands, like *jump* or *roll over* or *give Mommy a hug*.

Not that Jordy's heart had ever softened to our new bundle of joy. Saying:

That thing shits anywhere near my supper plate, it's out to the barn with him, Laraine.

Or:

Dad burn it, woman, coon-boy here is no more going to talk than he is to fly. Cuz whatever he is, he sure ain't no parrot.

Or:

How'd you expect your critter to learn his name when you keep calling him different every day?

Then late one dusk, both of us bone-tired, sitting at the dinner table:

Something I hesitate to bring up, knowing how sensitive you're likely to be.

Yawning. Then don't say it.

Jordy shrugged, barely able to lift his shoulder. Too late. See, Jack Leland says he knows this guy who travels with the carnival, has his own raree-show. Two-headed cows, a pig with horns, midget animals, that kind of stuff. Over in Gothingham the other day, word is he paid twenty dollars for a baby born dead, but had itself a bat-face. And given how we're over sixty days behind in getting our loan repayment to the bank—

Over my dead body, Jordan Elwood.

On his way out, slamming the door behind him, making the whole kitchen vibrate. Well, don't expect much more than a pauper's grave when we're living in the poorhouse, woman.

§

My monthly visitor now three weeks late.

§

As the heat continues, dust-devils dance out in the field, the sun looking swollen and red.

Mister White from the Littlefield Bank mounting the steps of our front porch, shaking his pomaded head. In his valise, the dreaded papers. Later, as he climbs back into his Studebaker, asking, That your nephew or something? Don't quite look right by my eyes, but I'm sure he's a treasure in other ways.

§

Say Mama, child. Pretty please with sugar on it? ('Cepting we can no longer afford sugar and are using sorghum.)

§

Know I always said I wanted kids, Laraine. Just never realized the baby stage would be so much less fun. Of course, this being no real child.

§

Stalked by nightmares, drifting off into half-sleep, milling stunted corn.

A multiplicity of children, all looking like Possum, tossed down into the cistern, mice twitching from their jaws, as Jordy cackles from above, beseeching the clouds for rain.

My son screeching mama mama mama.

Me back in the stirrups, Doctor Bradley talking in tongues of fire, saying (I think) You need an operation, Laraine. One quite typical for women your age.

§

But by far the worst nightmare came several days later and was all the more frightening because it was real, not a dream-scrap or induced by fatigue.

Intent on *ventilating* a few crows, Jordy had his 12-gauge Remington parked up against the porch and was loading his hunting vest with filled cartridges of birdshot. Me, I sat on the steps shucking peas into a colander as Possum bounced an old blue ball of Jip's up and down. When suddenly the ball caromed back at an odd angle, bouncing past Possum in the direction of the Remington. Which tottered and fell as Possum raced past toward the ball, the shotgun falling and discharging with a loud crack, somehow just missing my bounding child.

What the—? But far from being grateful nobody had gotten peppered with birdshot, Jordy flew into a rage. Stupid ignorant beast, you could have durn killed someone. And he began to beat Possum, striking him on the face and shoulders.

And then as my howling son reverted to all fours, scampering back lightning-quick to where I sat, fists raised protectively over his head, saying *Papa Papa Papa.*

Oh my God, Laraine, said Jordy, stopping dead in his tracks. You hear that? He talked! The little son-of-a-gun talked!

I was too stunned to answer. And not nearly as proud as I have should been, considering all the time I'd spent trying to teach the boy. Maybe even more than stunned. Flabbergasted and not just by the shotgun firing. *Did I even hear that right? Papa? PAPA? Was I really wishing now as I held my darling son so tight to my chest, he could barely breathe that he'd said nothing? That he'd remained mute forever?*

§

Worthless ingrate child.

§

Not that I don't still love you, Possum. But you hurt Mommy bad. See my tears?

§

Not Mama, but Papa Papa Papa Papa Papa?

§

Possum's perfect hand unclenching, releasing a fistful of birdshot.

§

I must confess I was not myself the next morning, otherwise I might have perhaps known better. Calling Isaac, but thinking maybe he'd let himself out, was out bouncing his stupid ball against the side of the house.

On the table I found Jordy's handwritten note next to his coffee cup. GONE TO THE BANK—BACK AROUND NOON.

Hmph, I thought. Kind of a long time for a trip that shouldn't take more than twenty minutes tops both ways.

And that's when I remembered something Maura and I used to do as kids, passing secret messages to one another in school. Passing on not the original message, but the paper underneath, which while looking blank—and therefore less likely to get us in trouble with Mrs. Lang, our teacher—could be shaded in with pencil, and the words retrieved from the indentations left-behind.

Diagonally, as I scribbled away on the notepad, the directions that Jordy had written down on the second sheet underneath began to emerge like ghost writing. TAKE A RIGHT ON GRAYSON BY THE OLD CIRCUS GROUNDS, THEN ANOTHER RIGHT BY THE CEMETARY.

Not no place in Littlefield, but Gothingham!

Possum, I yelled hurriedly, getting up. Going at once to the screen door. You outside, honey?

And that's when I became aware of the vehicle pulling into the yard, the familiar-looking station wagon, its right front fender bashed in so bad it was rubbing against the tire, making a burnt rubber smell.

Out jumping the university professor, the one who always wore a bow tie. Talking so fast I could barely understand him.

We need to use your telephone, ma'am. There's been an accident. Your husband—I'm afraid he's been hurt real bad, Mrs. Elwood.

Opening the door for him, hoping there was no one on the party line.

Dialing away like mad, waiting for the operator to pick up. But there's good news too, ma'am. Case you're wondering, your son looks to be barely scratched.

§

Actually, he did the heroic thing by swerving, said the military man, Captain Olsen, who continued to apply first aid in the form of khaki bandages torn from his shirt. Otherwise he would have hit us head on. The dust blowing and all, it was almost impossible to see anything until just before we collided.

Hearing now the ambulance in the distance. Still unable to look at Jordy's crumpled body and broken-melon face for more than a half-second. Wondering how we'd ever get to market or the co-op now with our pick-up truck overturned and smashed that way.

And your boy, ma'am! What a brave lad. Him even trying to help us free your husband from the wreck, we had to keep shooing him back. Hope to see the Army makes an allowance for him someday.

Yes, I said, still holding him tight as I could. He's a good one, all right.

Thinking to myself: I forgive you, Jordan Elwood. Just don't die on me, damn it.

My heart sinking deeper and deeper into an ocean of blood.

§

For three days it was touch and go, Jordy spending more time in the operating room than out, and me taking sleep wherever I could: in the barn, at the kitchen table, in the waiting room or back seat of the jeep, which continued to convey me back and forth between home and hospital. Fortunately, seeming to sense something was amiss, Isaac was on his best behavior. Or maybe he was just gentled by the new mother-child bond between us. Only on day four then did Dr. Bradley finally utter his first words of optimism, meeting me outside the room where Jordy lay in his plastered casts and bandages, his cocoon of red gauze.

Whew. I'm happy to report things are looking pretty stable today. I think we finally stemmed the internal bleeding and the penicillin seems to be combating the infection. Not that the road back for your husband won't be long and arduous or filled with challenges, Laraine. It will, and you will both need to be strong. You want to go in and see him now, you can. Just don't stay long or expect him to be fully conscious. I'm sure just the sound of your voice will be reassuring to him all the same.

The pitter-patter of my heart increased to thunder seeing him lying there, all broken up and splinted.

Taking up and stroking his left hand. Hello, darling, I said softly. Doc says you're starting to heal real good and should be out of here soon. Meanwhile, back at the farm, me and Isaac, we're doing the best that we can, sure enough, and if it's any comfort for you to hear the bank has granted us an extension.

Everything else, however, from the recent turn in the weather to the help we were receiving from the army base in Wichita to my nursing, I kept to myself.

But then just as I was about to leave, Jordy groaned, stirring beneath the plaster and gauze. Up fluttered his eyelids, opening, and recognizing me he seemed to smile.

Low rumble of something I had to lean in to distinguish.

To hear him in the depths of that room say only one word: *Mama?*

The Sightflower

Brian Trent

I. The Stranger

*D*riving along the lonely tunnels of the salt mine, Gabriel Sobon gripped the steering wheel tightly, feeling an inexplicable thrum of anxiety. He slowed the truck to make an especially narrow turn; the mine flooded with the scarlet hue of his brake-lights. His ID badge jingled at his breast-pocket.

Fifty-six years of driving these gray, ghostly tunnels, bringing quarried salt to the crusher station six-hundred-and-fifty feet beneath the desert! More than a half century of life...and now the last run on his last day had arrived. Gabe breathed deeply, his chest burning like a raw wound.

"Poppy?" his granddaughter Amanda asked, sitting in the seat beside him. "Are you okay?"

"Sure, honey," he muttered.

"Honestly?"

Gabe looked at her. Amanda's gaunt, sixteen-year-old face seemed to float like a mask in the cabin's blackness. "Retirement's got me nervous, that's all." The girl watched him, unconvinced, her eyebrows furrowed in concern, so he hoisted a smile onto his white-bearded, leathery face and added, "Your grandpa will be fine. What do you think of the salt mine?"

"It's like driving on the moon." She touched the window, fingers splayed against blackness and the occasional glow of work-lights festooning this labyrinth beneath the Roswell desert. "Do you think we'll have tunnels like this on the moon, when we colonize it someday?"

"I don't know, sweetie. Maybe."

"People will work underground there, too."

"Sure."

"It's fun to think about, isn't it?"

"It is."

"You're quiet today, Poppy."

Gabe patted her knee. "I was just thinking that a girl your age should be hanging with her friends at the mall, or going to see a movie. Anything other than accompanying her granddad on his last day of work."

"I wanted to *finally* see where you work! A secret salt mine beneath Roswell? Count me in!"

He chuckled. "It's not secret! Don't go making Roswell sound any weirder than people already think it is…um…"

His words died in his throat, as made another turn into another tunnel and saw someone standing there—a lonely, tall, very slender someone in the middle of the road.

Gabe quickly applied the brakes; the truck squealed and creaked and halted. The headlights illuminated a man in a black suit, black tie, black pants. Less like a man, he thought, than a man-shaped darkness in the tunnel, blocking his route to the crusher station.

Amanda stared. "Poppy? Who is that person?"

"I don't know." Gabe lifted the CB from his mirror-mount and radioed the docking station. "Jeremy, this is Gabe. Any inspectors onsite today, over?" The seconds lengthened like the shadow stretching behind the mysterious stranger. "Jeremy, are you reading me? Does anyone copy, over?"

"Poppy, he's walking towards us!"

A chill spread along Gabe's spine like the tickling of spider legs. *Could it be? After all this time?*

"Hide in the back sweetheart," he urged. "Hurry!" His granddaughter pulled herself out of the seat, her useless legs dangling as she crawled into the back of the cabin to nestle down near her folded-up wheelchair.

The approaching stranger reached his passenger door and opened it. "Mr. Sobon?"

Gabe studied the man from his neatly-parted hair to his suit to his onyx-black shoes. "Who wants to know? And how'd you get down here? Trespassing is forbidden in the mine."

The man flashed a badge. "Federal agent. Name's Kace."

Gabe raised an eyebrow. "Federal agent? But…what does a federal agent want to talk to *me* about?"

Kace's oddly elongated face made no expression. His eyes were large and dark and cold, like portals of shaded glass. "About the alien you discovered, Mr. Sobon."

§

Idling in the truck, surrounded by the blasted-out cavern of gray-white rock salt that was some quarter of a billion years old, Gabe tried not to think about his granddaughter hiding in the back. His heart gave an ominous, pained thud that he could feel in his wrists.

"I found the alien seventy years ago," he said, measuring his words carefully. "Why are you asking me about that now?"

The agent climbed awkwardly into the cabin. He was almost too tall to fit; the man hunched over, arms trailing to the floor. "You found it when you were about…eight? Nine?"

"Eight-and-a-half."

Agent Kace produced a small notebook and flipped it open. "August 18, 1947. Roswell PD responds to a call that a local boy has found a body by a creek. Police describe the body as 'unusual' but don't elaborate in their report. Do you remember what was unusual about it?"

Gabe scratched his beard anxiously. "I remember it had no shoes on," he said.

"Oh?"

"Some animal had gotten at the shoes. Chewed them up, so that they were just tatters around his ankles. Coyotes will do that, you know. With the shoes gone, I could see that he had feet like hands."

Kace blinked. "Excuse me?"

Gabe killed the headlights, casting the world around them into primordial blackness interrupted only by lonely work-lights. "The feet had freakishly long, flexible toes, obviously meant for grasping."

"You're sure?"

"Does that sound like something a kid would forget?"

"Go on."

"Well, the man's face was strange, too."

"Explain."

"I don't think I can. It wasn't exactly deformity, but…if you were in an elevator with this guy, you'd get the heebie-jeebies standing next to him. You ever see some of these computer-animated cartoons nowadays?"

"Yes."

"My granddaughter watches them all the time. Sometimes they don't do the faces right. The eyes are too big, the features too…unreal."

Agent Kace said, "You're talking about the Uncanny Valley."

Gabe shrugged.

"Could it have been a mask?"

"No," Gabe breathed in the smell of diesel and salt. "And his hair was *really* strange. Coarse like a boar's bristles."

"Anything else?"

"I was scared, so I ran home to my parents. The police came, and then some government men, and suddenly Dad had a new tractor and Mom had her teeth fixed and I got to go to college." He absently jingled the truck keys. "And there's something else, too."

"Yes?"

"Well, it's not about the body. It's about you."

Kace glanced up from his notepad. "Me? What about me?"

"Remember I said that body had strange hair? And the features were a little off?" Gabe leaned back in his seat and folded his hands in his lap. "You have that look, too, Agent Kace."

II. Inquiries and Lies

Receiver: Third World Quarantine
Sender: Agent Kace na'loketl

Databurst: This is why we never close out threat audits. You said that since we recovered the body seventy local years ago, there was no cause for concern. You said it didn't matter that we couldn't find the Sightflower. You said the Sobons were backwoods bumpkins. That's three times you were wrong. Run a global search-and-scrub of the girl's post. I've got them both in custody and am commencing interrogation.

§

The creek was ten miles from the salt mine, and the dwindling sun made it a place of deep shadows blossoming from beneath rocks, trees, and brush. Gabe glanced around wonderingly, his thoughts steeped in a strange fog. He realized he was holding his fishing pole, the bait already tied.

A few meters away, Amanda leaned forward in her wheelchair by the creek's edge, gripping her own fishing pole in her strong hands. Since the tumor had metastasized to her spinal column and rendered her legs useless, her hands had become calloused and rough. And the ensuing chemo had rendered her head smooth as a cue-ball; sunlight played like flame in the blonde locks of her wig.

Agent Kace studied the creek. "*This* is where you found the body?"

Gabe blinked, noticing how the sun sparkled on the water and on the granules of salt that dusted the three of them; even his reflection in the creek showed his beard like a penumbra of glitter around his mouth. "Yes."

Kace pointed towards the girl. "What's wrong with her?"

"High-grade brain tumor. She started getting headaches two years ago, and an MRI scan found it. Metastasized to her spine and Lord knows where else. The chemotherapy hasn't shrunk the goddam thing. She'll be dead in a year."

"I'm sorry."

Gabe regarded him harshly. "Are you indeed?"

"Mr. Sobon, seventy years ago you found a body here…but you found something else, too, didn't you?"

"Did I?"

"There would have been an artifact with the body. Hand it over, and our business is concluded. I'll leave you and the girl here, and you'll never hear from me again."

"That's what I'm afraid of."

The agent stared dumbfounded at him. "What?"

Gabe snarled, "We're not even on Earth right now! Sure, it *resembles* the creek behind my house, but this is one big hallucination!"

Kace looked stricken. He started to speak.

Gabe cut across the first syllables out of his mouth. "You tell me how a fourteen-year-old cancer patient is such a threat that you had to *pull us off planet Earth? I'm* the one who found the body! If I found anything else, then *I'm* the one you should be abducting…not my granddaughter!"

Agent Kace rubbed his neck in a nervous motion. "How did you know we're not on Earth?"

Gabe folded his arms across his chest. "The water isn't right, for one thing. I've been fishing here all my life, and the water never flows this fast. Also, the trees are wrong. A storm knocked down that pair of maples last summer, yet here they are, risen from the dead! I think it's clear that we're in some video game or something, but you've recreated the environment using outdated information. How am I doing?"

Kace sighed. "Quite, quite well."

"Also, my memory of getting here is fuzzy. I remember you finding my granddaughter in the back of the truck. I remember punching my time card at the mine, talking to my supervisor Jeremy… cutting my retirement cake…but it's all hazy. I think you spirited me and Mandy out of the mine, and fed us false memories. Admit it!"

"I admit it."

The old man snapped his fishing rod forward, casting a line. "Do better than that. Let me catch a five-pound bass right now. Go on!"

Instantly, the line bent. A moment later he was wrenching a thrashing fish from the stream, water flinging from its scaly, desperate convulsions.

Gabe watched the fish dangle on the line. "We can't eat this, right?"

"I can make it so your brain *thinks* you're eating it." Kace sighed impatiently and took the rod from him. "So, about the body—"

"The police confiscated it seventy years ago."

"Yes, I know. Roswell police contacted the FBI back in '47, and the body—one of *our* field agents—was put into cold storage and carted off to a secret hangar. My people infiltrated the place and took the corpse. But there was a problem." Kace squatted by the stream, regarding the velvety mud. "The Sightflower. Our researcher would have had one on him, yet there was no sign of it anywhere at the hangar, and no reference to it in any human files. We scoured the woods where you'd reported the body. Started thinking it had been irretrievably lost, that perhaps floodwaters had washed it away. But it wasn't lost, was it?"

Gabe felt his stomach clench.

Kace's horse-like face with its large dark eyes was unpleasant enough without having to see it frown. "*You* had pocketed the Sightflower as a boy and didn't tell anyone…until last month, when you started showing it to your granddaughter."

Gabe flushed. "I don't know what you're talking about."

They were far enough away from the teenager that she couldn't overhear them, but suddenly she began waving her arms. "Poppy!"

"What is it, sweetheart?"

"The fish aren't biting today! I tried three different kinds of bait!"

Gabe glared at the agent. "For Chrissakes, would you let her catch a goddam fish?"

The alien nodded. A moment later, Amanda squealed in delight as she pulled a wriggling trout from the water.

"I want to show you something, Gabe," Kace said softly. "Look into the stream."

Gabe stared at the glassy water. A glowing computer screen appeared on the rippling currents.

It was the image of a website. A message board thread that Amanda had participated in; Gabe immediately recognized her avatar—a mermaid—and he began reading the post she'd made. Apparently, the website's community had been discussing the probability of alien life in the universe.

Gabe tasted blood and realized that in his apprehension he had fallen back to a childhood habit of chewing his lip.

The post read:

We won't find life in cold Martian deserts where the atmosphere has been stripped away. Life started in the sea and we'll find it in other seas. Titan, Enceladus, and Europa. Someday we'll have research labs on those moons like a network of igloos. Researchers will take submersibles out to deep-sea thermal vents, and they'll find strange life crowding those sources of heat and nutrients. You just wait! Three moons, three unique ecosystems!

Kace touched the water, dissolving the computer screen. "Titan, Enceladus, and Europa," he said. "And she *described* the bases we have there. How could a sixteen-year-old girl know such things?"

Gabe dipped his hand into the stream; it felt icy cold to his touch. He rubbed the slimy rocks at the bottom. "She shouldn't have posted that message," he said with great resignation.

"No," Kace whispered, "she shouldn't have."

III. *Flying Saucer*

Receiver: Third World Quarantine
Sender: Agent Kace na'loketl

Databurst: Mission Status—I've confirmed that Gabe Sobon did steal the Sightflower as a boy and still has it somewhere. I've confirmed, also, that he let his granddaughter use it! They've both been looking straight into our labs! This is why we never let our guard down with Homo sapiens! They are as dangerous as their reputation. Will report again once I have the SightFlower in my possession.

Receiver: Agent Kace na'loketl
Sender: Third World Quarantine

Databurst: Do whatever you must. And get rid of them—both of them—once you're done.

§

The creek vanished in a whirl like melting crayons, and Gabe gasped at his new surroundings. He was still squatting, arm extended to touch the slimy rocks of the creek, when he abruptly found himself in a room that seemed carved from black diamond. A massive viewport overlooked the blue world of Earth from space, scattered clouds drifting above the American southwest.

Amanda yelped at the shift in visuals. She spun her wheelchair around to face them, hands still closed around a fishing pole that had vanished.

"What's happening?" she cried. "Poppy! What's happening?"

"Everything's okay, honey," Gabe insisted.

"But that's.... that's *Earth!*" She pointed. "We're looking at Earth *from space!*"

"Yes," Kace said flatly. "We're in geosynchronous orbit above Roswell, New Mexico."

Amanda gaped at the sight, rolling her wheelchair towards the viewport. She looked small against the vast blue planet. Then she stiffened. Tears sprang to her eyes and she turned back to them. "I'm *sorry!* Poppy, I'm so sorry!"

Gabe rushed to her, cradling her and glaring at their alien abductor. For his part, Kace calmly strode towards them, saying, "You peered through the Sightflower, Amanda. You used it to spy on my people, to watch our bases throughout the solar system."

Gabe snarled, "I showed it to her *one* time! After her last prognosis, I just thought...I wanted her to see something special! I wanted her to have *some* joy before the end!"

Kace crouched, vulture-like, before her. "Your grandfather stole something that didn't belong to him. I need to know where it is."

The girl met his pitiless gaze. "What's your real name? Kace isn't the name of an alien."

"Kace na'loketl. I figured Kace would be easier."

"Mr. Kace na'loketl, I love your research labs! How *does* the Sightflower work? I look into its petals and see three different research bases, on three different moons."

"The petals are quantum-entangled receptors for real-time viewing, regardless of distance. My people use them to connect to all our colonies throughout the solar system."

The teen gave an audible gasp. "You have *other colonies?* Where?"

Kace stiffened. "Hidden."

"But we could visit them in this... um..."

"Flying saucer."

"A flying saucer?" scoffed Gabe. "Is *that* what you call it? Seems awfully bourgeois."

"That's not what *we* call it!" the alien snapped, his deeply black eyes narrowing. "I'm trying to use your own terminology. To make you comfortable."

"Don't patronize us!"

"In English, the closest translation would be 'cloud carriage.'"

Amanda smiled at this, letting the words roll off her tongue. "Cloud carriage. I like that! Can we visit Europa in your cloud carriage? Europa is my favorite! A whole ecosystem clinging to the underside of ice-floes!" She clapped her hands together like a child about to find out contest results. "And I love how each day, the Europan ice cracks open in the sunlight and those things go scampering on their fins across the surface! Do you think someday they'll evolve into land-dwellers? Anyway, I *love* Europa! Can we go? Please!"

Kace gave a stony look. "No."

"Why not?"

"Because humans will *never* be allowed to leave Earth. The whole planet has been quarantined from Sol society."

Gabe spat. "We've landed on the moon! We've sent probes into space!"

"You landed on the moon, yes. We allowed it as an experiment, to see if your people might..." Kace trailed off. "Let's say you met our expectations."

"What the hell do you mean?"

"You landed on the moon—something that should have elevated your species into a new way of thinking and view of the cosmos. Instead, you shrugged it off and went right on with your wars and pollutions and nuclear arms race. So, we decided to keep you right where you are. You'll *never* be allowed off-world again. We will *never* allow it."

Amanda looked away and rubbed her eyes, as if she'd gotten a particle of salt in them.

Gabe's heart broke to see her expression. "So, we're just a bunch of backward savages to you, huh? Lemurs for you to study from afar?"

"Wolves would be the better analogy. Where is the Sightflower, Mr. Sobon?"

"I'm sorry!" Amanda cried. "I'm very—"

"Don't apologize," Gabe barked, his ire meant for the alien. "Tell me, Agent Kace, how a young girl's post on the goddam Internet threatens your mighty civilization?"

"Because we can't have you people watching us. You are far too dangerous."

"Fine. Cure my granddaughter, and I'll hand you this Sightflower on a silver platter."

"No."

"Where's your sense of humanity?"

"A strange thing to ask a visitor from space, don't you think?"

"Maybe," Gabe growled, "if you were an alien jelly or winged millipede or something like that. But you people *originated on Earth*, just like mine did! I'm no scientist, but I won't believe that your appearance is the result of some miraculous, coincidental parallel evolution! No, if there are aliens out there—real aliens—then they'll *look* alien. But you...you're a primate of some kind. A cousin of the human race!"

Kace was silent.

"I'm right, aren't I? You people started off on Earth."

"Yes," replied the alien, who wasn't so alien after all.

"So how did *your* people get into space while the rest of have been stuck here, languishing with plagues and poverty and war?"

"War," Kace roared, "is *your* own fault! Shortly before the Toba eruption there were *many* tribes of hominids. Some looked upon the world and said, 'We'll make things better for all.' Others gazed upon that same horizon and declared, 'I will subjugate others, control them, and use them how I like.' *Your* priorities have always been aggression over altruism."

"I'm asking *you* for altruism. Cure my granddaughter, and I'll give you the Sightflower. Everyone wins."

"I can't."

"Bull."

"What I mean to say is, yes, we have the technology. No one in *our* society suffers from cancer. But if an Earth girl miraculously was cured of her condition? That would raise too many eyebrows, even for a town like Roswell." The agent paused, seeming to struggle with some decision. "However, I *can* extend her life. Grant her another five years. Ten, maybe. That wouldn't make *too* many waves."

Gabe said, "That's the carrot. What's the stick?"

"I have orders to eliminate you and your granddaughter if you don't cooperate."

"That won't help you find the Sightflower."

"Perhaps not. But it will silence the two people who know of it."

"You're a cold bastard, Kace. We are no threat to you—"

"*You've always been a threat!*" Kace shouted. "You always figure out ways to *be* a threat! When *our* people were working for the betterment of tribes, yours were devising better tools for murder and conquest! You're always plotting, always conniving, always planning some destructive strategy!" Kace struggled to get his temper under control; he settled into an icy, timeless hate. "Give back what you've stolen."

Gabe looked into his granddaughter's eyes. "Ten more years…"

Amanda tugged on the alien's sleeve. "You can really do that?"

"Yes."

"Will you?"

"Only if your grandfather cooperates."

"And if he does… you'll let us go?"

Kace's eyes were large and cold. "Of course."

IV. *Inhuman*

The black coffin sealed shut around his granddaughter, and Gabe felt a thrill of terror. He had long ago resigned himself to the fact that he would outlive her—that he'd be setting her body into a coffin someday and watching it lower into the ground. His final view of her was the alien sarcophagus closing around her worried face. Her empty wheelchair lay parked near the viewport, pale blue light sparkling off its wheels.

"She'll be fine, Mr. Sobon," Kace said softly, standing beside him. "We don't harm children. Not even the ones of your troublesome species."

Gabe anxiously rubbed his beard. "You really can extend her life?"

"I can."

"Will you? Or is this another of your illusions and lies?"

"No illusions this time," Kace sighed. "But yes, I suppose this is indeed another lie. I told you that I could extend Amanda's life by another five or ten years, but that's not true."

"You son of a—"

"I'm curing her."

For a moment, Gabe wasn't certain he had heard the alien correctly. "Curing her? Why would you do that?"

"For reasons you wouldn't understand." Kace paced slowly around the black sarcophagus, the machine humming with energy. Surrounded by the cloud carriage's dark walls and strange protruding shapes, Gabe wondered how he had ever thought Kace was human;

the freakishly slender body and elongated face and eerie eyes seemed to become even more pronounced, like a shape stretching along the warped surface of a funhouse mirror. "The machine is repairing Amanda on the cellular level. When she emerges in the next couple hours, every trace of cancer will be expunged from her body. I'm fixing her right down to the DNA."

"You said—"

"I know what I said!" Kace snapped, but the anger died quickly and, somehow, he managed a smile. It was an especially unpleasant expression, making him resemble a leering Venetian mask. "Many of us are not indifferent to the sufferings of our long-lost genetic cousins. Empathy is in our blood, alas. I'm curing your granddaughter…and I'm doing it in defiance of my own orders." Kace's smile turned cold. "Nonetheless, even compassion must have its limits. Fulfill your end of the bargain. Tell me where the Sightflower is, right now."

Gabe met the alien's gaze. "On the shelf in my closet."

The alien blinked. "What?"

"It's on the highest shelf of my bedroom closet."

"*That's* where you kept an alien artifact for the past seventy years? *In your closet?*" Kace spoke into an implanted bead at his wrist, uttering a liquid and otherworldly language. There was a tense moment of silence, during which Gabe glanced worriedly to the coffin enclosing Amanda.

Then another voice spoke from Kace's wrist, and the alien visibly relaxed, his long arms dangling.

"My people have just confirmed the Sightflower has been recovered. Right where you said it was." He shook his head. "Strange place to stash it."

"What happens now?"

"I'm still curing Amanda."

"But what if she tells people what she's seen?"

"She won't be able to. I'm wiping her memory of this entire encounter. She'll wake up by the creek. The real creek, back in Roswell. She'll remember the trip to the mine, and then will think that she spent the rest of the day fishing with her grandfather…" Kace extended his hand.

Gabe grudgingly shook the alien's hand. Something sharp pierced his palm.

He cried out in surprise and pain.

"…except that her grandfather will have suffered a fatal heart attack."

Gabe staggered backwards, clutching his chest. His heart stuttered, like an engine stalling for lack of fuel. He collapsed into Kace's arms.

"I am sorry," Kace said, holding him. "Amanda will live, but *you* have seen far too much for far too long. Like your species, you're just too dangerous."

Gabe stared into the alien's dark eyes, seeing himself reflected in those tar-black depths. It was peering into the tunnels of the salt mine, he mused with the last of his strength. A view that was endless and gloomy and cold.

"Goodbye, Mr. Sobon."

Receiver: Third World Quarantine
Sender: Agent Kace na'loketl
Databurst: This will close out my report on the Sightflower investigation. Gabe Sobon has been eliminated. His granddaughter's memories are erased. Worries over. Case closed.

V. Missing Time

The elevator rattled and squealed up the narrow mine-shaft like the dumbwaiter of a condemned hotel. If the OUT OF ORDER sign wasn't enough to dissuade an absent-minded miner from taking it, then the rusted stuttering passage of the car through crudely-hewn rock-salt was enough to make anyone hit the red STOP button and reverse course.

Not that the controls would even activate without the right ID badge, handprint, and retinal scan keyed to personnel of Operation Overthrow.

The elevator doors slid aside, and Shift Supervisor Jeremy Hunter emerged to stare at the intruder the mine's security guards had found lurking about. A teenage girl with long blonde hair.

"Mandy?" Jeremy said in surprise. "Why are…how are you…?" He stared at her legs, at the absence of her wheelchair. She was leaning on a cane.

But she was actually standing!

Amanda Sobon smiled slightly. "The doctors are calling it a spontaneous remission. They're calling it a miracle."

"Mandy, this is incredible—"

"Just like the local police and medical examiners are calling my grandfather's death a heart attack."

Jeremy bowed his head. "I'm so sorry, Amanda. Your grandfather was a friend and an important person here. His death was—"

"His *murder*, you mean."

Jeremy frowned. "Murder? He had a heart attack."

The girl peered hard at him, tucking a stray lock of her wig behind one ear. "It's a lie, Jeremy."

He glanced to the security guards, then gently took her arm and steered her towards the elevator. "What do you know, Mandy?"

"Not a lot, and my memory is fuzzy. I remember fishing at the creek. Remember turning and seeing my Poppy on the ground. Like he dropped dead from heart failure."

"That's what the coroner—"

Amanda shook off his grip. "When I saw him there, unresponsive, I screamed and wheeled over to him. He needed an ambulance. My own phone was back in the truck, but he had his in his pocket. So, I grabbed his phone, and as I went to use it, I saw this." She held up the smartphone so that Jeremy could see the VOICE MEMOS icon.

"Mandy, I don't understand…"

"At some point towards the end of his final shift, he set his phone to record. Had been recording for hours, hidden away in his pocket. You'll want to listen to it, Jeremy. You and the people you *really* work for."

Jeremy stiffened.

Amanda held his gaze. "A few months ago, after my diagnosis, Poppy wanted to do something special for me. He showed me something he'd found as a kid. He showed me the Sightflower." She saw Jeremy's astonished face and added, "I was dying, and he must have figured there was no harm in spilling the secret to me. How he used the artifact growing up, seeing all those alien cities around the solar system. How he learned that Earth was being quarantined. How he decided to finally tell the local authorities what he'd found." She leaned on her cane. "Thing is, *this is Roswell*. You can't cover up a… *cloud carriage* crash, and the discovery of alien bodies without local authorities being in on the secret. When my Poppy came forward with a piece of workable alien tech, he was brought into the conspiracy. How am I doing?"

Jeremy swallowed hard. "You're as smart as he was."

"On this phone's recording, you can hear him telling the alien that he kept the Sightflower in his closet, but that wasn't always the case. It was usually kept *here*, in this mine, wasn't it?" She looked meaningfully at the elevator shaft. "I always thought it was strange, how Poppy the salt truck driver sounded suspiciously like a scientist to me. This place may be a real mine, but that's just the public face. There's more going on beneath it, right?"

"Much more than that. It's where we…"

"Where you study the alien menace. Where you reverse-engineer their technology." She cocked her head. "Your people figured out how to make your own Sightflowers now, haven't you? That's why the original was so easy for him to smuggle out for me. You and this…"

Steel came to Jeremy's eyes. "Operation Overthrow."

"Operation Overthrow. I like that."

Jeremy smiled. "You looking for a job, kid?"

Together, they stepped onto the elevator and descended into darkness.

The Infiltrator

Joe Vasicek

The Infiltrator clacked his mandibles in greeting as he ascended the latticework of the council chamber. The high queen of the advance expeditionary force hive waited for him there, surrounded by attendant daughters who attended to the control stations and holovid projector that hung from the ceiling. The high queen's antennae were folded back in solemnity, her eyes dark and pensive.

"Welcome, child," she said, acknowledging the Infiltrator with a sweep of her forelimb. Though the Infiltrator was not one of her children, the title was nonetheless a mark of respect, and he took it as such, his eyes glowing a contented turquoise.

"My queen," he said, lowering his carapace in a sign of deference.

"Let us dispense with the formalities and speak clearly," said the queen. She gestured to the seat nearest her throne, and he installed himself in it promptly. "I presume you have already familiarized yourself with the data gathered by our scouts on the alien race you are to infiltrate?"

"I have," said the Infiltrator.

"And you have reviewed your mission objectives?"

"Yes. I am to observe the target race in their natural habitat, coordinating with our scouts already embedded in the system to gather data that cannot be obtained through telescopic instruments and radio interception alone."

"Correct," said the queen, dismissing a worker drone who offered to regurgitate a drink for her. "But do you understand the full significance of your mission? The importance we have placed on your success?"

The Infiltrator preened his auxiliary antennae nervously. "I understand that it is important enough for you to brief me personally on it, my queen."

"Indeed," said the queen, clacking her mandibles in mild irritation as her eyes glowed yellow. "Make no mistake, Infiltrator. The target species represents one of the greatest existential threats we have ever encountered. In only ten thousand revolutions of their local sun, they have progressed from the barest inklings of sentience to spaceflight and atomic weaponry, all while waging war on themselves unceasingly. They are more vicious than the K'plath, more cunning than the Ch'nuri, and quite possibly more intelligent than even ourselves. It is only by the grace of the Great Queen Herself that they have yet to discover the secrets of faster than light travel, but when they do…"

The queen rasped her vestigial wings and shook her head in horror. All around the chamber, the worker drones did the same.

"Forgive me, my queen," said the Infiltrator, "but these larger matters are rightfully your domain, not mine. I don't understand why I should be concerned with anything other than the mission which you have sent me to fulfill."

"Because the information that you will glean is of critical importance, not only to our continued dominance of this sector of the galaxy, but perhaps to the very survival of our species itself. Understand, we are not speaking of hypotheticals. The target race *will* ascend to the stars, and if we are not prepared when they do, their ascension may well mark our doom."

The fact that the hive queen herself feared this species made the Infiltrator shiver with fear. Ichor rushed to his eyes, making them glow a deep and scintillating purple.

"I understand, my queen," he said, flattening his antennae in deference. "I will not fail you."

"That remains to be seen," said the queen, waving the worker drone back to her. After swallowing the regurgitated drink, she turned her attention to the Infiltrator again. "You are not the first Infiltrator we have sent, though thankfully none of your predecessors were discovered before they expired. Our advance scouts saw thoroughly to that."

"I understand that the transformation I am to undertake is… significant," said the Infiltrator.

"Yes. Quite. The aliens' physiology is unlike that of any other race we have encountered. Your carapace will have to be softened; your mid-limbs absorbed into your thorax; your abdomen shrunk to almost nothing. It will take extensive gene therapy and body modification, and even then, you will never fully be able to pass as one of them."

"But I will be able to hide within those woven shells of plant and animal fibers that they call *clothes.*"

"Indeed," said the queen. "It is a curious alien practice, but one of the few things that will work to your benefit. So long as you keep yourself covered, we should be able to alter your appearance sufficiently well so as not to attract unwanted attention. However, the one part that the aliens rarely if ever cover is also the hardest part for us to alter. I am speaking, of course, of your eyes."

The Infiltrator rasped his mandibles ever so slightly. The eyes of the target species were so alien that he found them even more striking than their lack of proper antennae, or the profusion of fine hairs across the creatures' soft, fleshy skin. Instead of protruding from the head, they were recessed within the aliens' internal carapace itself. Instead of changing with the aliens' mood, they maintained a constant color, and never glowed.

"How am I to infiltrate this alien society if my eyes will betray me?"

"That is something that none of your predecessors were able to discover," the queen admitted. "However, there is a special covering which these aliens have designed to shield their eyes. Observe."

The holographic projection flashed to show the alien form he was to undertake, complete with the fibrous layers of outer coverings that were to make up his disguise. The fabric looked gray and worn, with sizable tears in places, but taken as a whole the shell was uncompromised. Even the claw-like manipulators at the end of the upper appendages had their own individual coverings. A loose wrap covered the neck and singular mandible, while the eyes had a special instrument comprised of two black plates set in a squarish metal frame. At first, the Infiltrator thought that the plates were designed to shield his eyes entirely, but then he realized that they were visors, made of tinted glass.

"That is…acceptable," he said, preening his antennae rather nervously. "How substantially does this disguise differ from the appearance of most individuals in this species?"

"We don't know," the queen said tersely. "That is why we are sending you."

His eyes glowed a deep blue, but he gave no other sign of fear. "I take it I am to land in an unpopulated part of the planet, and weave my way into their society from the fringes?"

"No," said the queen, her eyes glowing suddenly red. "Your predecessors already tried that, and failed spectacularly. Our scouts report that they now have a legend, called *sasquatch*, as a consequence of this tactic."

"But…are you saying I must land in a populated area? Not on the fringes of their society, but the very heart of one of their hives?"

"I am indeed," said the queen. "It is, ironically, the best way to avoid suspicion."

The Infiltrator suddenly understood why so many of his predecessors had failed. It was, of course, unthinkable to refuse an order from the hive queen, but he feared his own failure more than his own death.

"Do not fear," said the queen, her eyes turning turquoise once again. "I know your skill, Infiltrator. Your legendary accomplishments with the K'plath precede you. Where others have failed, I have no doubt that you will succeed."

The Infiltrator clacked his mandibles, and his eyes glowed yellow. "I will not disappoint you, my queen."

§

The body modifications were more painful than the Infiltrator had anticipated. In addition, the gene therapy failed to take effect after his next molt, so he had to wait another full cycle before he was able to shed his old carapace for the one the geneticists had designed for him. It felt so soft and fleshy, so vulnerable and exposed. Perhaps that was why this species had become so warlike.

As he waited for the changes in his body to take effect, he studied as much as he could about the aliens' culture and language. Much was still unknown, but from radio and telescopic observations, the scientists had pieced enough together for him to feel confident that he could pick up the rest in the field. Unlike the worker drones, he was a quick and adaptive learner, a trait that had served him well on all of his previous missions.

There were no teleporters on the planet's surface, and no scientific outposts close enough to make for a practical landing zone, so the Infiltrator had to be inserted by planetfall. The capsule was built to disintegrate shortly after use, but the atmospheric entry itself would doubtlessly attract no small degree of attention, especially so close to one of the alien hives.

The insertion itself was flawless. The flames of reentry roared all around him as the capsule made planetfall, but it protected his tender new body as designed.

Upon landing, he emerged only to find himself at the bottom of a shallow body of water. His new lungs were unaccustomed to breathing in such an environment, but with a little exertion, he rose to the surface and took a deep breath of the oxygen-rich air.

These aliens do not submerge themselves in water without first removing their clothes, the Infiltrator thought to himself. *I should stay hidden until my own clothes have fully dried.*

He sought cover among some flora by the water's edge. A trail of smoke still hung in the air, and some of the larger plant specimens had been bowed over by the blast. On the far side of the body of water, a crowd had already begun to gather. Though it was dark, many of them carried illumination devices, with which they began a disorganized search.

Chills shot down the Infiltrator's fleshy new back, and his eyes glowed blue beneath his darkened shades. *I cannot stay here,* he realized. *If I do, then surely they will discover me.*

He passed quickly through the nearby forest, tearing the fabric of his outermost layer of clothes as he ran. At one point, he tripped and nearly smashed his eye shades from the fall. The prospect of losing them filled him with a jolt of fear, and for the briefest moment, his vision turned purple. Thankfully, though, the shades had landed on soil, not stone, and were still intact. He stopped for a moment to catch his breath before moving on.

Emerging from the forest, he passed over a long stretch of blacktop and followed it toward the glowing lights of civilization. Occasionally, a ground vehicle passed him, headlights glowing bright in the darkness. None of them slowed to inspect him, though, and the occupants stared straight ahead without so much as glancing his way.

The disguise is working, he reassured himself, lifting his shades so as to give him a clearer view in the darkness. *They hardly even notice me.*

At that moment, one of the vehicles slowed in front of him. The ichor in his veins grew cold.

"Hey, buddy," one of the aliens called from an open window. "You look terrible. Need a lift?"

"No," he rasped, covering his face from the light.

"It's okay, buddy," the alien called back. "I'm not going to hurt you. I just—holy crap!"

It was, of course, his eyes. The Infiltrator fled from the blacktop as fast as his modified legs would carry him, vanishing into the underbrush. A harsh squeal sent shivers of fear down his fleshy back, but the ground vehicle took off at speed, without any sign of the alien within.

The Infiltrator waited nearly a full minute before resuming his voyage, this time near the edge of the trees. Though the shades made it difficult for him to see, he was careful to keep them close over his glowing eyes.

$

The planet's solitary moon soon rose over the night sky, offering some light by which to travel. Unfortunately, the Infiltrator could not tell whether he was coming closer to alien civilization, or going farther away.

Just as he began to wonder whether he should turn back, he came across a set of parallel rails made from a crude iron alloy. His eyes turned from blue to green; according to his cultural research, this alien infrastructure was designed to transport cargo and fuel. More importantly, the vehicles that used them were mostly unmanned, offering an opportunity to travel undetected into the very heart of one of the alien hives.

He walked along the rails until one of the large cargo vehicles passed him from behind. It was going just slow enough to run alongside it, and as an empty cargo container passed him, he leaped and grabbed hold of the doorway to pull himself inside.

For the next several hours, he rested fitfully. His soft, fleshy skin was not well suited to the hardness of the container floor, or the chilly native air. Moreover, the cargo vehicle jolted him quite uncomfortably, making sleep uncomfortable. He pulled his torn and shredded clothes tight against his skin, wondering at the fact that the aliens had not evolved to be more specialized to the environment of their own homeworld. Was this, then, why they had fashioned these clothes like second skins? Or had the clothes themselves altered their evolutionary path, making it indispensable for these aliens to wear them?

As thoughts like these troubled his weary mind, fatigue began to overcome his fragile, new body. The hardness of the container floor seemed less of an inconvenience, and even the jolting seemed to disturb him less. Recognizing the need to regenerate his strength, he surrendered to his exhaustion, hoping that the aliens would not discover him as he did so.

§

"Hey, you! What are you doing in here?"

The rude words were accompanied by a shove that brought the Infiltrator immediately to his senses. A wave of dizziness soon followed, and his vision blurred until he saw a bright light with an alien face peering down at him.

"All right, buddy, put your hands where I can—what the hell?"

My eyes! the Infiltrator realized, his mandible clattering beneath the loose garment wrapped around his neck. His vision turned a warm, frightened purple, laced with traces of crimson.

Several things happened at once. The alien made a loud, high pitched call, no doubt to alert any others in the area. At the same time, it fell back out of the doorway, its light pitching wildly. Without thinking, the Infiltrator bolted, putting as much distance between himself and the alien as possible.

It was still dark, and that at least gave him some cover as he ran. But to his dismay, there were no trees or underbrush in which to hide, only several dozen pairs of long, parallel rails, stretching endlessly in either direction. It appeared that he'd arrived at some sort of loading and unloading station, and the loud rumble of engines filled his soft, fleshy ears.

This must be one of their hives, he thought as his panic began to subside. But the sound of a commotion behind him made him realize that he was not out of the clear just yet. The alien who had discovered him had gathered others to assist in the pursuit.

His eyes a dull yellow, he quickly scanned his surroundings. A wire fence surrounded the compound, with coils of sharp barbs wrapped around the top. In his pink, fleshy form, climbing through those barbs was out of the question.

He dashed towards the nearby vehicles and soon found himself in a maze of containers and equipment. The compound was far larger than he had expected, and was arranged almost like a maze. Thankfully, that worked to his advantage, and his pursuers soon lost track of him.

As they split up to search, his eyes fell on a section of fence that had been pulled up, allowing passage through a crudely dug-out channel in the dirt underneath. He crawled through and passed over another blacktop that stretched like a canyon beneath several large structures that stretched high overhead.

Every semblance of nature was gone, and in every direction, artificial lights banished the darkness of night. The Infiltrator realized that he had entered one of the aliens' hives.

§

The hive was strangely inactive, though. The aliens in this part of it must have been sleeping, which told the Infiltrator that he had yet to enter the heart of it. In all likelihood, he was still in the outskirts.

I must seek out the heart if I am to fulfill my mission, the Infiltrator told himself. *Also, I must learn how to interact with these aliens without them becoming alarmed at me.*

Pulling his shades close against his eyes, he followed the blacktop around a corner, toward the sound of a small crowd. The aliens had gathered around a fire in a large metal canister, which he recognized as a storage device for carbon-based fuel. Their clothes were old, gray, and torn, very much like his own.

What a perfect opportunity, he told himself.

A few of the aliens turned to regard him as he joined their small group, but most of them seemed to pay him little mind. There were a few grunts as they shifted positions around the fire, but for the most part, they accepted him peaceably.

All except for one.

"Hey," a large alien asked from across the fire. His skin, though fleshy, was black instead of tan. "Who's the new guy?"

None of the others responded at first. This only seemed to agitate him.

"I said, who's the new guy?"

"Dunno," said the alien to the Infiltrator's right. He moved away from him ever so slightly.

"He's no friend of mine, Jack," said another of the aliens. Unfortunately, this did little to placate the first.

"Who the hell are you?" he said, walking around the circle to confront the Infiltrator directly. He looked straight at him, pasty-white eyes set deep in his creased sockets. The Infiltrator flinched and looked away. Only the shades prevented the black-skinned alien from seeing through his disguise.

"I'm talkin' to you, buddy. Who are you?"

"Just leave him be, Jack. He ain't hurtin' no one."

"No way, man. Who is this punk?"

The Infiltrator's ichor warmed, and his eyes turned blue. He didn't know how to respond to the alien's dangerous posturing. Only one thing was certain: that ignoring him wouldn't work.

"Not...want...problem," the Infiltrator vocalized slowly, taking great pain to enunciate each word. The scientists hadn't had much success in replicating the aliens' vocal capabilities, and his fused mandibles made the words sound awkward. That was why he hadn't said anything until now.

"Yeah, I'll bet you don't," said the alien, not pacified in the least by the Infiltrator's feeble attempts at communication. "And that's another thing—where do you come off wearing those shades at night?"

Without warning, he lunged forward and grabbed the Infiltrator's tinted eye coverings. The Infiltrator snatched them back almost immediately, but by then it was too late. One of the other aliens let out a high-pitched warning call, while the others raised their upper appendages in threatening, warlike postures.

The Infiltrator ran from them as quickly as he could manage. Blue and indigo clouded his vision, mingled with the violet of despair. Even to those whose clothes matched his own, his eyes still betrayed him.

§

The light of dawn was growing on the horizon, and the artificial lights of the hive were gradually blinking out. The Infiltrator noticed with no small degree of alarm that alien activity was increasing. Keeping to the shadows, he managed to evade their notice, but that was at best a temporary solution. If he could not find a way for these aliens to accept his presence, then his mission would undoubtedly end in failure.

His eyes darkened, flecks of violet clouding his vision. Everything about this place felt unfamiliar to him, and it was difficult not to feel discouraged. He longed for a quiet place where he could rest, away from the harsh artificial environment that these aliens had constructed for themselves. Unfortunately, there was none.

The alien activity increased markedly with every passing moment. He sat down against a wall, on a hard, *gray-top* floor. With dismay, he realized that there was nowhere left to run. He was quickly surrounded, first by dozens, then hundreds of aliens passing him in either direction. The most he could do was stay still and stare at the ground, until he was inevitably discovered.

A minute passed, followed by another. Tentatively, he lifted his eyes. To his surprise, none of the hundreds of aliens who passed him even attempted to make eye contact, even when they passed within easy reach of where he sat. A few seemed to keep to the far side of the *gray-top*, as if consciously trying to avoid him, but none of them gave him any scrutiny or regard.

Have I somehow managed to disappear?

The Infiltrator glanced down at his gray, soiled clothes, confirming that he hadn't turned invisible. But to the masses of aliens who passed him, he might as well have been. It was the strangest thing, considering how different his appearance was compared to those who now surrounded him. Where his clothes were dirty and torn, theirs were neat and clean. Where he stooped near the ground, they stood tall and proud. Males and females, old and young—all seemed almost to conspire to ignore him.

It's working, he realized. *They've accepted my presence.* His vision returned to its normal color as his eyes lost their frightened glow.

A young male approached him with a squarish piece of green fabric clenched between his fleshy claws. "God bless," he said, giving it to the Infiltrator. For a moment, his mandibles twitched as he wondered if the alien expected a response of some kind. But the young male turned and left without so much as giving him a second glance.

The Infiltrator silently observed the aliens until the golden-yellow sun set in the sky. And when night came, he installed himself on another patch of *gray-top*, regenerating his strength for the next day of his mission. There were so many things to see, so much useful information to glean. The hive queen and all her scouts would truly be pleased with his work. For though he walked in the midst of them, listening to their speech and observing their alien ways, so long as he played the beggar no one ever looked into his eyes.

The Man with the Alien Aura

Mike Adamson

*D*octor Janice Weatherly sighed in the pre-dawn gloom.*
Red digits glowed in the dark, 5:43. Sunrise was due around 6:00 at this time of year, the day would be hot and dry.

The woman ran a hand through her tawny, shoulder-length hair. The motel was just outside Trinidad, Colorado, traffic on Interstate 25, a background rumble of trucks. Soft breathing from the other bed told her her companion was thankfully still sleeping, and she frowned into the gloom. They would be at their destination today.

Not Roswell, but close enough. Just a place in the parched country that Alan Hardy must reach.

Must reach. It was quite literally life or death for him, and as a psychiatrist she had taken her patient under her wing. She was the first to admit it was not the most professional conduct, thus why she was traveling in a cheap, second-hand car, in casual clothes, spending cash and staying off her mobile. At all costs, she did not want to draw attention.

They had left Spokane, Washington a few days earlier, and the only colleague she had confided in, even peripherally, had criticized her handling of the case. She was worried, but so far there had been no interference. Perhaps it was *her career*, as he had said, but the time for doubt was long past. All or nothing, she wanted to see what hid within Alan Hardy, and, if he was right, reaching that remote point in the middle of nowhere would indeed liberate the demon on his shoulder—and him from it.

§

He was a troubled young man; twenty-six, attractive enough in the modern way, with dark hair that seemed to have a life of its own, and a once quick wit and native intelligence that had been blunted, beaten down, by troubles. He had started college late and dropped out in senior year, unable to concentrate or commit. He had lost friends, a relationship, had wandered from car wash to supermarket to bar, one nothing job after another, and been referred to Janice following a breakdown of some kind in which he raved about *the other*.

The other had become the defining motif of his life, for, he claimed he shared his head, his body, his skin, with another identity.

This was not schizophrenia, it fit no specific pattern, and all expenses met by his parents, Janice Weatherly had investigated his case for weeks using the standard methodology—immersive discussion, medication. T*he other* had subsided a little, but its presence was always felt. Eventually she had tried hypnosis, and it had been the most frightening episode of her entire life.

As a qualified hypnotherapist she had required no assistance, and taken Alan into a mild trance in the quiet of her offices. She had regressed him to the last year in college when he had been doing well, and tracked his life forward from that point. His parents were proud of his education, his girlfriend had been in all ways happy with him, but then something had happened. In the session, he shied from the focus of matters, had become uncomfortable, and it took several more sessions to draw close to the event.

That was when the deeply-entranced young man began to speak of the night of the falling star.

He had taken an interstate trip during the summer break a year back, visited friends in Great Falls, Montana, then went on to see others in Billings, taking the scenic secondary roads across the Badlands. The country was wide and parched and lonely, but he had his mobile and his car was in good repair. The problem had been when the star fell, when he was crossing in the blue night, the territory between Hobson and Harlowton, not a long stretch, but lonely—lonely enough for things to happen out of sight of anyone else in all the world.

It came down silently. He saw it from the corner of his eye and turned to look in time to collect an impression, an intense, bluish light surrounded by green ionization, towing a tail of red. It disappeared into the wastes with a flash and he had braked hard, came to a halt with heart thudding, wondering what he should do. His first thought was *satellite burn-up*—a piece of space debris. A meteorite was another matter, but both might be valuable, and as an inquisitive, energetic young college man, he was more than ready to be first on the scene. He tried his phone to report it to the nearest sheriff's office, but was out of coverage area, and dropped his SUV into four-wheel drive, to turn off the road across rough country, heading for the landing point.

In the quiet of Janice's office, he had told her, distressed despite her calming words, that a few miles from the road he had found burning debris and smashed pieces of what seemed to be a vessel of some kind. He had left his car, taken a flashlight and his phone, and photographed the scene. He could recognize nothing, all was twisted, seared by re-entry, but a single part seemed less damaged, a panel open like a hatch, and sprawled below it was a shape…

It might have been humanoid but was burned terribly, too badly to make out much detail by flashlight, and he had photographed it with trembling hands, his phone flash painting wild shadows among the flames. But when the thing moved, he froze with terror, and there the account become doubly difficult, both for him to repeat and for Janice to credit. For this was not a mortally injured astronaut, but something clearly not human. It was larger than a man, with too few digits upon its hands, and a skull of bizarre form…

Paralyzed with shock, the young man had watched it rise in its agony, extend a hand to his skull and cup his forehead, then… All became nonsense, for in a burst of light and pain the figure dissolved, vanished as if it had never been, and from that moment forth *the other* had ridden along in his mind and soul, guiding his hands at times. Without comprehending, he had taken a device from within the cockpit and manipulated controls, and a soft violet ray played over the remains of the spacecraft. One by one, the pieces disintegrated, flaring up as their mass was converted in some chemical or molecular reaction, as if metals were burning utterly away. And finally, he set the device down and stepped away, and a moment later it also self-destructed the same way.

He returned to his SUV and sat for a long time, shaking with internal conflicts, before the power guiding him compelled him to delete the evidence from his phone. Then he drove mechanically, and by the time he was back on the blacktop, all memory of the crash was fading from his mind.

The traumatic stress of reaching into those memories, despite deep trance, was severe, and she brought him back a step at a time. She had considered instructing him to not remember the events, but before she could do so, something utterly beyond her experience as a hypnotherapist had occurred.

"You are an impediment to me," a voice had said, issuing from Alan Hardy's lips but in a timbre and modulation far from his own. "You threaten my survival, and I will not allow it."

She was stunned, rocked back for long moments, but gathered her composure, ready to press a contact in her chair arm that would summon her practice security if she felt physically threatened. "Who are you?" she asked softly.

"I am that which you have compelled the being inhabiting this vessel of flesh to recall. Against my will and his."

"What do you want?" Her question seemed feeble in her own ears.

"To be allowed to operate without hindrance." The words were peremptory, brusque. "You are faced with a conundrum, something outside your accepted normality." For a moment it seemed the entity studied her, though the young man's eyes were closed. "But you are trying to comprehend your universe, with diligence and competence, and I cannot fault you for that." His lips twisted in a suggestion of a smile. "Aren't you going to make notes?"

She had glanced at the voice recorder on the coffee table between them. "I'm not even sure of my own sanity at this point."

"Then let me help you. I must reach a point far to the south of here by a time a week from now. Either the entity with whom I share physicality will reach it alone, or it will be via whatever assistance he can attract. You wish to help him? Then help me, and you will achieve the same end."

"Why should I believe you?"

"I am leaving you no choice. But I will furnish you proof, as I sense you are driven by tangible evidence, despite your science being an inexact one." She sensed a hint of scorn in the word. "Do you have an ultraviolet light source?"

Her mind raced and she recalled the insect-zapper in the bathroom off her office, and when she described it the patient smiled through closed eyes and rose stiffly. She rose, backed away, opened the side door and watched as, eyes still closed, Alan Hardy passed with ponderous step into the small bathroom. "Turn out the light," he grated, and with trembling fingers she did so.

The shock could not have been greater if she had been dreaming wide awake. The soft ultraviolet glow from the bug-zapper illuminated something that was not there. A crackling, shifting, hazy field surrounded Alan's body, and in it she saw substance, the outline of something very different overlaid upon his form, like a projection, two slides in the one carrier—substance and ghost.

And the ghost was simply not human. The cranium was arched backward in a kind of horn or mass, and the limbs were of differing proportion, the hands too large, and Janice was quietly glad she could make out nothing of the face, for what mask of horror she might have perceived was beyond her at that moment.

"Do you believe your own senses?" was the flat, quiet question, and she nodded, swallowing on a dry throat. "Then, will you help me?"

Janice had stared at the alien outline, fighting back panic, trying to view the matter objectively, and at last let out a shaky breath. "I guess someone has to be first to learn, well, *anything*." Almost without conscious thought, she nodded. "What do you need me to do?"

"Take us to a place in the south."

"Where south?" Visions of the southern hemisphere danced in her mind as she switched on the light and beckoned, and the apparition faded as Alan Hardy's body left the UV. As he returned to his seat, she took a driving map from a drawer of her desk and unfolded it. "Can you show me?"

To her relief, a hand went blindly to a spot a few states away and tapped repeatedly. *Monument Canyon, New Mexico.*

"Why do you need to go there?"

"Freedom," was the single word of reply.

§

In the dark motel room, Janice let her thoughts drift over the case, replaying the facts as she had a thousand times. Psychiatrists had treated those who had taken part in UFO encounters for generations, ever since the celebrated Hill case of 1961, and she smiled as she recalled her past skepticism, the obligation to approach the things Alan Hardy had told her with the cool tolerance of her profession. Until that point, she had known in the security of her position, that he was expressing a psychosis, and helping him to understand it was her only goal. Then she had seen the alien hiding in his aura with her own eyes, and her whole world, her universe, changed.

They had four-hundred miles to go, and today was the day on which the alien had specified they would each be liberated. By evening, they must be in the desert country by Monument Canyon, and then... Then she would see what was meant, and how good an alien's word was. She had staked everything on it, hers and Alan's lives in all probability, certainly her reputation and professional standing. It was an exciting notion, to be dealing with something utterly unknown, and a source of unutterable frustration that she may never commit these events to paper; but better frustrated than incarcerated and medicated as a lunatic, as she would have done with Alan or anyone else who spoke of such matters without evidence—and she would have none. Even her own recordings and notes were now under lock and key and she had decided to bury the case file as if it had never existed.

She rose and parted the slats of the blind to find first daylight outlining trees and cables, and birds were singing now. She pulled on jeans and shoes, a clean shirt, and studied her driving atlas—anything to avoid using her phone, which would flag her location. Alan still slept, and she was glad *the other* was leaving him alone: tractable, scared, but going with her of his own free will. The entity had instilled in him an instinctive need, though not the actual facts. It had given her the barest bones of the matter, more inference and implication than statement. She deduced that it—he, she—clearly was not meant to be here, otherwise why eliminate the debris of the craft?

Alan woke around sunrise, and Janice brought them back breakfast from a diner nearby, hash browns and bacon with tall coffees, then they packed up and were on the road by seven, traveling south on Interstate 25 through rolling green hills.

The day was hard and bright, and Alan rested fretfully, watching the country go by as they crossed the state line into New Mexico, the last state of their journey. He sighed and relaxed visibly the closer they came, as if his passenger was also relaxing. The road seemed to stretch forever as they headed into the rugged country, the dry basin south of Raton, and Janice drove steadily, a little below the state limit. They had time, pulled over for gas in Maxwell, picked up road food, avoided conversation... It had become an art, and if asked, she was traveling with her nephew to see family. Anything but the truth, because the truth was beyond anyone's handling. She had the oil and water checked at the gas station; the car was far from new and bought for convenience, and the worst thing she could imagine was a breakdown on a desert blacktop a hundred miles from where they needed to be.

Hold together, she thought to herself, almost praying, as the specter of being stranded so close preyed on her mind. Alan seemed oblivious of the danger, often he was silent, withdrawn, as if just marking time. In such moments, Janice understood more of the weight he carried, the intrusion, invasion of his mind and self, and had begun to formulate her approach for helping him through recovery, once he was free—once they were all free of his possession.

About 10 a.m., they took US Highway 84 south of Las Vegas and were headed more directly for their destination. The psychiatrist had to smile when she acknowledged that the nearest town to Monument Canyon was, of course, Roswell, New Mexico. They would be looking for a motel before dark, due around 8 p.m. this time of year, and she prayed there would be no cheesy, plastic flying saucers and tacky neon signs, but beggars could not be choosers and they were keeping a deliberately low profile.

They took an hour for lunch at a truck stop in San Ignacio, and Janice reassured Alan with a quiet smile. Time was on their side, and all they need pray for was the verity of an alien's word.

§

The desert was hot and bright, and the wind moaned through scrub trees and thorn bushes as evening gathered in flashes of magenta-and-gold cloud. They had taken State Highway 13 south from their motel in Roswell, and with half an hour of daylight remaining, turned off on one of the access roads into the scenic wilderness: the tangle of gullies and canyons that characterized the landscape westward to the Mescalero Apache reservation. This was wild and beautiful land, a maze of ridges and stream-cut gorges, and Janice cruised slowly on the gravel track, waiting for Alan to react. He asked her to pull over as fingers of light marked the dying sun. He got out of the car and walked a little way to the edge of an overlook, standing for a long while as if sensing the world around them. She saw him framed in the end-of-day, and had the overwhelming impression *the other* was very close beneath the surface now. And when Alan returned his eyes were not his own. He rasped, "Continue," and a chill went through her. Yes, the entity was very much in control now, and she did as it asked.

Another few miles, and she was driving with highbeams, the bizarre shapes of saguaro appearing from the twilight at the roadside, and the tension between them wicked. At last, Alan raised a hand and she pulled in, killed the lights and switched the engine off. Silence... Just the chirp of insects out in the dark.

"May I ask a question?" she whispered.

Eyes made strange by possession turned to her and, after a long pause, the entity spoke. "Ask," it said simply.

"Do you mean us any harm?"

Oddly, a smile gathered around its mouth. "No. Nor are we here to be of benefit to you. We are gatherers of information. We observe to understand what drives an emergent intelligence and to see if social evolution on this world can be any different from a thousand others."

"There are that many intelligent species out there?"

The eyes blinked slowly. "Every species is intelligent in one sense or another. Moral value does not attach directly to intellect in either direct or inverse proportion." The words were grunted and she had the impression they were given grudgingly. "We shall continue to observe, and should your kind manage to avoid self-annihilation from any of a dozen causes, we may initiate formal contact. At this point, you are far from ready for the responsibilities that would attend such meeting."

They sat in silence, staring out at the luminous desert night as great, white stars glowed over the rough ridges. At last Janice asked one last question. "Do you intend to allow Alan and I to live? If so, will we be allowed to remember these events?"

"We are not wasteful," was the guarded reply, the rasping voice from the young man's lips. "There is no call to extinguish the being who has unwillingly hosted my essence, nor yourself. Memories are a burden, but I know my host well enough, after a year in his aura, to know he would relish the truth. Yet the price to his mind would be high, unless his impressions were verified by another. Are you prepared to provide that validation?"

Janice nodded slowly. "I know I cannot speak of it to anyone other than Alan, and wouldn't try. But it is a privilege to *know* we are not alone in the universe."

"Then perhaps we may leave those memories intact. But be aware, there are opinions beyond my own to contend with."

Then they sat in silence for a long while, 9 p.m. went by, and the night was shot with the odd meteor, glimmers here and there from traffic on roads far away. But at last Janice felt the hairs rise on her nape, as if something stirred on levels she could not normally perceive, and Alan's body moved in the gloom at her side. "Come."

They stepped out of the car, and made their way through the not-quite darkness under the stars fifty yards from the car, and Alan—the entity— raised a hand to the night sky. He stood immobile for a long while, and she imagined him to be calling, communing in some way, and when he lowered his arm she felt a sudden cool breeze stir around her. It built gradually to a chill rush of air, and she looked up to find an amorphous shape blotting out the stars.

Oh my god, this is it. It's real... Her thoughts became disjointed as the shape enlarged in absolute silence, and a sensation of static electricity made her skin itch, her hair stir, and she stepped back a pace or two. The great thing came softly to earth and hovered just above the surface, and momentarily an aperture appeared, opening like a cameras lens to emit a soft blue glow. And out of that glow stepped two figures which approximated the shape she had seen in the energy field surrounding her friend, far away and a week ago.

Alan's body turned to her and the guttural voice spoke softly. "I thank you. My kind thanks you. I have hidden a year on your world until our next mission was due to arrive, and now I may unburden this unwilling host. Farewell, and keep to your oath. For only you will suffer should you break it." He stepped forward and tensed, became like spring steel as if the entity drew in its strength, then, in a strange and eerie iridescence, the aural ghost became visible, overlying the human body. It drew away, like an insect casting an outgrown skin, and Janice saw the alien, fully formed, step away from the host, leaving only a tendril attached to his torso. Then the tendril withdrew in a snap of bright light and Alan cried out, falling to his knees, while the alien took on physical solidity, resolving into a tall, angular, quite-frightening being, like those who waited, outlined in the glow from the hatch.

They stepped forward and the castaway turned to look back. They conversed subtly, not in words, barely in gesture, but Janice felt they were speaking. A hand was raised by one of the pilots and her heart sank for she felt their memories were to be taken—leaving them as so many who had encountered the strange: lost and troubled, subject to scorn and conspiracy theories.

But the outcast pressed down the outstretched arm, and they conversed for a few moments as Janice knelt by Alan and assured herself he was well, found him looking up at the beings with wonder with his now entirely human eyes. Then the entity he had hosted so long placed a hand where its heart should be and made a very human half-bow to them, and the three withdrew into the blue glow. The portal closed and, without a sound, the vessel lofted away, directly upward, until it was lost to their gaze among the summer constellations.

§

For months after her return from a mysterious ten-day absence from her practice, Dr. Janice Weatherly looked after Alan Hardy, and reported to his parents that he was doing well. She assigned his breakdown to college stress, relationship difficulty, the general anxiety of life in so troubled and uncertain an age, but expected him to make a full recovery. She negotiated with his college for his resumption of study, and was delighted to see him return to his full potential.

Yet, for years to come, they would meet once per month for therapeutic conversation, and in the confidentiality of the doctor-patient relationship none ever guessed that the therapy went both ways, for each needed the validation of the other: they were mutual witnesses to the strange and fantastic, and the proud bearers of privileged knowledge. They knew they were not insane, and now viewed many others who claimed alien encounters in a kinder light.

Certainly, there were troubled people, those seeking attention, the misguided and the delusional; but, among them, Janice and Alan were now quite sure, was a small and solid core of those who really did know what they were talking about.

They *knew*. They could not share their knowledge with a soul, but great satisfaction came from looking at the night sky and knowing that life throbbed among the stars.

Reconnaissance Mission

Steven R. Southard

While renovating the Jefferson Hall Library at West Point, a staff member found several loose pages tucked into a volume of poems by Ovid. While historians are still authenticating those handwritten pages, what follows is the full text of the manuscript.

*O*ut of the Stygian sky they came. Lights, brighter than any star, moved at a velocity exceeding that of any bird, traversing to and fro above our desert campsite. My skin tingled as I dreaded what these mysterious, darting illuminations might signify.

"Douse the fire," I whispered, and the men of my squad obeyed. We sat together in the darkness, my nine men and the Spanish trapper, gazing at the inexplicable array of colored lights as they careened overhead. Unlike a lamp, candle-flame, or star, they did not flicker, but gleamed with an unnerving and unvarying intensity.

"Some Indian trick, perhaps?" Private Glendinning asked.

"Impossible," replied the Spaniard.

"*Die Mexikaner*?" Private Metzengerstein's voice held a fear I shared.

The trapper snorted. "Even less likely."

"What on Earth are they?" I asked, not expecting anyone to know.

Private Dupin answered with his usual air of certainty. "They are not from the Earth, Sergeant Major."

Not from the Earth? "What do you mean?"

"See how the lights move together?" Dupin asked. "They must be affixed to some conveyance, a carriage that sails the heavens as a ship voyages the seas. See how they change course at intervals and assume various compass directions? No kite or hot air balloon moves that way. That aerial ship must come from the Moon or some other celestial body."

When the meaning of his words sank in, my pulse and breath quickened.

"A Moon ship? *Ach*, I'm ready." Metzengerstein began loading his musket.

Without a sound, the lights vanished, streaking over the horizon to the southwest.

§

Three months prior to that encounter, I served in an artillery battery at Fort Moultrie in South Carolina. At the age of nineteen, I'd already attained the rank of Sergeant Major. The battery commander had even recommended I apply to the Military Academy at West Point.

The Army seemed the perfect place to live a life of adventure and to prove my mettle. I delighted in having found a suitable vocation, one in which I could enjoy a most satisfactory career. This remained true up until the day in Mid-March of 1829 when Second Lieutenant Howard called me to his office.

"Sergeant Major," he'd said, "I'm recommending you for a secret mission. Unless you accept, I can tell you nothing about it, except that it involves danger and will take eight or nine months. Every man on this mission had to volunteer for it. If you decline to join them, it will not affect your record."

He'd spoken the words *secret* and *danger*, but I heard the words *adventure* and *excitement*. "I accept, Sir."

"Are you certain?"

"I am, Sir."

He smiled. "Very well." He strode to a wall and pulled a curtain, revealing a map of North America. "You'll join a reconnaissance platoon under Lieutenant Bransby, headed here." He pointed to the eastern portion of Nuevo México. "The platoon will observe the Méxicans and the Apaches, and report whether either group is conducting operations that represent a near-term threat to our United States." He pointed at me. "You'll observe only, not shoot unless fired upon. Since you'll be within the sovereign territory of México, you'll not be wearing uniforms. If you're discovered, our government will disclaim any knowledge of you. Do you have any questions?"

"When do I leave, Sir?"

"The day after tomorrow." He wished me luck and dismissed me. I thanked and saluted him, but he spoke again as I reached the door. "Sergeant Major?"

"Yes, Sir?"

"If you find Eldorado, bring back as much gold as the wagons can carry."

He looked serious, but I smiled, said "Yes, Sir," and left. I took his remark as a joke, for I was a solemn and rational young man, with no time for frivolities such as myths or legends.

§

During the fifteen-hundred-mile trip westward, Lieutenant Bransby's thirty-man reconnaissance platoon passed from some of the greenest and most verdurous sectors of the Earth to the brownest, driest, and hottest locale on this side of Hades. Hunting became more difficult as we advanced, rivers less frequent. Horses had to content themselves with tawny, scraggly desert grasses when our supply of hay ran out.

At least the men of my assigned squad were competent. Most of the soldiers had emigrated from Europe and spoke English poorly, but my familiarity with Old World languages eased this difficulty. Three of my subordinates deserve special mention. Red-haired and jovial, Private Glendinning could shoot an apple from a tree at two hundred yards. Blond and impulsive, Private Metzengerstein proved himself a master horseman. Private Dupin rated low in all Army skills, but possessed an uncanny prowess in deductive reasoning, an ability I valued.

A week after fording the Pecos River and roaming eastern Nuevo México, we had seen vast herds of bison but neither Méxicans nor Apaches. Lieutenant Bransby ordered the platoon's three squads to split up so as to reconnoiter a greater area, and to rendezvous in one week. He and his platoon sergeant accompanied the other squads, leaving me in sole charge of mine, an indication of their confidence in my leadership.

My squad included ten men altogether, twelve horses, and one supply wagon. We journeyed south to our assigned sector. To ensure we remained unobserved, I sent two scouts ahead on foot, each of whom used hand signals to indicate whether the squad could advance undetected.

At one point, Dupin motioned for a halt and summoned me. Arriving by his side, I crouched behind a row of yucca plants and saw an elderly man struggling with ropes and pulleys some fifty yards ahead.

"He's a trapper," Dupin whispered. "He caught something in his pit trap and can't extract it."

"Is he alone?" I kept my voice low.

"Yes."

"He's no threat. We'll back up and circle around him to the West."

The old trapper stood up and looked in our direction. "*Hola, Señores.* I know you are there. If you help me hoist this bison, I will share its meat with you and take you to water."

How the deuce did he detect us? I held a finger to my lips, silencing the scouts.

"Come now," the old man shouted. "I would be a poor trapper if I did not know every sound and smell in this desert, eh? Show yourselves, and let us strike a bargain."

We were supposed to remain unseen, but we'd failed. Assuming he was alone, this old man did not seem a threat. Moreover, I sensed from his accent, his clothing, and his bearing that he was Spanish, not Méxican, and therefore unlikely to reveal us to government authorities. I took a chance and stood up with my musket trained on him, and ordered my scouts to do likewise. "How can we trust you, sir?"

I saw his wide smile even from a distance. "And how am I to trust *you, Señor*? After all, I am one and you are many. It seems we must either kill, avoid, or trust each other. I propose we work together, since each of us has something the other needs."

That seemed logical enough. Walking toward him, I saw he wore clothing consisting of poorly-stitched coyote hide. His face had been wrinkled and browned by age and the desert sun. Something about his pointed beard and proud stance reminded me of the conquistadors of old.

Halting within a few feet of him, I asked, "What do you have that we need?"

"In addition to the food and water I mentioned, I can serve as your guide. I know this land, including the locations of Apache villages and Méxican towns." He looked at me for a reaction.

I remained deadpan. "What do you want in return?"

His face lit up. "Since you speak English, you must be from the *Estados Unidos*. Take me with you when you return home. From there, I can sail to my beloved Spain."

"I can't promise that." I shook my head. "But I will ask my platoon commander in five days."

"Very well. I will guide you until then." He stuck out his hand. "I'm Fortunato."

I shook it. "I'm Edgar."

We helped him raise the beast's carcass from his trap and load it in our wagon. An hour's hike brought us to a meager rivulet running beside a dilapidated structure. With the men filling water skins and the horses drinking, Fortunato pulled me aside. "Come with me, Edgar."

He ushered me into the house, really a crude cabin with such cracked adobe walls that I feared it would collapse at any instant. "Sit, amigo," From a dust-covered cabinet, Fortunato produced a bottle and two unclean glasses.

"You're not just a trapper." Glancing around his one-room cabin, I'd noted maps and prospecting pans. "You've been searching for Eldorado."

He followed my gaze. His imposing stance gave me, once again, a momentary impression of a knight or conquistador. He laughed and sat down across from me. "There is no Eldorado. It's imaginary. *Sí*, I spent thirty years searching for it across forests, mountains, and deserts. Eldorado is fiction, Edgar, poetic nonsense. But *this*…" he held up the bottle. "This is real. Amontillado, the world's finest wine. I have but a few last drops, and these I share with you."

"No, Fortunato, thank you." I held up my hand. "I must not enjoy wine while my men drink only water."

"Very well." He raised the bottle to his mouth. He swished the liquid around before he swallowed, his eyes closed and his smile ecstatic.

"Ah," he sighed. "I am old, Edgar. I must end my adventuring and return to Spain. There I shall spend my final days savoring real pleasures like Amontillado, not dreams like Eldorado."

That evening, my squad made camp near Fortunato's hut, and that was the night we beheld the ghostly lights moving across the sky, those lights theorized by Dupin to belong to a craft steered by Moon-people, lights that terrified me to the depths of my soul.

§

At dawn, I felt no desire to explore the regions toward which the lights had disappeared, and declared we would reconnoiter to the north-west. No one questioned my decision, so we broke camp and moved out, employing scouts as before. I felt comforted having an experienced guide along.

By mid-afternoon we'd seen no living creatures except birds, snakes, and large spiders. We entered a place of uneven ground and increasing scrub brush vegetation.

Fortunato halted his horse and sniffed the air. "Something here is not right."

A ring of dust exploded around us. Shadowy figures sprang up from concealment. My steed reared and by the time I calmed him, I saw Indian braves all around, aiming their bows and arrows and shouting at us. My two scouts had been similarly surprised and were walking back toward us, each followed by an Apache.

We had all drawn our own pistols and muskets. I feared whoever fired first (most likely Metzengerstein) would cause numerous deaths on both sides. "Stand down, men!" I shouted. "Await my orders."

These Indians wore a minimum of clothing, all shades of tans and browns, all decorated with beads and tassels. Their garments fit loosely, allowing free movement for hunting.

Among the nine Apache men, I saw a single female standing with her bow trained on us as well. She was the most beautiful, angelic woman I had ever beheld, a Diana of the Desert whose age must have neared twenty years. Her clothing neither emphasized nor hid her figure's perfection. From the soft curve of her jawline to her full lips to the deep coffee brown of her eyes, her face surpassed in feminine loveliness the ancient statues of Aphrodite. Two braids of her black hair descended to her breasts, hair that revealed a blue tint in certain angles of light, like a raven's feathers. Nevermore will I look upon a raven without recalling this princess of the plains.

"Edgar."

"Hmm?" From some lesser universe had come the sound of Fortunato's voice.

"They want to know when you white men will leave their territory."

"Who is she?"

"The woman? That is Liluye. It means Singing Hawk. But listen…Edgar!" He snapped his fingers in my face.

I turned to him. "Yes?"

"If you tell them when you're leaving, maybe we can all live past the next few minutes."

"Ah, sorry. Tell them we mean no harm. We are passing through and will not stay long."

Fortunato spoke, and the Apache leader nodded. At a word from him, all the others relaxed their bow-strings and lowered their arrows. I ordered my men to lower their firearms. Following the practice of Lewis and Clark, I further demonstrated my harmless intent by offering gifts from our wagon including knives, some spare shirts, and a couple of tinder boxes.

The Indians seemed impressed with these. After they conversed with Fortunato, he turned to me. "They thank you, and have offered for your group to join them at their camp, a half-day's ride away."

Private Dupin asked, "Did they see strange lights in the sky last night?"

Fortunato conferred, then answered, "They did, but thought you white men caused them. I told them you didn't, and they said it must be the sky spirits, then."

We rode toward the Apache camp, Fortunato's horse next to mine. He leaned close to my ear. "Forget about Liluye, Amigo. She is spoken for."

I felt disappointed, not surprised. For me, beautiful women have always been unattainable, a glimpse of Heaven permitted only briefly to me. During our ride, I stole many opportunities to gaze at Liluye, the Singing Hawk. Even her exotic name set my heart afire, with its two liquid 'l' consonants and its mellifluous vowels, a name to whisper with love and adoration.

§

The Apaches led us to their hunting party's camp, a flat area near a narrow creek where they spread their blankets. My men and I helped them prepare the fire and the meal.

As the sun went down, we dined on delicious bison meat and learned the Apaches had been well aware of our platoon's *covert* arrival from the start. While coyotes howled in the distance, we swapped stories with them, learning some of their ways while we spoke of the modern wonders of our country. I kept glancing at Liluye. The night seemed to magnify her loveliness, the campfire glow to liven her features.

"*Was ist das?*" Metzengerstein grabbed his musket. "Did you hear something?"

"No," Dupin said. "It's the *absence* of something. The coyotes stopped."

The silence of the desert deepened. The Indians looked at each other, then suspiciously at us.

"*Begorah*," Glendinning pointed. "Here come those bloody lights again."

All of us turned and observed, over the southwest horizon, the same array of multi-colored lights as before. This time they did not cavort about, but maintained a beeline toward us. The ominous approach of these colored, star-like points caused my former dread to return. My pulse quickened; my stomach felt hollow; my backbone shivered. Frozen to the spot, mesmerized by the spectacle, I stared with growing distress.

Soon they flew close enough for me to see they formed a single flying object, as Dupin had reasoned. Nearer came that aerial shape, which bore no resemblance to a hot-air balloon. Longer than a naval frigate, it looked like an enormous golden bug, a shiny beetle with jointed legs jutting from each side. It flew with neither wings nor gas bag, leaving me to wonder how it moved and stayed aloft. I abandoned the notion of a carriage containing smaller beings. This could only be a lone, whale-sized creature, a titanic flying organism.

I blinked and rubbed my eyes. Perhaps some new species of firefly flew only inches from my eye, and, due to the properties of proportion, I had mistaken it for an animal the size of the Egyptian Sphinx a quarter mile away. But, no, I'd made no such mistake; Glendinning and the others were seeing it as well.

Too late, I realized our own light might have attracted this mammoth moth. "Douse the fire. Quickly!" My voice emerged in a soft falsetto. Dupin and some of the Apaches smothered the flames, but the giant creature slowed to a stop and hovered right above us.

Terrified beyond comprehension, I wanted to run but my legs would not move. Perhaps the same fear-induced immobility afflicted the rest of our group, for they all remained in place.

Excepting Private Metzengerstein. He grabbed his musket and ran to where his horse strained at its lead rope. He mounted his charger, aimed his gun skyward, and shouted, "*Stirb, verdammtes insekt!*"

"No, Metzengerstein!" I yelled. "Hold your fire." I held out hope the bug might fly off and leave us unmolested.

Against my order, he fired his musket and began reloading. The ball bounced off the insect's shell with a metallic clang.

The golden bug swiveled in the air until its narrow front part faced its attacker. A thin, red tongue of flame lanced from its proboscis, setting both Metzengerstein and his horse ablaze. Before I could do anything for him, his horse bolted and galloped into the night, with the unfortunate soldier still astride it, flames streaming behind. Eventually, the glow of that fire and the sound of his screams subsided in the distance.

Still in shock, I looked about our group to ensure no one else brandished a weapon. The Indians lay prone, arms stretched forward.

Several of my remaining men knelt in prayer. Fortunato and I sat and shielded our eyes from the glare of the bug's illumination.

The insect began descending and beneath it a cyclonic wind picked up, whirling the desert sand. The force of this vortex whipped our clothes and flying grit stung our faces. I recalled what I'd read of tornadoes, waterspouts, and the frightful Maelström of Scandinavian regions. My hands provided scant protection against the lashing wind and punishing sand. We moved inward toward the center of the violent whirlwind, which lessened our torment without alleviating it.

As if to punish us further, the accursed golden beetle emitted a new and perplexing light. White in color, this beam radiated downward a few feet with undiminished strength and then ended abruptly in a sharp edge, unlike any known category of light. This luminous blade began sweeping to and fro with its upper source fixed, like a clock's pendulum. The beam lengthened as it swung in ever-descending, inexorable arcs. Was the lower knife-edge of this ray a solid scimitar blade destined to cut us all to slivers? I stopped breathing and stared in petrified horror at the wedge advancing lower, ever lower toward me.

Soon the oscillating photonic axe swept just above our heads and we shrank from it, flattening ourselves upon the ground. Then it swooped lower still, cutting through a few of the others with no apparent detrimental effects. The beam swept through me and I felt nothing but a momentary vibratory sensation, a brief tremor speeding along my limbs.

I saw the flat-edged light ray pass through Liluye, and stop. Rather than sweep through her, it lingered, bisecting her body with a fine line of light. It widened into a cone, its apex at the bug and its circular bottom enveloping the beautiful woman.

She rose to her knees, wide-eyed, glancing all about and shaking. I heard her cry out and flail her arms, then her body began ascending. The enormous insect had deployed no filaments or webs, merely the cone of light. The beam that had done little to me began pulling the unfortunate woman skyward.

"Liluye!" Springing from my spot, I lunged toward her. I entered the cone and reached for her moccasin-clad feet. I grasped one of her ankles but could not pull her back to the Earth.

Instead, I ascended along with her, borne aloft by some invisible force. To my utter shock, nothing below me supported my weight. I slowly rose as if hoisted by an unseen hand.

Still holding Liluye's ankle, I glanced upward. A hole had opened in the bottom of the insect, a white rectangle of blinding illumination, too bright for my eyes, and the conical beam was drawing us into it.

§

I awoke to a somber blue light, darker than a Carolina sky and more uniform in hue. I lay supine on a smooth, cushioned surface. I tried to move, but could not. My head, trunk, and limbs seemed pinioned in place despite lacking any visible restraints. I could shift my eyes but only perceived a limited sector of the room. My attempts to move brought on no pain, nor did I experience any discomfort while lying there, but my forced immobilization brought on a new wave of distress.

I heard music, or a form of it. It sounded like the diminutive tinkling bells celebrants tie to horse's tails at Christmastime. Something felt alien about the tune; a melody not built upon any musical scale I recognized. Listening closer, I realized the bell tones themselves rang in the opposite manner of a standard bell. Instead of the usual impact noise followed by a diminuendo fading to silence, these sounds emerged from nothing, swelling until they reached an abrupt and jarring end. Those anti-bells, if I may so term them, were pleasant—if foreign—to the ear and helped calm me.

A being appeared and leaned over me. This personage wore a hooded robe and I saw no face within the hood's dark opening. Colored black, the robe bore an abstract and unusual design. At length I construed the design as irregular splotches of a dark reddish hue, star-like patterns surrounded by elongated teardrop shapes, as if someone had simply splattered a red liquid upon the black garment.

What if *my own blood* had somehow spilled on this individual's clothing? What was the creature, even now, doing to me? Throughout, it remained silent and I felt no pain, yet I knew nothing of what the entity was up to.

A second being joined the first, looking like its twin. I had been wrong to think I'd entered a titanic insect. Dupin had deduced correctly at the onset; these frightful creatures had taken me inside some hitherto unknown aerial vehicle.

The character of the music altered, from tiny dinging sleigh-bells to a larger, clanging variety sounding much like annoying cowbells. Also, inexplicably, the room turned purple. The beings had not conveyed me to a different room; the very walls and ceiling had changed hue. I should have felt astonishment at this, but too many things had shocked me on this day for a room color change to merit special distinction.

My first black-hooded attendant shifted position and by glancing to that side, I saw a second bed a few feet distant from mine. On it lay Liluye. Sweet Liluye. She rested, as I did, facing up. Her eyes may have been open, though I could not tell for certain. I called out her name, or tried to, but no sound emerged and it would have been drowned out in any case by the clanging of the anti-bells, whose chaotic discordance grew more irritating by the minute.

Another of my mysterious, robe-clad attendants arrived and once again the room changed color, this time to a deep, rich green. The illumination came not from any visible candles or oil lamps. Somehow the green light emerged directly from the room's walls and ceiling.

Though I felt nothing, the two standing by my bedside kept busy with their unfathomable tasks. I caught occasional glimpses of thin arms and oddly-shaped metallic implements, though their objective remained unknowable.

A fourth Moon-person arrived and blocked my view of Liluye. Once again, the room changed color, this time to orange. Once again, the tone of the anti-bells deepened and sounded more depressing. Unlike the 'ding-dong' of Earthly bells, these lunar anti-bells rang in a *nid-nod* manner. Their incessant *nid-nodding* had progressed to a cacophonic din I could neither silence nor ignore.

Now another color change, to white. Now more attendants coming and going, busily working in the region of my torso, doing things I could not see. Yet I felt no pain other than faint pressures, as if fingers were touching my chest.

When the room changed to violet, I felt no surprise, only curiosity at the purpose of these changes and how many more lay in store. That led me to ponder why these Moon-beings would trouble themselves to voyage to our orb in the first place. Why undertake this journey? Perhaps, it occurred to me, they had embarked on nothing more than a reconnaissance mission, just as our platoon had done.

Next came the most unusual and sinister change. The walls and ceiling turned utterly black, yet a red light shone from some unseen source. By now the dirge-like *nid-nod* tolling of the anti-bells, apparently the size of cathedral bells, had become a maddening pealing, a clashing of tones that will linger forever in my nightmares.

While the deafening death-knell of those Moon-gongs assaulted my ears, I saw one of the black-robed beings reach down into the region of my chest. With utter stupefaction and horror, I watched as this creature lifted up what looked like a human heart, deep purple in the crimson light, a heart still beating and dripping blood. So ghastly and hideous was this act, I didn't pause to wonder how I could be consciously witnessing it. I tried to cry out in anguish, in protest against this barbaric savagery, but I seemed incapable of uttering noise.

At the edge of my vision, I saw the Moon-being place the life-organ—my own heart—into a cabinet embedded in the wall. Even after this hooded butcher shut the door, I swear I saw the cabinet door pulsing, throbbing, beating with the same rhythm as my heart.

I screamed an inner scream only I could hear, then passed out of consciousness.

§

"The smelling salts are working. He's waking up."

"Aye. His eyelids fluttered a wee bit."

"*Gracias a Dios.*"

Somehow, I awoke. I lay on the ground, my men and Fortunato leaning over me, with several Apaches in the background. The campfire—apparently relit—blazed not far away.

Horrid memories then returned and I sat up and looked down at my chest. My shirt, though drenched in sweat, appeared intact. I placed a hand on my breast and felt a steady, rapid beat. I still retained my own heart! The beings had returned it, or never taken it but caused me to believe they had.

Looking up, I saw the clear sky holding nothing but stars and a full moon. "Where?" My voice scratched.

"Flown away, Sergeant Major," Dupin said. "They sent a light beam down, returning you to us. Then they sped that way, toward the Moon."

"Liluye," I peered past my men, seeking her among the Indians.

"I'm sorry, Amigo," Fortunato looked down. "They did not return her."

I shouldn't have cried in front of my men, but did so.

After I calmed down and dried my eyes, Private Glendinning asked, "Sergeant Major, are you a'right?"

Though I assured him I was, I have been asking myself that question ever since. A mile from the site, we found and reverently buried Metzengerstein's body. We then returned to the rendezvous point, having agreed to say nothing of the strange Moon-craft. I told Lieutenant Bransby that Private Metzengerstein had died of a snake bite. As to Fortunato, I eventually convinced the Lieutenant to allow the Spanish trapper to accompany us eastward.

Am I truly all right? I returned to Fort Moultrie, received my appointment to the Military Academy, and reported here. But I am a man wholly different from the one who entered that aerial vehicle, perhaps doomed to remain different from all others. My mind writhes in constant torment from dark nightmares, evil forebodings, and ghastly apparitions, all more real to me than everyday Army life. I feel driven, obsessed with the craving to write about these dreadful and gruesome phantasms. I must capture in words my sorrow and ever-increasing grief over the loss of the beautiful, unattainable Liluye.

In a bizarre way, I have kept my promise to Lieutenant Howard. I found the legendary Eldorado, or a version of it, and returned with a wagon-load of its riches, secreted within the blackest shadows of my mind.

Write, write, I must boldly write or go further insane. I see now that West Point is no place for me. I do not belong in this gray prison. Whatever I am meant to accomplish in life, I will not achieve it here.

E. A. Poe
~~Cadet, Third Class~~
January 1831

An Unmapped Island

Brock Poulsen

*E*ntry 1:
    Having settled into my cabin, I proceed with a record of my findings. By way of introduction, my name is Ferdinand Nehemiah Weaver, and in the wake of recent tragedy in my life, I have joined the crew of the *HMS Marjorie* for scientific purposes. I am a Biologist by education; I graduated from Oxford at the age of 22 and began my study of living creatures on, and around, the British Isles. When the opportunity arose, I joined this ship to sail into unexplored regions of the vast Pacific, in search of hitherto unexplored islands and unusual fauna.

    I have brought with me my copy of *On the Origin of Species* by Charles Darwin, and few other belongings: a shaving kit, a locket that belonged to my deceased wife and which contains a lock of her hair, and—though I hope against the necessity of its use—a pistol given to me by my late father. As for the crew, they are prepared against the possibility of trouble in every conceivable way. Captain Jean Goddard, a black-skinned Frenchman, is tall and thin and speaks English with a boldness that inspires confidence in his crew. His first mate is older and skittish, with a pale face that has crisped in the sun, and is called Harrison Reginald Holt. The rest of the crew has been aloof to my presence. I suspect they will not concern themselves with me if I stay out of their way.

    This volume will chronicle my findings during my journey aboard Captain Goddard's vessel, with the hope of some significant discovery.

Entry 3:

The opportunities for scientific inquiry have been sparse. The only living things I've encountered are the seagulls—which are not, as subjects, ideal—and my fellow crew members. If I were a neurologist, perhaps I would be permitted to plumb the workings of their minds. Alas, I will have to wait for more suitable creatures. I have been engrossing myself with study of Darwin's volume; however, I long to make my own observations and conjectures, rather than merely to read about them.

I don't care for life on a sailing vessel, if I am honest. The constant motion has me feeling perpetually uneasy and regularly nauseated. The food is bland and comes in meager portions that hardly sate my appetite. Beer, however, is in ready supply, and serves at the very least to allay my grief. I am doing my best to adjust, but I fear the weeks ahead of me will be difficult, more so without a topic of study.

We have been at sea for weeks, having to a large degree followed Darwin's route. I have expressed my desire to the Captain and crew to follow in Darwin's footsteps, but I have suggested that it may be necessary to stray from them literally, in order to pursue them scientifically.

Entry 7:

There is news! Early this morning, just as dawn was lighting the seas, the ship listed sharply starboard, and there were shouts from the deck. Something unusual had been spotted in the distance. I ran to get a look, and could scarcely make out the shape against the horizon. But its color is what has me intrigued: it is richly green, certainly meaning the presence of life.

I hope for an island, but the captain assures me this is unlikely. These waters have been thoroughly mapped, and no such bit of land appears on any of his charts. More likely, he says, it is a tangle of driftwood and algae that has thrived in the friendly springtime sun.

Regardless of its makeup, I look forward to a closer examination. A structure of its size may have biological peculiarities of one type or another.

Entry 8:

We reached the island—though Captain Goddard is loathe to hear me to call it such—last evening, and have spent the intervening time drifting in its orbit. It does seem unlikely for such a remote location to have much in the way of animal life. I remind myself of Dr. Darwin's finches, and I take heart that there may yet be discoveries in store.

The captain and crew have expressed a desire to draw closer to the structure, a notion I heartily endorse. It may be they are as anxious as I to see our journey's purpose, or they may be eager to see it foiled; in either case, tomorrow I shall have more answers.

Entry 10:

The thing, which for convenience's sake Captain Goddard has started calling an island, is rather larger than we originally estimated. It is several kilometers in diameter, and roughly a circle. The surface rises no higher than our bulwark at any point, remaining mostly level, if overgrown to varying levels with vegetation, including trees.

Much to my dismay, however, we remained on the ship, due to a lack of serviceable locations from which to approach. Efforts to plumb the ocean floor have been curiously unsuccessful; where the crew expected to find a rising ocean floor, they found none. Their efforts were repeated several times, each time drawing closer to the island, and each time with the identical result. I am Tantalus, with my heart's desire almost within arms' reach, yet just beyond my grasp.

Tomorrow we shall see if this poor Tantalus can take to a crowded longboat, and obtain that which he seeks.

Entry 11:

Today was an exceptional day. With little urging, Captain Goddard agreed to my request, and sent me to the island with several members of his crew. They persisted in their attempts to gauge the ocean's depth, again without success. The ocean was clear enough that we could see into it a great distance. Were I a geologist, I would posit that the island rose from the ocean floor at an enormous speed compared to the usual, resulting in a much steeper slope. But perhaps I presume too much familiarity with my colleagues' fields. The lack of discernible depths does trouble my shipmates, and many have taken it as a bad omen.

I prefer, instead, to think on the scientific possibilities. I will document my findings to the best of my ability, to preserve my first impressions of this anomaly.

First setting foot on the island's lush green surface, I was struck at its unusual texture. It seems—at least on the beach where I stood—to have a thick layer of moss concealing either the sand or rock beneath. It is comfortable to walk on, and contributes to the impression that this island is a bit of jungle, different from its kin only by its odd location.

Many different varieties of trees are present, which seems unusual. My theory is that their seeds reached this remote speck of land on air or ocean currents, or in the droppings of seafaring birds; it would not be unheard of in the least.

Animal life, however, doesn't follow the same pattern. I am unlikely to see anything larger than insects and birds here, but I will make the most of whatever we discover.

Entry 12:

There is life on the island. Several of the men thought they heard something moving deeper in the greenery, so I'm holding out hope for animal life. The trees are varied and well established, some bearing a fruit that resembles a hard pear. I am glad to have something other than hard tack and dried lamb for my evening meal.

Entry 13:

There were more odd noises today as we explored the island further. An unusual insect is prevalent: it has a greyish pink carapace, like a shrimp, and alternates between the water and the trees.

After some inspection I realized they were not insects; rather they were krill, or some mutation thereof. No, not a mutation: an evolution, for they all bore the same changes. Hundreds, possibly thousands of generations had preserved alterations in this line of the animal, allowing them to thrive above and below the ocean's surface. Fascinating, to say the very least!

That the island is old is no surprise; there is soil, meaning the decomposition of plant life, which takes a great deal of time. But to host an evolutionary progression this drastic is something else entirely. They lack the aesthetic appeal of finches, but these krill may be just the kind of thing I have been seeking.

Entry 14:

Any elation I may have felt yesterday has evaporated. Holt has gone missing. I and the rest of the crew fear the worst. His hat and boots are still by the fire, but the man himself is nowhere to be found.

I fear he has wandered into some remote portion of the jungle and fallen into a sinkhole, or become injured and unable to return. It's not the type of danger any of us were expecting when we came here. Our mission now seems to have changed, and we must locate Holt.

The men are getting nervous. We've as yet found nothing to suggest it, and no one will speak it, but another possible explanation is that something much larger lives on the island. The men are vigilant, and will be posting a watch tonight as we sleep.

Entry 15:

A strange man, perhaps 25 years old, came into our camp this morning, shocking all of us. He communicated in French well enough, though perhaps isolation on the island has warped his memory. He was utterly nude, and claimed to have been here for a few days. It can't have been more than a week, perhaps two, since he became stranded.

I tried to learn more, but he was gone in the next second, back into the thick jungle. We will attempt to locate him in the morning, to learn more of his survival. I would have expected him to be more grateful to see us. Perhaps he is of limited mental capacity, and fails to see how dire his situation was before our arrival.

We will also find out what has become of Holt, and hold this man accountable if necessary. The rest of the crew has assured me of this fact.

Entry 16:

We found the man, not far inland from our camp, and discovered his name to be Sonny. He has no shelter, furthering my suspicion that his time here has been short, but we loaned him enough clothing to ensure his modesty. We are all suspicious that he was involved in Holt's disappearance, but there is no evidence beyond the circumstantial. If he was involved, and if his mental faculties are not to be trusted, then I fear we may have to deal harshly with him. I don't fear for our safety; the crew are smart and prepared enough to deal with one unarmed, naked man. But I wonder after Holt's fate.

It seems inconsequential now, but I am continuing my study of the krill. Their habits—their very existence—are fascinating to me. They seem to have a home toward the center of the island. With any luck our explorations will take us closer to their nesting grounds, so that I can gather samples and make observations of this rather alien species.

Entry 17:

The island continues to reveal new secrets. During the night, the trees began to glow with a soft green light. Upon closer inspection, small insect larvae dotted the branches of the trees, their thoraxes emitting a faint light. What the evolutionary advantage of this would be, I have no guess. More likely it is a mutation that has survived in the absence of any bird or rodent predators. In any case, it is a fascinating part of the biome.

Unable to sleep, I left the camp to explore the nearby area. I headed toward the interior of the island, thinking it more likely to contain a diversity of life. Within moments, I heard footsteps behind me in the jungle. Thinking it to be one of the crew answering nature's urging, I did my best to evade them, ducking into a thick copse of trees as they drew nearer. The glowing larva were, mercifully, not to be found in my hiding place, but they illuminated the area just outside it, giving me a view of my compatriot.

I watched as Sonny walked by, naked and streaked in dirt. His hands hung at his sides, clutching like claws, and he looked around with a puzzled expression on his face. He seemed agitated by the place as much as by the pursuit, looking nervously at the trees around him, and within a moment he moved on. I noted that the trees here were the tallest I'd seen anywhere on the island, and grew straight up into the sky, spaced at regular intervals. It seemed too unlikely an arrangement to be natural.

Making a note to return to the place in the daylight, and after waiting what I considered a sufficient time for Sonny to leave the area, I at last returned to the camp and my bed. My sleep was restless, and I startled awake at every sound until at last dawn arrived.

Entry 18:

Sonny visited us early, and his memory seems to be returning to him in fits and starts, today summoning a recollection of service in some branch of the military. He recounted serving on a ship, though his description suggested that the vessel where he served was quite old.

Useful memories were in short supply, and we are still no closer to learning the island's secrets, or the cause of our companion's disappearance. Each moment I spend among the island's trees troubles me further. I never thought I would long to return to the ship, yet here we are. There is a similar tension in my crewmates, especially when Sonny is nearby. He has an odd affection for us, which unnerves me when I consider him as the most likely culprit behind Holt's disappearance.

Entry 19:

Today the rest of the crew voted to explore further into the island, with the desire to find Mr. Holt's whereabouts. I decline to say *his body*, though that was certainly the implication at the outset of our search.

We found something far stranger. At what I estimated to be the center of the island, we came upon a small hill, grown over with dark green algae. There was an indentation in the algae near the base, resembling an animal's burrow. At the base of the indentation, naked and content, was a baby.

Entry 20:

I must admit to being entirely perplexed. The child seems to be in perfect health, based on a cursory examination. He seems well-nourished, a fact I cannot explain. If Sonny and the baby had been stranded here for even a few days, I would expect to see signs in the child of inadequate food, yet we met Sonny several days ago, and he claims to have been here several days prior to that.

Despite my adherence to the scientific method, I cannot help but wonder if something is happening here that is outside of scientific knowledge. My mind begins to speculate if there are forces from beyond at play.

Entry 21:

Sonny informs us that the child's name is Harry, though he cannot explain to my satisfaction how the child came to be on the island healthy and uninjured. Harry is old enough that he can subsist on fruit, but before much longer we will need to return to the ship, and return the baby to civilization.

But after much pondering, I have become resolute in my conviction: I will solve the mysteries of the island, or die in my attempts. I am, after all, a scientist searching for the truth—no matter how strange. Tonight, I will return to the center of the island, to where we found Harry, to discover the reason for Sonny's fascination and constant returns. I will take only my wife's locket for bravery, and my pistol for protection.

Entry 22:

I waited for my traveling companions to be comfortably abed, and then stole away for the heart of the island. The luminescent larvae assisted with my journey, lighting the way until I came to the hillock. I stood at its base for several minutes; though I'd reached my destination, its purpose still eluded me. Its very presence suggested to me an unnatural origin.

After I'd made my third lap around the area, I heard behind me the familiar chittering of the krill, growing to an alarming volume.

There must have been a thousand of the creatures, writhing on the lush jungle floor, charging unitedly to the dark indentation at the hill's base. The whole mass disappeared into the opening within a few moments, and then, emerging from the ensuing silence, was a noise.

The hill itself began to hum. Its surface seemed to vibrate, an effect I at first thought I was imagining in the weak light. Upon placing a hand to the flora, I discovered it was indeed moving to a degree, in addition to feeling warm beneath my palm. Some reaction was taking place, I assumed, though as to its nature I could hardly guess. I took several steps away as the humming increased in intensity; I began to recall scientific papers regarding geysers and the like, and attempted to take shelter in a location from which I could still observe the structure.

The sound reached a peak, then began to wane. Within another moment there was an end to the noise, and from the cavern spilled some hundred or so of the mutated krill. They were in almost every way identical to those I had just seen, only I noted several peculiarities. Some had a blue crest standing up from their head, while others had a similar crest on their back. Others had eyes that seemed too large for their bodies, or even extra limbs.

I should like to propose that beneath the hill is a large krill habitat, where the creatures live and breed, and what I saw was simply two groups passing in and out through the same entrance. What I am less equipped to accept, or even to hypothesize, is that which my own eyes showed me this evening. For it seemed to me that this hill—this island, perhaps—*consumed* the bodies of the first group of krill, and then, through some process anathema to science, *spawned* the second group from their biological ingredients.

I am ill to consider it, and found no comfort in discovering this secret purpose. I attempted to record the event, but must confess the singularity of the experience caused me great distress. I retreated to a copse of trees some distance away, though the hill was still within my sight. Without a doubt, I was witnessing an event of significant scientific importance, and strove to record the details with accuracy.

It was only moments later that I saw Sonny approach the mound, and the peculiarity only worsened. The young man placed his arm, up to the shoulder, into a hitherto unseen orifice in the hillside. Again the structure came to life with its humming sound, though it lasted not as long this time. Sonny withdrew his arm as naturally as if he'd just been shaking hands with a stranger, and began to speak. It seemed he was addressing the hill, though I could ascertain no response. I'm beginning to suspect the hillock is somehow sentient.

After a time, Sonny concluded his errand, and left the area. I nearly slept there in my nook from sheer exhaustion, but instead dragged myself back to the safety of camp.

Entry 23:

I confronted Sonny today. I found him in a moment when we could be alone, and told him frankly that I had seen his visit to the center of the island, and demanded to know the purpose of the hill, and the island as a whole.

In all my days I could not have imagined a more fanciful story than the one which Sonny casually related, as we sat together in the shade of a fruit tree.

Upon my revelation that I'd seen the krill disappear, and his interaction with the hillock, Sonny's disposition changed from his normal jocular aloofness to one I would describe as clinical. With a firm hand on my arm he took me aside to an isolated location.

He explained to me that the mound of algae at the center of the island concealed a machine of great scientific importance to his people. A people not from our world. When I pressed him regarding what world he meant, he clarified that the machine had come from another planet entirely.

Evidently my scientific curiosity outweighed my astounded disbelief, and I urged him to go on. At the heart of the island is a sort of mechanical brain, sent from the stars by scientists. Its purpose is to simulate generations of mutation and adaptation, and catalog the results. When it landed in our ocean, it began collecting biological material and reproducing it, building first a covering of algae. As it encountered varieties of life, it replicated them as well, eventually resulting in the floating mass on which we now sat. A sister machine, he told me, was sent to the rocky deserts of the American Southwest.

Sonny proudly informed me that he was the most complex form of life this machine had yet created, allowing the machine's "brain" to use his own mind to communicate its purpose and history. When I pressed him for details on how long ago he actually came to be here on the island, he gave me the same answer he always had, corresponding to approximately the same time our party arrived.

I was beginning to dread the answer we were approaching. The machines reuse biological material, this much I understood. I asked Sonny where his diagrams—as it were—came from, and he answered that *we* had brought them to the island.

Sonny, I asked, what is your full name? Sonny cheerfully answered that he was called Harrison Reginald Holt, but as a man in his twenties he'd been called "Sonny" by his friends.

Realization dawned on me, and I said the child's name aloud. Harry. The baby is also called Harrison Reginald Holt, I asked Sonny, and he nodded with a childlike satisfaction.

He explained with the enthusiasm of a proud engineer how the machines recorded the structure of an individual organism, and could use raw elements from their environment to construct the creature at any point in its life, even retaining its memories.

By this time my head was positively spinning, but I couldn't relent. I pressed Sonny for more information; for the purpose of the machines. He told me that they were sent by a biologist to study the progression of Earth species. The machines could, with equal ease, disassemble and recreate organisms. Perhaps someday the alien scientists would visit Earth, to collect their machines from the desert and tropical climes where they'd been installed and witness our planet's lifeforms firsthand. But Sonny was mute on the details. My heart nearly leapt from my chest. A colleague of my own and of Charles Darwin, a universe away, with the same goals. To be able to see Darwin's principles of growth and change, even though they were the result of alien intervention, demonstrated before my very eyes, was a spectacular privilege.

I am going to sleep now, though I am certain it will elude me. Tomorrow we return to the ship, and I fear I'll have nothing but my own writings to show for the island's discovery.

Entry 24:

Today I woke with a purpose, while the rest of the crew were preparing to leave, loading supplies into the longboat. I assured them I'd be along shortly, then went in search of Sonny, my locket held tight to my chest and my pistol at my side.

The machine requires very little information to create a living creature whole cloth. Sonny himself is not the first version, he tells me, only the version the machine chose to keep.

My hopes are confirmed when I show Sonny the lock of hair from Elizabeth, my beloved wife. He assured me the machine can bring her to me, just as I remember her, and there is nothing I long for more. Though I know it in my black heart to be abominable, yet I press on. Life, and in the moment I feel I must quote the visionary Mary Shelley, has been an accumulation of anguish without her.

Once again we will be together, after so long apart. It will be, for her at the least, as if not a moment has passed. She will find me a grateful husband, and this our paradise.

Final Entry:

I cannot return to society with Elizabeth—knowing what I've done. To say that people would not understand seems laughably inadequate.

Instead I am sending my journal back to the ship, along with a man who is as much me as he is not. Indeed, he is Ferdinand Nehemiah Weaver, just as I am, but younger, without the knowledge of this cursed place and its sister desert site.

Likely the island will never again be found, and if indeed not, let these words be my legacy: I have chosen the arrival of a peculiar happiness over the possibility of a traditional one.

The Taking of Alice Burrows

Christopher Wheatley

*I*t begins on a late spring morning, on a parched stretch of New Mexico highway, twenty miles from the city of Roswell. Ted Hawksberry stands by the side of his battered Chevrolet, which is parked half-off the road. The towering sky runs the spectrum of blue, from deepest cerulean to the color of Ted's eyes. From the far horizon, broad strands of cirrostratus unravel like caterpillar tracks, shielding the massed ranks of sagebrush from the power of the raw sun.

Ted stares out at his homeland through the dark, adaptive lenses of his prescription glasses. The familiar anxiety that he feels is a comfort, the irony of which lends a grim smile to his mouth. Folks will tell you that Hawksberry never smiles at all, but then folks are never present at the places where he stops to watch and to wonder.

The voice talking into his ear is that of Ted's former teacher, Doctor Phelps. "Still not answering your phone," is the first thing that it says. "I'd like you to stop by the university. There's a visitor I want you to meet. From Santa Fe. It's hard to explain. They'll be here till Friday. Try your very best to make it."

Ted turns the phone off and replaces it in the glove box. He has no further work today and nothing else to do. The high clouds seem untouched by the hot breeze. The highway, in both directions, is dead. To go and see Phelps requires an effort that Ted is not sure he can muster. For an extended time he stands still, eyes closed, trying not to think or to feel.

§

The Roswell campus of the Eastern New Mexico University is a square-lined and unobtrusive spread of buildings. The best you could say about it is that it looks neat. Ted parks his Chevrolet and traces a route along familiar stairwells and corridors up to the doctor's office. He feels like an intruder amongst the bright and bustling students. No, he feels like a ghost.

The office door is open. Doctor Phelps perches on his desk, with one grey-trousered leg hanging loose. He wears a dark sweater over a white shirt, the very picture of a college lecturer. His shoulders seem a little rounder, the lines on his face a little deeper. When Ted arrives, Phelps is talking to someone who is out of view.

"Why, here is the man himself," exclaims Phelps, a little too quickly, standing and smiling and beckoning Ted in. "Perfect timing. This is Miss Sarah Hutchingson. She's down from Santa Fe."

Sarah Hutchingson reminds Ted of the campus building, neat and clean and a little impersonal. She is in her mid-to-late-twenties, extremely thin, with hair as red as the New Mexico dust, and a shot-gun spread of freckles across her face.

Ted shakes her hand and does his best to smile. He feels that, on him, the expression looks strained and mocking.

"It's a pleasure," says Sarah, and she seems to mean it.

"Drink Ted?" says Phelps. "No? Take a seat." He raises his hand to his chin. It is a gesture that Ted has seen many times before, back in his classroom days. It signifies that the doctor is about to launch into some fresh topic of import.

"I think that the best thing is to be straight-forward. How about I kick things off and then pass you over to Miss Hutchingson?"

Sarah nods.

"Last Wednesday, that's right isn't it? Last Wednesday, I had a call from Miss Hutchingson…"

"…Sarah, please."

"Last Wednesday, I had a call from Sarah. She's part of an archaeological dig, a joint-leader, pardon me, of a site out near Blackwater Hill. A place called Hunter's Nest."

"I know it," says Ted. His heart begins to beat quicker. He licks his dry lips.

"Well here's the strange part, Ted. Now we don't know if this is some elaborate practical joke."

"All the tests point to it being not," says Sarah. "If I thought this was a prank then I wouldn't have taken up your time. Either of you."

Phelps throws up his arms. "Fact is we just can't explain it."

"Explain what, doctor?" Ted hears himself say. It was a mistake to come, he knows that now. A mistake.

Sarah stands and crosses to the table. She removes from a cardboard box a circular object, around eighteen inches in diameter. The object is made of dark red clay, about a half inch thick. Its surface is etched with a spiral design running from its center to its outside edge.

Ted's gaze switches from the object to the doctor and back. He leans forward to take a closer look, not because he wants to, but because he feels it is expected. The disc has an indefinable air of great age.

Sarah pauses, unsure. "It's a least five hundred years old," she says, "probably older. One of my students joked that it resembled one of his dad's old vinyl records. I ran with the idea, purely as a learning exercise. Supposing there *were* audio information on it, I asked him, then how would you retrieve it? When we got back to Santa Fe he had a go."

Doctor Phelps stares hard at the point of his shoe, his arms crossed.

"You found something?" says Ted.

"My student used a precision laser to map the micro-contours on the disc's surface," says Sarah. "It's important to stress that we can be very sure that these grooves are contemporaneous with the disc itself."

"Except logically, that can't be so," says the doctor.

"The sound we retrieved," says Sarah, "is messy but clearly discernible. It's a voice. A woman's voice. If you'll allow me to play it, then you'll understand why I'm here."

Ted feels unable to move. His mind is a fog. He nods, slowly.

Sarah places her phone upon the desk. After a short pause the audio file starts to play. There is crackling and a fizzing and *her* voice. Alice. She sounds changed, damaged, but it is unmistakably her voice and it reaches right into Ted and it twists his insides.

"My name is Alice Burrows," she says, "I am a Ph.D. student in acoustic engineering and this is a message for Ted Hawksberry. He will be a student at Eastern New Mexico University, Roswell, between the years nineteen ninety-four and nineteen ninety-nine. Doctor Philip Phelps will be his mentor. If you find this, please pass it on."

Ted lets out a sob. He leans forward in his chair. Sarah looks to Phelps, who shakes his head.

"I am going to leave this message," says the voice of Alice Burrows, "at Blackwater Hill, where we had our first date. If Ted thinks to look, it will be there."

"I didn't look," says Ted, sitting back. He is dimly aware of the concern on Doctor Phelp's face.

"They took me," says Alice, "just like we talked about. I know where I am, but I don't know *when*. I think perhaps sixteen hundred A.D. At one time we were in Egypt. Then the African continent. I'm not sure what they wanted with me, Ted. They did things. They've changed me. I think that they needed to take parts of me and now they have left me alone."

"Alice," says Ted.

"Don't blame yourself," says the recording. "My memory comes and goes. In a moment more, I may have forgotten. I know you will have done everything that you could. I built a machine to record this, Ted, but I can't play it back. I don't remember any more. I love you, Ted. I love you. I..."

Then there is only static.

"That's where the recording ends," says Sarah, softly.

"I need a minute," says Ted, standing up.

"Want me to come with you?" says Phelps.

Ted shakes his head. "I'll be back."

§

He bursts through the fire-door into the parking lot and takes great lungfuls of air, as if rising from the depths. He puts his fingers to his face. He leans against the wall and with shaking hands he takes out a cigarette.

He remembers.

It begins on an early spring evening, on a parched stretch of New Mexico highway, twenty miles from the city of Roswell. Ted Hawksberry stands by the side of his pick-up truck, which is parked half-off the road. Alice Burrows, in shorts and T-shirt and sunglasses, white streaks of sun-screen on her forehead and cheeks, leans over the hood of the truck, looks up from the spread-out map and grins.

"This is it," she says. "This is where it happened."

"Here?" says Ted, smiling back. "This is where those old folks saw E.T.?"

"They didn't see any aliens," says Alice, standing, with her hands on her hips. "They saw a UFO. Right after their car engine cut out. That's what we call a Close Encounter of the Second Kind."

"That's what I call one too many cocktails at Tony's."

Alice sticks out her tongue. "You sure you're up for this?" she says.

"Camping out in the middle of nowhere all night waiting for spaceships? Sure."

"You forgot to mention," says Alice, "the scintillating company of your beautiful girlfriend." She opens the trunk and begins to unpack. "Plus, we have sleeping mats, binoculars, coffee and a luxury-selection of tinned biscuits. Good enough for you?"

"What sort of biscuits?" says Ted, and ducks as a rolled sleeping mat sails through the air.

The remainder of the day they spend hiking, just for the sake of it. From time to time Alice pauses to examine the ground or to take a photograph.

"Tell me again about your grandfather," says Ted.

"You've heard it a thousand times," says Alice. There is a smile upon her lips. They both know that Ted will coax it out of her anew.

It takes all of ten minutes.

"My grandfather grew up in Roswell," Alice begins, as they walk on, with their lengthening shadows going before them. "He reckoned that even before 'forty-seven the aliens were around here. This is a special place for them, he used to say, something in the ground, or in the mountains. 'It's like catnip for kitties,' he said. 'There's a lot of history here, a lot of *accumulated* time.'"

"That's a new detail," says Ted. "Accumulated time. What does that mean?"

"I don't know," says Alice. She stoops to pick up a pebble, rolls it around in her palm as they walk. "I only just remembered he said that. 'History is like an energy.' That's another of his sayings. When you look around at this landscape, though, you can see what he meant. Can't you?"

Ted shudders. Something about that thought makes him uneasy.

"Anyhow," continues Alice, "the story is that on the night that my grandfather proposed to my grandmother, he took her out to Blackwater Hill and they saw..."

"Here it comes," Ted interrupts.

"You want the story or not?"

"I do."

Alice lets the pebble slip back to the ground. "They saw a spaceship—a glowing blue light in the sky, and they watched it for at least ten minutes. At one point it came so close that it lit up their car with its beams. Grandfather thought it was trying to tell them something. Or to understand something *from them*. That was the night that my grandfather proposed and my grandmother said yes and now, fifty years later, here I am."

"You left out the good part."

"Why is *that* the good part?"

"C'mon," says Ted. "Let me hear it."

Alice rolls her eyes. "Well," she says, "Grandfather told me that he felt something change inside of him. In his..."

"Yes?"

"You're a pig," says Alice, and she begins to run, kicking up dust as she swerves between the shrubs, laughing and half-screaming as Ted starts off in pursuit.

Later, when the sun has gone and the moon reigns, they recline on their backs in a small clearing amongst the sagebrush, basking in the unparalleled display of the clear, star-bright universe. Ted feels the warmth of the coffee cup which is balanced on his chest, the warmth of the earth beneath his body and the warmth of Alice Burrows as her head snuggles into the nook between his shoulder and his neck.

"What if we did see them?" says Ted. "What difference would it make? I ask in all seriousness."

Alice turns to look at him. "It would make *all* the difference," she says. "It would mean that we weren't alone. It would force people to sit up and pay attention. Maybe we'd stop fighting each other. Maybe the world would finally grow up."

Ted is silent for a time, then, "maybe," he says, but he does not believe it.

"All through history," says Alice, after a pause, "there have been stories of strange objects in the sky."

"So, they keep coming back?"

"Maybe," says Alice, "maybe not."

"What do you mean?"

Ted feels Alice shrug. "Some people believe that the aliens travel through time. That they take things from one era and transport them to another. Some people believe that the Earth, for them, is just like a big laboratory."

Ted begins to speak, to say something amusing, to make Alice laugh, but for some reason he lets it go.

They look up in peace at the celestial blanket, while the world turns, the coffee grows cold, and tiredness creeps into their bones.

Ted awakes to flashes of bright blue light and, he thinks, a distant scream. The first things that he sees are the stars, for it is still night. He sits up, and seeks to distinguish between what had been in his dream and what is real. His hand reaches out for Alice, but the mat on which she had been sleeping is empty. A blue-white light flashes again, illuminating the night beyond the slight rise to the east. Then comes a woman's scream, for sure, this time.

When Ted crests the hill, breathing hard from the sprint and trembling, he sees, on the flat plain before him, beneath the high dark sky, a landed spacecraft. It can be nothing else. The vessel is shaped like two soup-bowls pushed together, silver, with a curtain of blue light under the rim of its *disc*. In its side is an open door, and from this extends a ramp, which drops down around ten feet to the ground.

Two aliens are propelling Alice Burrows toward the opening in the ship. A third stands at the point where the walkway meets the earth. The aliens stand larger than a man. Their bodies resemble the trunk of a tree, thick and round. They have no heads but there are dark indentations where eyes or a mouth might be. Their legs are like branches, their upper appendages a mass of root-like protuberances. They may be wearing dark clothing. Ted finds it impossible to tell.

He runs, without thinking. Ted charges at the thing at the base of the ramp and comes up hard up against it. Leathery vines wrap around him, pinning his arms, encircling his torso. Ted struggles, using his elbows and his knees to leverage himself away from the thing.

The alien roars, a deep and animal-like sound. Its two companions, standing at the door to the spaceship, with a limp Alice between them, pause and turn. The creature that holds Ted calls out again, softer this time, and then once more. It seems to Ted that the thing is speaking directly to him. It relaxes its grip a little, but not enough so that the Earthman can get free.

It speaks again. Then it turns its head toward Alice and back to Ted. The two things holding the woman move a little way back down the ramp.

Ted understands what the creature is trying to communicate. *We can let her go*, it is telling him, *we can let her go if we take you instead.*

Ted lets his muscles relax. The grip on his arms loosens. He takes one step back, then another. He holds up his hands. He shakes his head. The thing which held him calls out again and Ted watches as the two other beings bundle Alice in through the doorway and out of his sight.

Ted let his arms fall. The alien who had held him seems to regard him. There comes a low gurgle from somewhere in its trunk. Ted feels a cold sickness in his stomach and an icy numbness in his head.

Slowly, the creature turns and makes its way up the ramp. The door closes. The lower half of the craft silently begins to rotate. White-blue lights pulse. With a loud hum the spaceship lifts up into the inky, star-flecked night. In a moment, it is a distant star, moving through the heavens, and in a moment more, it is gone. Ted, leaning against the wall in the parking lot at the University, remembers it all with agonizing clarity. His trembling hand guides a cigarette to his mouth. He takes a deep drag, and then lets it fall.

"I'm sorry Alice," he says. "Forgive me. I love you."

Five hundred years ago, high up in a cliff-side, in the mouth of a man-made cave at Tsankawi, the thing that used to be Alice Burrows sits and looks on as the lowering sun transforms the world into a deep-red and black landscape of grasping shadows. It wonders whether its message will ever be delivered. It wonders, from time to time, whether the world that it came from and the man that it loves are anything but a creation of its broken mind.

It wonders, but never for very long.

When Cows Pray

Annelise Knoot

*T*o *Whom it may concern,*
I don't know you. Bet you never made it all the way out here in the grasslands. Have you ever been to Roswell before? I guess it doesn't matter because you're here now. I've never written a letter quite like this before, to someone I do not know. My lawyer tells me you'll have read one like it before, but I have some doubts. Anyway.
I bequeath to the state of New Mexico, the Praying Cows Ranch.

My lawyer said that would be enough. A quick note and signature, leave it in the house, top drawer of my writing desk and he would find it and bring it to you. I'd call you Mr. Bankman, but in this day and age you could be a bank woman and then I'd seem rather foolish and old fashioned, so I'll keep with Whom. I'd like to detail the place, now that I'm setting down for a formal account, so you know what you're getting. It's a thousand acres. You might be surprised by that, if you're just looking out the window. Most of it extends beyond the mountain range, but it's all mine. Now yours. If you do divide it up, I'll understand. There're thirty cows still in the pasture. They're not going, and I won't sell them. My lawyer tells me it's better to let you make all the decisions once I'm gone, but I feel it necessary to make this one request.

Don't kill the cows.

§

Macy grew up on the ranch with her Ma and Pa back before Roswell really made it on the map. She helped Pa with the cows and Ma with the cooking. Not even a decade on this earth, she had already experienced life in all forms. Cows born, cows dying. Swollen rivers forded under the lash of Pa's whip, the sour tang of fear as cows were led off to the butchers.

Pa was a bit of a fire demon. *Pyro-technic* was the phrase used in the police report, but she never felt it captured the fear he inspired. Pa liked to explode. With anger? Sure, so did every other man from here to Tumbuktu but Pa liked to explode everything.

In the yard, he sighted down the barrel of his shotgun at a keg of black powder. Macy watched from the porch, fear already tickling her legs, preparing to run. The shot came and peppered the barrel, igniting little fires that winked out in the blast of gunpowder. Pa's whoop was echoed by a shatter inside. Ma stumbled out with a broken crystal decanter in hand.

He yelled at Ma, bellowed and lowed like the bulls with their heavy horns and peaked backs. Macy didn't need more warning and fled quick and faster still when Pa started swinging.

She found refuge on the fence posts, watching the herd. Lovely, docile creatures. Mothers with their sons and daughters. Quick pink tongues licking the tips of their calves' ears. Soft eyes and softer noses. Macy leaned into their presence and prayed quick and fast to God that Pa would be settled by the time she went back.

A cocoa brown calf mooed at her and she rubbed its knobby head. *Rosiedear.* The calf was an orphan and Pa had let Macy nurse her, tie a bell around her neck rather than brand her side with a blackened number, and give her a name. He promised Rosiedear could grow old on the ranch so long as Macy took care of her.

Dinner was set on the table and Ma was showing midnight bruises. She tugged her sleeves down to hide them even though the evening air was hot and still. Macy washed up, scrubbing hard to disperse the lingering smell of cow pat on her bare feet and joined her parents at the kitchen table.

Pa led them in grace and thanked God for the meal they were about to enjoy, then spooned a heap of mashed potatoes onto Macy's plate with a wink.

"Eat up, squirt."

He was back to the calm. Macy relaxed into the meal and Ma eventually thawed enough to chat about the neighbor's new baby. Pa shook out the newspaper, leaning back with a glass of brandy Ma had fetched him.

"Would you look here." Pa cut right through Ma's conversation, but she stopped without complaint.

He flattened the paper and pointed to the headline. RAAF Captures Flying Saucer on Ranch in Roswell Region.

"What is it?" Macy asked, leaning across the table. The front strings of her dress dipped into the mess of gravy on her plate.

Pa smacked her. The scolding followed just as fast to take better care of her clothes and Ma escorted her swiftly from the kitchen. They stood over the rain barrel just outside the backdoor. The dog panted on the stoop, sparing them the laziest glance to see if they had brought any table scraps.

Macy sucked back tears as her mother dabbed her cheek with a damp cloth. "What was it though, Ma?" She persisted through her sniffles.

"That newspaper mumbo jumbo? I've no idea. Certainly nothing worth bothering your head over."

But it certainly was. The Arrosas from two homesteads over came the next day for lunch, full of chatter of the alleged flying saucer. Their eyes slid easy as water over Macy's bruise and they sent her with the little Arrosa boys to play.

"My daddy says it's the government." Mark Arrosa said, stomping his heavy boots after the mice squealing beneath the straw. "Yeah, they're making weapons. They've got a whole army base hidden away in the mountains and this was a test subject that got out of hand."

"What's it do, though?" Macy asked, running her fingers through a mare's knotted mane.

"Could be a new type of rifle." John Arrosa said, following his older brother around the barn.

"Don't be stupid. Rifles don't fly, planes do."

"Maybe they want to make a gun that could fly that doesn't need people in it!" John protested.

"You never listen, stupid." Mark shoved his brother down and he landed with a huff. "The saucer didn't have any guns in it. Stop making stuff up."

"What do you think it was for then?" Macy asked, offering John a hand which he ignored, blushing furiously. "You don't think the government made it?"

Mark shrugged. "Maybe. Maybe not. But my uncle? He's one of the ones who found it and he got a good look at the smashed pieces. And those pieces?" He leaned closer and lowered his voice, drawing the other two in. "Weren't made from nothin' found on earth."

The Arrosas left before dinner and soon enough the neighbors from the south were over with similar news. Macy listened from her bedroom, ear pressed flat to the cracks in the floor as the adults discussed the mystery.

"Well if you eliminate all the usual suspects, seems to me the only reasonable answer left is that it's from up there."

"Nothing up there but Heaven. You trying to tell me that God sent that mess down here?" Pa's voice rumbled.

"Never said that. But how can you know there isn't something up there? Don't you ever look at the stars and wonder? Mrs. Montez. You must think there's something, or at least the possibility of something else out there."

Macy pressed her face harder against the floor but could not make out her mother's soft reply.

"She doesn't need to be thinking about anything beyond the state of our house. We're busy enough here taking the herd out without talk."

"You're no fun, Joel. There could be tiny spacemen running around your own backyard and you're too busy whipping cows to care."

"Of course I don't care about that blasphemy. There's no such thing as aliens."

Pa's fist hit the table, making the dish's rattle.

After a pause the neighbor said, "Well. That's probably enough chat for me tonight. Best get home to the little woman. Always a pleasure Mrs. Montez. Joel. Alright, have a good night."

Macy ran to the window to watch the neighbor's retreat, imagination brimming with his words. Aliens. People from space? What would they look like? What would they do? And could they really be just outside?

The alien speculation grew and soon Macy and the Arrosa boys were traipsing around the grasslands and fields searching for signs of the supernatural. Rosiedear followed, her forelegs hobbled so she couldn't take off without them. The boys loved her, and kept running back to show Rosiedear an interestingly shaped rock and ask her opinion of its potential alien qualities. Rosiedear licked whatever it was and gave the boys' arms a wash for good measure, reducing them to giggles.

"I heard my uncle saying that he saw weird lights in the sky last night, over by the foothills."

Mark dropped the juicy tidbit just as the sun was beginning its descent and Macy's stomach rumbled for lunch.

John wheeled around so fast he almost tripped in his too-large boots. "What? When was this?"

"After you went to bed, idiot. He was talking to dad about it. The lights woke him up and he looked outside and saw this column of fire, so bright it turned everything it touched to daylight!"

"Really?" Macy asked, amazed.

Mark nodded impressively. "Really. Then he said he blinked and it was gone. But!" Mark glanced around and beckoned Macy closer.

John pouted and sat, pulling off his boots to rid them of rocks.

"He could still hear this sound. This low buzzing sound echoing off the rock and all the cows stopped mooing and turned and watched the mountain. Every. Single. One."

Bzzzzzzzzz

"What's that?" Macy shrieked, spinning so fast she smacked into Mark and sent him skidding backwards down the dusty ridge.

She scanned the sky for a saucer, imagining dinner plates winging through the air. The weird sound sputtered out as she turned to John.

He pulled a piece of grass from his lips and cried with laughter. "You should'a seen your faces!" He pressed the grass and buzzed again.

Mark, brushing dust from his pants as he climbed back up the ridge, swore and pelted his younger brother with rocks. The boys took off running, chasing each other down the hill.

Macy waited, her ears still piqued. She had thought… There. Snatched back just as quick by the wind, a low hum.

Mark yelled for her and Macy saw the boys collapsed in a panting, laughing pile. She grinned and without another thought followed, kicking great clouds of dirt up behind her heels.

Catching her breath, Macy asked, "Do you really think there could be an alien here? I mean, if your uncle saw *that*, it must be true, right?"

"Come off it, Macy." Mark said, giving her a playful shove. "My dad said Uncle Louis was probably five cups in when he saw this so-called *light*. Probably just the sun comin' up and he was fool enough to stare at it."

"But that noise…"

"It was just John being stupid. Don't let it bother you."

"Yeah, sorry, Macy." John said, sharing an apologetic grin. "I was just trying to scare you." Then John frowned, staring back up the ridge. "Where's Rosiedear?"

They called and shouted and mooed, climbed all the way back to the top of the ridge and cupped their hands around their mouths shouting for the calf, but there was no answer. Macy slumped on her knees staring at the empty grassland as tears began to slide down her cheeks.

"She's never wandered off before."

"Wasn't she hobbled, too?" John asked, scanning the ground. "She couldn't have gotten far— Oh!" He jumped forward and grabbed something from the ground. It jingled as he picked it up.

Rosiedear's bell.

Pa was livid. As soon as the boys left for home, he withdrew his belt and snapped it across the back of Macy's legs. She yelped but didn't run. That would make it worse and he'd stop soon enough.

He whipped the leather two more times, then refit it snugly through his belt loops and sat on the stoop beside her, brushing away her tears. "Hey, now. Why don't you go fetch a firecracker from the shed, eh? We'll set it off and maybe Rosiedear will see it and come home. How does that sound?"

Macy leaned into his hug, then limped off to fetch the explosive.

That night, Ma rubbed her daughter's bruises with lotion as Macy rattled off the day's events, her voice winding down as it came to Rosiedear's mysterious disappearance.

"Do you think the aliens got her?" she asked in a whisper.

Ma's hand stilled. "Where did you go getting an idea like aliens in your head, missy?"

Macy shrugged, not wanting to get the boys in trouble.

Ma heaved a sigh and kissed the back of her head. "Don't go saying that to your father, whatever you do. There's nothing up in the sky but God and the angels. Now say your prayers and be quick to bed. Pa wants to start moving the herd tomorrow."

Macy didn't sleep well, racked by dreams of cows wandering off into blazes of bright light. Twice she woke up covered in sweat with the blanket tangled around her feet and she swore she heard a soft buzzing, but exhaustion pulled her under before she could work up the nerve to investigate.

The next morning, Macy prodded at her porridge, head too full of sleep to feel hungry. Pa stomped into the kitchen, eyes bloodshot.

"What's the matter?" Ma asked, towelling her hands off on a dishcloth.

He skewered her with a look that shot stiffness into her bones. Macy froze, careful not to let even her spoon clatter. Pa sighed and the moment passed.

"There're nine cows missing."

Ma followed him into the yard to recount, skirting the edge of the hired hands puffing cigarettes, eyes shadowed by broad brimmed hats. Macy stood at the window, spoon still clutched in her hand and the porridge cold and forgotten on the table.

Aliens. Aliens had taken the cows, just like they had taken Rosiedear.

Milling too close for comfort, the cows bellowed their distaste almost drowning out the shouts of the swarming adults. Pa turned to yelling at the cowboys who took none of it, flicked their cigarette butts at his feet and stomped out of the yard.

Ma wrapped an arm around Pa's waist and he tugged her close, pressing a kiss to her head. They whispered words Macy could not hear and walked out across the yard.

Pa set up a schedule for the night. The Arrosas couldn't come because two of their cows had also gone missing, but the Wagners, who raised pigs, had been unaffected and were there with shotguns in hand. Macy kept pushing her shutters open to watch the pairs of men and their thin beams of torchlight patrol the corral but had them shut just as fast by her mother.

The next morning found a group of disgruntled ranchers at the table drinking black coffee and filling the house with smoke and ash from their pipes. Pa walked around the table, adding a shot of brown liquor to each mug. Macy stayed out of sight while Pa thanked them for coming, shook hands with each at the door as they finished their cups and slid the bolt home when the last was gone.

"And?" Ma finally asked, and Macy thought she was very brave to do it. Pa reeked of liquor and sweat, and his eyes were redder than ever.

"Nothing. No one saw anything. But we counted again this morning and there's two more gone. Ed said he thought he heard sommat, but that old man couldn't tell a dinner bell from a foghorn."

Ma shrugged. "Maybe they escaped through the fence. Did you have the men check it all?"

"What are you saying? That I can't run my own ranch?"

Ma blanched, the apology swimming on her lips but Pa kept on, his voice menacing. "You think I would have missed something that obvious?"

"No, of course not, I just meant it's a lot of land to cover and maybe one of them missed something. Everyone was tired by the end of the night."

"I checked the fence. I checked it all. And now my own wife is telling me I must have missed something." He tossed his head back and laughed.

Macy giggled uncertainly. She hoped the storm had blown off, but Ma paled even further and she stopped.

Pa rubbed his neck, still chuckling softly and crouched by Macy. "You hear that, Macy? Your Ma thinks I must have missed something. Do I ever miss anything?" His eyes slid back to Ma.

§

Macy sat by the cows, her back against a fence post, toes in danger of being trodden on by the four-hundred-pound animals. They were quiet. Unusual after being kept in the corral all night. Their tails swished, batting off the occasional fly stuck to their flanks, and they blinked slowly, muzzles lifted to catch the breeze.

She shivered and lifted her head from her knees. Her eyes felt dry and crusty. The violet sky had darkened fast, but when she turned her head, she could still catch the whiff of gunpowder coming from the house. She clasped her hands together and stared hard at the empty sky, praying with all her might.

"Please, God," she whispered, and several ears flicked her way. "Let Ma wake up in the morning. And let Pa sleep. He needs some rest from all that fire."

The cows' breath clouded in the cooling air, sending their own hot prayers to the heavens. And that's when Macy heard it.

Bzzzzzz

High overhead, not circling like a bird but hovering dead-set against the sky, was a saucer. Macy gasped and stood, adrenaline coursing through her shivering body. Round as a plate, and twinkling with little orange lights, it sank through the air toward her.

The cows were calm. They watched the object curiously, nostrils flaring, but impossibly quiet, even as the buzzing rumbled closer. The saucer stopped fifteen feet above the corral and its center split open. White light flooded out engulfing the cows and illuminating their rippling browns and spotted whites, their wet noses and full lashes. Every member of the herd stared at the floating *thing* with what Macy could only describe as awe.

The beam centred around one large white heifer. Without any discernable sign, its hooves lifted daintily from the ground and it floated into the air. Macy felt her panic ebb. The insistent calm of the cows told her that whatever was happening, it wasn't dangerous. She squinted at the source of the light, eyes tearing up at the intensity of its holy fire.

The screen door squealed and banged shut back at the house. Macy tore her eyes off the miracle.

Pa ran across the dusty yard, shotgun swinging up to his shoulder. He yelled something and Macy stumbled back from the fence posts and the warmth of the cattle's spirits.

CRACK! Buckshot spattered the floating cow's thigh and blood rained on the ground. The cattle tossed their heads, the first bellows piercing the night as fear rocked the herd.

Macy shrieked at her father, "Don't shoot, Pa! Don't kill the angel!"

But either he didn't hear, or he didn't care. He shot again, light bursting out of the muzzle and pinging against the heavenly light. Tiny fires ignited around its rim and, illuminated, the saucer was much smaller than she had thought. Macy wondered how a cow would have even fit, but the thought was fleeting.

Pa shot again and again. The *thing* fell out of the sky and so did the cow, landing with a crack and thump. Pa ran for the saucer and Macy went for the cow. She ducked under the tossing heads, the cows' screams of murder clear in the night. Kneeling next the fallen animal, she ran her fingers against its soft face, watching its life fade.

Pa screamed. He'd never yelled like that before, not in anger, but in fear. He staggered back from the crash and stared around, his pupils dilated and useless against the dark.

"Macy?! Macy!"

She didn't want to go to him, didn't want to see his face in the light of another fire. But she couldn't disobey him either. She walked over on stiff legs, the cow's blood soaking her skirt. Pa grabbed her and pulled her close. She could hear his heart beating like a drum beneath the sweat on his skin.

"I thought they'd taken you," he coughed into her hair.

He turned them both to survey the wreckage. It stank and Macy wrinkled her nose. Burning oil and hair and a dusty-cold that burned her nostrils. The craft had split open and there was *something* tangled in the wreckage. Pa's breathing calmed and he gave her shoulder a reassuring squeeze. He took a step closer.

"Don't," Macy whispered, trying not to watch as he poked the drooping limb with the butt of his gun.

"Call the station, Macy, the Arrosas too. And Minister Diego. He'll need to see these devils."

The only devil she could see was the twisted shape of his jaw in the firelight, his words echoed by the mourning cows. Without thought, she stood in front of the screen door and opened it on the kitchen, on pieces of the still broken chair scattered across the floor. Something dark and sticky stained the hardwood she couldn't seem to focus on. Ma should have come down by now. No one could sleep through all that noise.

"Please, God." And she thought of the herd's angel, dead in her front yard.

Bzzzzzzz.

Macy turned just in time.

The craft glowed white hot. Pa threw up his arms and with a poof of fire, the saucer doused the ground in flame six feet across. He caught the full blast. His bones blackened and fell in with the aliens.

Grabbing the receiver, Macy dialed the fire department.

§

Sirens came, spattering the ranch in red light. A few reporters weren't far behind, hoping for a scoop of the supernatural, but all anyone found was Joel Montez's body, burned and blackened. The victim of his own explosion, the Arrosas decided. Everyone knew he played with fire. They found Mrs. Montez tucked into bed upstairs, though her face could have been a stranger's.

"Must've gone too far after what happened to his wife. Regret."

"Poor Mrs. Montez."

"He deserved it after what he did—"

"Now don't go speakin' ill of the dead."

"Dad." Little John and Mark watched from behind the police line as the neighbors helped douse the remains of the blast. "Where's Macy?"

§

I think if you searched, you could find the story in the *Roswell Daily Record's* archive. Overshadowed, I'm sure, by other sensations, but it's there. You're probably wondering what I did with *their* bodies. The only thing I could. I buried them. Pulled them out of the wreckage and laid them in my wheelbarrow. The cows followed me in procession and stood in a ring, watching me bury them. They're hard to describe. Bovine. It's the best word I found over the years. Not unnatural mind, more *pre*-natural. Something that existed from Before.

Speaking to you now, after you've read this, I hope you understand my request. The herd has seen something special. They've lived and birthed and died with the belief that their angels will come back and shine His holy light on them again. Take them to join Rosiedear wherever she is now.

If you still don't believe me, then go look for yourself. Go see the cows. Even as I'm writing this, as night falls and they huddle up for sleep, they're looking up to the sky to pray.

About the Editors

Kelly A. Harmon is a best-selling author and an award-winning journalist. She is a member of the Horror Writers Association and the Science Fiction & Fantasy Writers of America. She is a former newspaper reporter and editor, and now edits for Pole to Pole Publishing, a small Baltimore publisher.

A Baltimore native, Ms. Harmon writes the Charm City Darkness series, which includes the novels: *Stoned in Charm City, A Favor for a Fiend, A Blue Collar Proposition,* and *In the Eye of the Beholder.* A stand-alone novel, *Blood Soup,* was winner of the Fantasy Gazetteers Award. Her short fiction has been nominated for a Pushcart Award and short-listed for the Aeon. It can be found *Gallery of Curiosities Magazine, Beyond Steampunk, Occult Detective Quarterly, The Best Indie Speculative Fiction Volume 1,* and more.

She is co-editor with Vonnie Winslow Crist of Pole Publishing's first three Dark Stories anthologies: *Hides the Dark Tower, In a Cat's Eye,* and *Dark Luminous Wings,* and Pole to Pole's first five anthologies in the Re-Imagined series: *Re-Launch, Re-Quest, Re-Terrify, Re-Enchant,* and *Re-Haunt.*

Visit her website at http://kellyaharmon.com, or connect with her on Facebook.

§

Best-selling author, Vonnie Winslow Crist, has had a life-long interest in reading, writing, art, science fiction, fairy-tales, folklore, and legends. A member of the Science Fiction & Fantasy Writers of America, Horror Writers Association, Society of Children's Book Writers & Illustrators, and Pen Women, she has won awards for both her writing and illustrations.

Ms. Crist's books include *The Enchanted Dagger, Murder on Marawa Prime, Owl Light, The Greener Forest,* and *Leprechaun Cake & Other Tales.* Her speculative stories can be found in *Amazing Stories,*

Chilling Ghost Short Stories, Lost Signals of the Terran Republic, Cast of Wonders, Killing It Softly 2, Coffins & Dragons, Deep Space, and elsewhere.

Editor of The Gunpowder Review, Ms. Crist co-edited with Kelly A. Harmon Pole to Pole Publishing's first three Dark Stories anthologies: *Hides the Dark Tower, In a Cat's Eye,* and *Dark Luminous Wings,* along with the first four anthologies of Pole to Pole Publishing's Re-Imagined series: *Re-Launch, Re-Quest, Re-Terrify,* and *Re-Enchant.* For more information, visit her website: http://vonniewinslowcrist. com/, FB page: http://facebook.com/WriterVonnieWinslowCrist, or http://twitter.com/VonnieWCrist.

Also Available in the Dark Stories Series

Hides the Dark Tower
Dark Stories #1
http://poletopolepublishing.com/books/hides-the-dark-tower/

In a Cat's Eye
Dark Stories #2
http://poletopolepublishing.com/books/in-a-cats-eye/

Dark Luminous Wings
Dark Stories #3
http://poletopolepublishing.com/books/dark-luminous-wings/

Available in The Re-Imagined Series

Re-Launch
Science Fiction Stories of New Beginnings
Re-Launch reminds readers that new beginnings rarely go as planned and danger waits for the unwary on all worlds.
http://poletopolepublishing.com/books/re-launch/

Re-Enchant
Dark Fantasy Stories of Magic and Fae
Re-Enchant takes readers down twisted walkways to discover strange and magical places, people, and creatures.
http://poletopolepublishing.com/books/re-enchant/

Re-Quest
Dark Fantasy Stories about Magic and the Fae
Re-Quest takes readers on fantastical quests filled with adventure, magic, and danger.
http://poletopolepublishing.com/books/re-quest/

Re-Terrify
Horrifying Stories of Monsters and More
Re-Terrify reminds readers that monsters hide in the shadows and even the bravest person should beware of the dark.
http://poletopolepublishing.com/books/re-terrify/